I0665035

Crushed Ruby

JANE BLYTHE

Copyright © 2020 by Jane Blythe

All rights reserved.

No part of this book may be reproduced in any form or by any electronic or mechanical means, including information storage and retrieval systems, without written permission from the author, except for the use of brief quotations in a book review.

Cover designed by Q Designs

❀ Created with Vellum

Acknowledgments

I'd like to thank everyone who played a part in bringing this story to life. Particularly my mom who is always there to share her thoughts and opinions with me. My wonderful cover designer Amy who did an amazing job with this stunning cover. My fabulous editor Lisa for all the hard work she puts into polishing my work. My awesome team, Sophie, Robyn, and Clayr, without your help I'd never be able to run my street team. And my fantastic street team members who help share my books with every share, comment, and like!

And of course a big thank you to all of you, my readers! Without you I wouldn't be living my dreams of sharing the stories in my head with the world!

CHAPTER
One

July 28th
3:13 A.M.

It was dark in the back of the truck.

Although she couldn't see, she could hear her sisters crying.

She had been crying too, but now, Ruby Hatcher was more angry than scared. She was angrier than she had ever been in her life.

Her anger was focused mostly on her parents, who had just sold her and her four sisters to human traffickers for $225,000. It was supposed to be for a quarter of a million dollars; only the man had found out that she wasn't a virgin.

They'd found out because they had dragged her out of her bed in the middle of the night. They'd bound her hands behind her back, gagged her, and taken her down to the living room where her sleepwear and panties had been shoved down around her ankles and a finger pushed inside her.

Apparently, you could tell that someone wasn't a virgin by doing that.

She hadn't known that.

There was a lot she hadn't known, but she was only seventeen, and although she had heard of human trafficking, she'd never thought it was something that would happen to her.

Why would she?

This was happening to her right now, and she still couldn't believe it.

But believe it or not, it *was* happening.

She, her twin sister Amethyst, her older sister Diamond, and her two little sisters, Sapphire and Emerald, had all been restrained and thrown in the back of the van. They'd had metal collars clamped around their necks, the smooth cold against her skin felt like it was smothering her even though it wasn't too tight. The collars attached to chains which attached to a ring in the wall. The chain was short, and all she could do was sit with her back against the wall, her bound hands crushed painfully in between.

Ruby was alternating between vibrating with anger and vibrating with sobs.

She wanted to hit someone.

Preferably the men who had abducted her and her sisters—or her parents.

Her parents.

She didn't even want to call them that anymore.

What kind of parents sold their own children for money? Ruby knew that her father gambled a lot, and her mother had an addiction to shopping, but she would never have thought that they would do something like this. She wanted to scream. She could feel it bubbling up inside of her, trying to shove its way out except with a balled up rag in her mouth reinforced with duct tape wrapped around her head, the sound couldn't get out. Instead, it rumbled around inside of her, making her angrier by the minute.

Angry and afraid.

She didn't want to give voice to her fear just yet.

Once she gave into it, there would be no going back.

It would consume her, claiming every single piece of her until she was a slave to it.

Slave.

She'd heard of sex slaves before.

She was seventeen about to start her senior year of high school. In one of her classes last year, they had looked at the world of sex trafficking after one of their classmates had a cousin who had been a runaway and gotten mixed up with a pimp who had beaten her nearly to death after she tried to go home.

Is that what was going to happen to her?

Tears burned her eyes, and she fought to hold them back. She didn't want to let these men beat her, crush her, hurt her. The cops would come. They would rescue them. Going home wouldn't be an option, but she and her sisters would be okay because they had each other.

Ruby was enormously relieved that she wasn't here alone.

Together, she and her sisters would find a way out of this mess.

"Mmhmmhmm."

She looked toward the sound. She might not be able to see in the back of the dark van, but she knew the sound was coming from her sixteen-year-old sister Sapphire.

A moment later, she felt something nudge her foot. Then, another foot touched hers. Keeping that foot touching the others, she reached out with her other leg and poked Amethyst, who was on one side of her and Diamond, who was on the other, and then all five of them had a foot in the middle of the van touching one another.

Human contact.

Ruby hadn't even known how important that was until this very second. Her parents hadn't been touchy, feely kind of people. They didn't hug a lot, and there wasn't a ton of I love yous. She and her sisters fought like cats and dogs, but they also loved each other, and whatever hugs she didn't get from her parents, she made up for with her sisters.

Now, it was just the five of them.

Tears leaked out despite her best efforts to hold them back. If she could, she'd brush them away. Ruby didn't want these men to see her a sobbing, hysterical mess.

She didn't know how long they sat here like this.

There was nothing else they could do but wait.

Which sucked.

She wanted to do something; she hated feeling useless like this. Since they were all gagged, they couldn't try to come up with a plan. All they could do was simply sit here and wait for what came next.

She didn't even want to think about that.

It seemed that she wasn't going to have to wait long to find out.

The van pulled to a stop.

Ruby felt all four of her sisters tense, and she did too. There was so much fear inside the van that she could feel it. It was like an oppressive fog that circled around you, blocking out everything else and covering you so that you almost felt like you were part of it.

She didn't quite know what to expect when the van doors opened, and she supposed that she shouldn't have been surprised that several big, burly men clambered in, unclipped their chains, and dragged them out into the dark night. They were standing outside a huge mansion, and it seemed so incongruous with the reason she was here.

Unless it was a mistake.

She wished it was a mistake, but she couldn't think of a single mistake that could have resulted in this.

"Put the blonde ones in the east wing and the brunettes in the west," the man who appeared to be in charge ordered. "The oldest goes up to the north end with the other eighteen and overs; put the other two in separate rooms. I want that one ..." He pointed at Sapphire. "... prepped immediately. I have a buyer I think will be interested in her."

Her sisters all looked as shocked as she felt.

They were being split up?

She couldn't do this on her own.

She couldn't.

It was impossible.

Too bad it looked like she wasn't going to have a choice.

Ruby struggled as she and her twin sister were dragged off toward one side of the building, and Diamond, Sapphire, and Emerald were dragged off toward the other. She wanted them to stay together. They'd already been ripped away from their home, and now they were being separated.

Did that mean that wherever they were going to end up, it wouldn't be together?

Just hours ago, she and her best friend had been talking about all the possibilities for their future. All the fun of their last year of school, the prospect of college freedoms right around the corner, and then the whole world would be at their fingertips.

Now her future was filled with possibilities again—only not the ones she'd thought—and none of them were good.

They entered the house, and Ruby was shocked again when Amethyst was taken toward a flight of stairs, and she was taken toward a corridor that headed off to the right. She thought they were going to be kept together. The man had said to take the blonde ones somewhere and the others somewhere else, but it seemed like that wasn't the plan at all.

Amethyst's eyes met hers as they went in different directions, and she wondered if that would be the last time she would ever see her twin sister. They were close, like most twins were. Her sister had always been there. *Always*. Ruby couldn't remember a time when they hadn't shared a room or gone to school together each day. They were two halves of a whole, and she didn't want to face this without her twin at her side.

The tears threatened to burst out again as her eyes tracked Amethyst until she disappeared from view.

She was in shock and didn't pay any attention to where she was being taken. The house was huge, and there were so many corridors— they weaved down one, turned, went down another, turned again— until she didn't know which way was which.

"This one will be going off to Igor's when he makes his next visit. She's used," the man pulling her along said as he stopped in front of a door where another man was waiting. The way he said the word *used* made it sound like she was less worthy than her sisters.

But she wasn't unworthy.

So, she'd had sex, so what?

It wasn't just some meaningless thing that she'd slept with her boyfriend. They were in love, and they were going to go off to college together next year. When they graduated from college, they were going to get married and start their lives together.

"Igor is gonna love her." The man at the door whistled. He looked her up and down with an appreciative look that made her shudder. She didn't want this man touching her. She didn't want *anyone* touching her, but she had no idea how she was going to stop it from happening.

"He is," the man who had brought her here agreed. With that, he roughly turned around, removed the duct tape, and cut the plastic ties at her wrists. Then she was shoved into a bedroom where another chain was attached to her metal collar. It was a longer one this time that she guessed would allow her to roam the room but not get out the door.

"I'll be back later." The man from the door winked.

Then the door was slammed shut, and she was left alone.

Alone in hell.

A hell she had no illusion of ever escaping.

CHAPTER

Two

July 30th
4:22 P.M.

She stared at the ceiling.

The backs of her eyes burned from staring so long and hard.

There wasn't anything else to do here but stare into space.

Ruby hadn't slept since she'd arrived here at the mansion. There was a bathroom attached to her room; she had taken a shower and used the toilet a few times. But other than that, she'd just laid here and thought.

Or tried not to.

Thoughts of her sisters haunted her. Were they still here? Were they okay? Had they already been taken—no, not taken, but sold—to their new owners? Would she ever see them again?

The odds of that were not in her favor.

It was likely that she would spend the rest of her life with this Igor person, and that her life would not be particularly long. It hadn't really hit her yet that her life wasn't going to be the one she'd thought she would have. It wasn't going to be the life normal people had. There would be no college, no job, no husband, and no kids in her future.

The only thing her future held was pain.

More pain.

She had already had a lifetime's worth in the last two days.

Yes, she was seventeen, and yes, she'd had sex. She also knew there were other things people did with their partner, even if she never had done them. But some of the things the men here had done to her in just two days were things she'd never even heard of.

She'd been humiliated and raped and made to do things that no one should have to do.

Ruby didn't even feel human anymore.

The more they treated her like an object, the more she started to feel like one.

She was being conditioned to believe what they wanted her to believe about herself. She was here to be used and abused by the man who would buy her. She belonged to him; she was his, and there wasn't anything she could do to change that.

Whenever this Igor person arrived, she would be taken by him wherever he wanted to take her, and once she was there, she would do whatever he made her do. Until then, she was stuck in this room. The chain attached to the metal collar allowed her to use the bathroom and move about the bedroom, but that was it. She was a prisoner, and although she wanted to fight against it, she was already starting to think of herself as one.

She blinked, and her eyes stung. She wanted to go and wash them—maybe take another shower. Who knows, maybe if she took enough showers, she would eventually feel clean again.

Not that Ruby expected that to happen.

She didn't expect anything.

Nothing good anyway.

Ruby yawned. She was so tired, but she couldn't sleep. She was afraid that if she closed her eyes, the door would open, and one of those men would be back. The night she and her sisters were sold, the men had seemed to care which of them were virgins and which weren't. When they had found out she wasn't, they had paid her parents less for her than for her sisters. She had assumed that meant that they couldn't get as high a price for her when they sold her. Was that why the men here didn't have a problem doing whatever they wanted with her?

What did that mean for her?

What did Igor have planned for her if he didn't care that she wasn't a virgin?

Her brain hurt.

And her heart.

She felt so overwhelmed with questions. She wondered why her parents had done this. She wondered what had happened to her sisters. She wondered what was going to happen to her.

It was too much.

It was so much easier to just turn her brain off—to not think, to not feel, to barely even exist.

Maybe that was the answer.

Maybe there was a way to make sure that she didn't have to be hurt again.

Slowly, Ruby sat up.

She could do it.

She could end her own life.

That way, she would avoid whatever plan they had for her.

Her eyes scanned the room, searching for a way to do it. There were no medications in the bathroom cabinet, and there were no knives or other sharp objects in here. She knew because she'd looked when she was first locked away in here. They had removed anything that could be used as a weapon. There was the chain that ran from her collar to the far wall ... maybe there was something that she could to with that.

Before she had a chance to figure anything out, the door was swung open.

She tensed immediately and shrank away from whoever was there.

She didn't think she could take another round of torture.

But when she looked to see which of her tormentors had returned, she saw a new man was standing there. He was dressed in a black suit with a black shirt and a black tie. In contrast to what appeared to be his favorite color, his skin and hair were ghost pale.

Ruby didn't have to be told that this was Igor.

He fixed her with a black stare—his eyes were as black as his clothes —and then turned and barked at someone hovering behind him, "Get the girl, blindfold her, gag her, and let's get out of here. I have things to do today, and I just want to get her back to the house."

Two men—possibly the biggest men she had ever seen in her life— came into the room. One had a key and unlocked the metal collar, letting it drop to the mattress. He picked her up off the bed like she was nothing, stood her on her feet, wrapped a cloth around her head to cover her eyes, slapped a piece of duct tape on her mouth, then pulled her arms behind her back and tied them with a piece of rope. He kept hold of one end of the rope and began to pull her along so quickly she had to run to keep up with his long strides.

It hit her as they were walking along that she hadn't even fought him.

The fight had been beaten out of her in the last couple of days.

She felt like a zombie—technically alive, but no longer human.

She just no longer possessed the ability to do anything but be led about like a puppet.

Which, in a way, she supposed she was.

She belonged to Igor now and would no doubt be expected to perform whatever tasks he asked of her.

No one spoke as they walked through the house. The sudden rush of sticky heat said that the front door was opened, and after another short walk, she heard car doors open, and she was shoved inside. Unlike when she and her sisters had been brought here, this time, she wasn't put in the back of a van. Instead, she sat on a nice leather seat, sand- wiched between the two muscle men.

Ruby didn't know how long they drove, but it felt like an eternity. When the car finally stopped, she felt butterflies start fluttering in her stomach.

This was it.

She was about to find out what the rest of her life was going to look like.

Someone leaned over and pulled off the blindfold, and she found Igor's black eyes staring at her. He gave her an appreciative once-over, his gaze lingering on her face. "Your photos don't do you justice. You're a very beautiful girl. You're going to bring me in a fortune."

She was gagged so she couldn't reply, but he was looking at her like he expected a response. What kind of response was she supposed to give? Did he expect her to be happy that she was now his prisoner? Did he expect her to be happy that he was going to exploit her? Did he want her to be angry? To fight? Did he get off on that?

Ruby had no idea, so she went with a simple nod.

That seemed to be enough, and she was taken out of the car and found herself standing outside another mansion. It seemed like rich people had so much money that they thought they could just use it to buy whatever they wanted—including people.

Instead of taking her in the front door, she was led around the side and down a short flight of stairs to the basement. A huge metal door was unlocked, and the rope was untied from around her wrists, and the gag was removed. Then, she was pushed through the door, which was then slammed behind her.

Faces looked up at her, and people whispered.

She was the new girl in a world that they knew while she was completely in the dark.

She wanted to keep it that way.

She didn't want to know what this place was and what was going to happen to her here.

She just wanted the ground to swallow her up.

She wanted to disappear.

She wanted to cease to exist.

Ruby sank to the cold concrete floor and curled herself up into a tiny little ball. She couldn't really make herself cease to exist, but she could just block out the world and let herself fade into nothingness.

CHAPTER
Three

December 24th
10:38 A.M.

"Look ... there's a new girl."

Ruby looked up at the whispered words from the girl who had the bed beside hers and saw a scared young teenager standing by the steel door that opened to the outside.

An outside she hadn't set foot in since she had arrived here.

She missed the feel of the sunshine on her skin, the breeze whispering through her hair, raindrops drumming down, making that kind of sloshing sound and feel as they hit your skin or your clothes. Right about now, she would even take snowflakes fluttering through the air, and she hated the snow—anything to feel like the real world still existed, and she was still part of it.

Only she *wasn't* still part of it.

Her world had no part in the world that everyone else lived in.

Her world was this dank, dark basement and the rooms in the house above it.

"Maybe we should go say hi," Anna suggested, and Ruby forgot that they had been talking about the new arrival.

The girl looked to be around fifteen, the same age as Ruby's youngest sister, and was standing frozen in shock, staring at the room like she couldn't believe that she was really here.

She remembered that feeling.

She remembered when *she* had stood there scanning the large, open space. Two of the walls were lined with beds. On the wall at the far end, there were showerheads and toilets. Here you had to clean yourself and do your business with an audience.

She remembered when she had curled up in a little ball on the floor, wanting nothing more than to disappear.

She remembered when two of the girls had approached her, taking her over to her bed and explaining what this place was.

She remembered when they had offered her their friendship, and she had gladly accepted because it was all she had—the only thing to keep her going.

"Yeah, we should," Ruby agreed.

Together, she and Anna walked over to the girl, whose fearful eyes met them when they got close. The girl shrank back with nowhere to go but up against the steel door, and that wasn't going to get her anywhere. They should know. They all had, at one time or another, tried desperately to get through it and escape.

"It's okay," Ruby told the girl. It wasn't, of course, nothing about being in this place was okay, but she didn't know what else to say. *Hi, you just entered Hell*, wasn't the best opening line. "My name is Ruby, and this is Anna. What's your name?"

"C-C-Cordelia," the girl answered softly.

"Hi, Cordelia." She smiled as warmly as she could. Warmth was something that was no longer a part of her life. It was always cool and damp down here, and they weren't given many clothes to wear or many blankets for their beds. Most of the time, she was borderline freezing. The men who tended to them were pretty much the opposite of warm. They were cruel, and they treated them like garbage. And, most of the time, like their own personal toys. There wasn't a lot of warmth from any of the other girls, either. Most were depressed. Some suicidal. All of them were suffering, but they offered each other what they could, and those friendships were the only things that got her through the day.

All 148 days she'd been here.

One hundred and forty-eight.

It was a lot of days to spend as someone's prostitute and sex toy.

It was hard to believe that 150 days ago, she had no idea that when she climbed into her bed, she had just hours before her life would be all but stolen from her.

Christmas Eve.

Today was Christmas Eve. Instead of spending it preparing food for the following day's big family lunch or baking Christmas cookies, she was here. Instead of wrapping gifts for each other and stacking them under the huge Christmas tree in the living room, she was here. Instead of celebrating with her family, she was here—in this basement—along with two dozen other girls who had been sold to Igor.

She had no idea how she would be spending tomorrow.

While Ruby knew it wouldn't be exchanging gifts and eating a big lunch, she didn't know if the perverts who paid money to come to this brothel and do whatever they wanted—literally *whatever* they wanted— to the girls here so long as they paid for it, visited here on Christmas or if they have families they spent the day with, pretending to be human and not the monsters they truly were.

She wondered where her sisters were today. Who had they been sold to? Where had they ended up? Were they even still alive?

"My friends call me Delia," Cordelia said. "Well, they did," she added.

"Come and sit down, Delia, we'll find you a spare bed," Ruby said, and she and Anna led her to a bed just a couple down from theirs.

"There should be some clothes in the box at the end of your bed," Anna told her. "They probably won't be your size, but they're better than nothing."

Certainly better than things she would wear when she was sent to one of the upstairs rooms. In a few hours, someone would come and collect Delia and take her to a room where they would dress her up and take her photograph. Those pictures would then be used for the men to browse through the catalogue and decide who they wanted to pay to spend time with that day.

"Is there a toilet, you know, with a wall and a door?" Delia asked, her terrified and overwhelmed eyes still scanning the room.

Ruby had long since stopped being self-conscious about going to the toilet or showering in front of the others, although she remembered how mortified she had been at first. The first shower she'd taken here, she spent the whole time attempting to cover herself as best as she could, and she had held on until her bladder felt like it was going to burst before she had finally succumbed and used the toilet. But now, it was no big deal. At least they had a toilet, and the showers had hot water— which was nice.

Before she could answer, one of the men who worked here approached. "Ruby, you have a client." She hated how they called them clients. These men weren't her clients; they were her rapists.

She knew the drill. She'd done this hundreds of times in the 148 days she'd been here. Sometimes she might be required to service four or five men a day. Which was, she supposed, why she had ended up here. She wasn't a virgin, so the men her parents had sold her to probably couldn't get as much money for her if they sold her to someone who wanted a private collection. But here, no one cared if she was a virgin. All they cared about was that she let these men use her body.

And she did.

There was no way to escape. There were no windows down here and only two steel doors—one leading outside and one leading to the rest of the house. She was always accompanied by an armed man who stood guard outside of her and her "client's" room.

Ruby no longer felt like a person. She felt exactly like the sex doll she was. Lie there, try to let your mind wander, get through each day as best as she could—that was all her life was. To exist in this place, you had to accept that now, you were nothing.

Obediently, she got off the bed and trailed along behind the man. She paused while he unlocked the door and let them both out of the basement dormitory, then walked straight into the dressing room. Since she'd done this hundreds of times before, she didn't need to be told what to do. She went quickly into the shower, and using the hair products and body wash, she quickly scrubbed herself and her hair, then dried off. A woman was waiting to blow dry her hair and apply the appropriate makeup, then whatever outfit she had been ordered to wear was waiting for her to put on. Today it was a low-cut blue dress that matched her eyes, and a pair of white sandals.

Once she was dressed, she was escorted from the dressing room, up the flight of stairs leading to the main house. The place was gorgeous and expensively decorated, but despite that, to her, it was just a filthy house filled with filthy men who wanted to act out their filthy fantasies on helpless victims who couldn't fight back.

Some of the girls who came here tried to fight back, but all they got for their efforts was broken bones and black eyes and punishments that included not being fed for a week or more.

What was the point?

This was her life now.

She was nothing—just someone else's possession.

She didn't matter.

She wasn't important.

She was just a doll.

They stopped in front of the door where she knocked, anxiously waiting to see who was inside. Some of the men were nicer than others. Others liked to beat her or use toys on her. Some wanted her to suffer, while others just wanted sex. Some used her so roughly she would bleed, and others were gentle like they thought that the two of them were equally as invested in the experience. Some had weird fetishes, and some liked role-playing. But, one thing was always the same; she was to do everything she was asked without complaint.

When the door opened, she immediately recognized the man. He was something of a regular of hers. He had taken a liking to her and usually came every couple of weeks—often, more. Sometimes he brought her chocolates or flowers or other gifts, but what he wanted to do with her was always the same. As far as men went, he was one of the better ones to deal with.

"Hello, Ruby," he said as he closed the door behind her.

"Hello," she returned, keeping her gaze fixed on the floor. *Never make eye contact* had been quickly drilled into her upon arriving here.

"You look beautiful," he said, coming to stand before her and hooking a finger under her chin, tilting her face up so he could see it.

Her eyes met his for a brief second before darting away. She didn't want to make him mad, and just because he'd never hit her before, didn't mean he wouldn't.

"Let's go into the bathroom," he said, taking her hand. While the bathroom in the basement was filthy, and the one in the dressing room practical, this one was ornate, and she saw he had already run her bath, filling it with fragrant oils and bubbles. He undressed her, his fingers lingering on her skin, then he took her hand again and helped her into the bath. After removing his own clothes, he stood and watched her for a few minutes—his hand stroking himself until he was hard.

When he was ready, he joined her in the bath, sitting behind her. His erection pressed up against her back, he reached for the shampoo. Over the next thirty minutes or so, he washed her hair, then with soapy hands massaged every inch of her body. It wasn't until he was satisfied that she was clean that his hand settled between her legs and his fingers pushed their way inside.

Automatically, her body clenched at the intrusion, earning her a swift slap to her cheek, reminding her that while this man wasn't as bad as the others, he was still a monster, and as such, nothing to be messed with.

Ruby forced herself to relax and let him do what he had come here to do.

While one of his hands stroked her insides, and his other stroked himself, she let her mind wander away and wondered how many times you could let your mind go before you could no longer get it back.

CHAPTER

Four

Four Years Later

March 4th
11:56 A.M.

One thousand six hundred and eighty-one.

That was how many days had passed since she was sold by her parents and snatched from her bed in the middle of the night. She was taken to Igor's, where she spent the last four and a half years as one of his prostitutes.

The last four years felt like they had lasted an entire lifetime, and yet, at the same time, when she thought back to what her life had been before, it seemed like it was just yesterday that she'd been hanging out with her friends, swimming in the pool, and talking about boys and their coming senior year.

No longer was Ruby Hatcher a seventeen-year-old kid. She was now a twenty-two-year-old woman. Her birthday had come and gone the previous month and with it more thoughts of her sisters. If they were still alive, Diamond would be twenty-three now, Sapphire twenty-one, and the baby of the family, Emerald, was twenty—no longer a teenager. Her twin sister would also have recently turned twenty-two, and Ruby still felt the ache in her heart that came from not having her twin in her life.

That ache was pretty much the only thing she felt these days.

One thousand six hundred and seventy-nine days spent in this basement had taken everything else from her.

She was no longer afraid.

She was no longer angry.

She no longer bothered to make friends with the girls here. Anna had gotten sick a little over a year ago. Since their captors had refused to take her to the doctor, she had died down here. Delia was still here, and so were a lot of the other girls who had been here when she arrived, but many had since died.

Soon it would be her turn.

She'd get sick, or one of Igor's clients would go too far, hurt her too badly, and she would die.

Part of her wanted it to happen.

Part of her couldn't care less.

She didn't care about anything anymore.

"Ruby, you have a client."

She didn't even think about what she was doing. She just stood on autopilot and walked toward the door.

How many more times would she hear those words?

At first, they had filled her with dread.

Now they couldn't stir even the tiniest bit of emotion inside her.

She didn't care that she was going to be raped.

She didn't care if she was going to be hurt.

She just didn't care.

About anything.

The steel door opened, and she took her shower, then sat quietly as her hair and makeup were done. She didn't even look at the clothes that were laid out for her. She just put them on and followed her escort up the stairs and into the house.

"No, you're doing a house call today," the man said when she automatically started for the staircase.

A house call.

Those weren't common, but this wouldn't be the first time she had been taken off the property to cater to a client who preferred to use his own home. The last time she had been anywhere was over a year ago, and when she stepped out into the chilly outdoors, her skin immediately prickled as though it no longer recognized fresh air.

She was directed to sit in the back seat of a black car. No one bothered to restrain her in any way.

They knew she wasn't going to cause any trouble and try to escape.

And they were right.

She wasn't.

She was so pathetic.

Ruby was ashamed of herself.

She should be fighting back. She should be trying to take advantage of every single situation that presented itself and try to escape. She should be doing something. Anything.

But she didn't.

She just did as she was told, like the obedient little zombie that she was.

Tears blurred her vision, and surprised—she hadn't cried in over three years—she brushed them away.

She was a useless excuse for a person who deserved everything she got.

They drove for close to thirty minutes, leaving the quiet countryside where the brothel was located and entered the city. It had been so long since she had seen anyone besides her fellow captives, her captors, and the men who paid to spend time with her, that it seemed strange seeing people going about their lives. They were driving about and walking up and down the strip malls they passed. Parents played with their children in the parks. People laughed and talked; they looked so happy. She had almost forgotten that some people lived their lives doing whatever they wanted whenever they wanted to do it.

It was like she had been brainwashed.

She'd been conditioned to live the way she had been, and she didn't know that even if she somehow managed to return to the real world that she would be able to break their hold on her.

They stopped in front of a pretty colonial, and the driver got out and opened her door for her. People were milling around in the street and in their yards. She was tempted to scream out to them and tell them that she was being held against her will. They were so close. All she had to do was reach out, and all of this could be over.

But she didn't.

What she did do was walk up the front path and stand silently while her escort rang the bell.

She'd been brought to this house once before. The door was thrown open only ten seconds later by a man she recognized. This man had been to the brothel several times as well.

He was a violent man.

He didn't just want sex. He wanted to inflict pain.

"You have her for sixty minutes. I'll be in the car." With that, her escort turned and headed back to the car, and she was left alone with a man who would terrify her if she was still capable of feeling such emotion.

When they were alone, the man grabbed her and yanked her inside his house, jarring her shoulder in the process. He didn't waste any of his sixty minutes, immediately throwing her up against a wall. Her head hit the plaster so hard she saw stars. She bit her lip in the process and tasted blood.

Without giving her time to recover, he was on her again, his fingers curling around her throat as he slammed her head into the wall a couple more times before tossing her down on the hardwood floor. She landed with a bone-jarring thump. The man was on top of her before she could turn over. He crushed his mouth to hers, kissing her roughly as his hands roamed her body.

Fight or flight.

Both had been trained out of her, so she just played dead, went limp, and let him do what he'd paid to do.

Grabbing her roughly by the wrists, he dragged her to her feet and pulled her up the stairs. She stumbled several times, making him growl in frustration. On the second floor, he flung open a bedroom door and threw her onto the bed. Several pieces of rope had been cut and were waiting on the nightstand. He made quick work of securing her wrists and ankles to the posts of the canopy bed.

"Struggle," he ordered. He was breathing hard, and his brown eyes glittered with desire.

Struggle?

She barely remembered the meaning of the word.

"I said, struggle," he repeated, picking up a cane that was standing beside the bed and hitting her with it. Her clothes broke some of the impacts, but she still felt the sting. "Struggle!" he roared, hitting her several more times.

Ruby did.

She thrashed as hard as she could, ignoring the way the rope ate at her flesh, and her movements jerked her joints.

Pleased with her response, he climbed on top of her, hiking her mini skirt up around her stomach. He shoved her stockings down as far as he could with her legs spread eagle.

As he shoved himself inside her, Ruby let her mind float away.

It didn't go anywhere in particular. It just left her body.

The next thing she was aware of was the man cutting through the rope binding her right wrist, then tossing a knife at her. "Cut yourself free and go clean up. I'm taking a shower."

With that, he left the room.

Leaving her with a knife.

A weapon.

Her brain whirred, trying to think for itself for the first time in four and a half years.

She didn't know what to do.

Was this a chance at escape?

With her free hand, she cut through the rope at her left wrist and then both of her ankles.

She was free.

Should she stay here and wait for the man to come back?

Should she wait downstairs?

Should she take this opportunity and run?

Ruby was so confused. To most people, this probably seemed like a no-brainer. But, she'd spent the last four years as a prisoner. She'd been conditioned to think a certain way and beaten into believing she was nothing. She didn't think the same way as most people anymore.

Tentatively, she stood.

Her clothes were torn, and her hair disheveled. She knew that, at the very least, she was bleeding from her mouth because she could still taste blood. When her escort returned, he would no doubt have a change of clothes, so if anyone saw her as they walked back to the car, they would have no idea what had just gone on inside this house.

She could hear the sound of the shower running, but the man could come back at any second, and if he found her trying to escape, she would be in big trouble.

Slowly—as though they had a mind of their own—her feet started walking toward the door. They didn't stop in the hall—just took her down the stairs and through the house. She couldn't go out the front door. If she did, her escort would see her, and she didn't even want to think about what her punishment would be.

"Hey."

The voice startled her, and Ruby didn't even think about what she was doing. The hand with the knife just flung out and connected with the man who had obviously come looking for her when he found that she was no longer on the bed where he'd left her.

Blood.

She had cut him.

Her subconscious aim must have been perfect—she'd gotten him in the chest—because, from the way he staggered and gurgled and dropped to the floor, she must have got him right in the heart.

Terrified, she turned and ran.

If her escort came in to get her and saw what she'd done, she was afraid he would kill her. If she got away and got to the cops, maybe they would throw her in jail for murder.

Maybe she should just run and keep on running and never stop.

Ruby went out the back door, across the yard, and over the fence. She ran around the house in the next yard and out into the street.

It was lunchtime, and there were people about.

People.

Real people.

Not prisoners like her and not monsters like Igor and his men.

Just normal, regular people.

A car was driving down the street, and she ran out into the road, waving her arms and sobbing and screaming. "Help!" she cried. "Please help me. Please. I need help."

~

2:02 P.M.

Sirens.

Ruby heard sirens.

The cops were coming.

That meant she had really done it.

She had really escaped.

When she'd flagged down the car, the driver had stopped and given the fact that she was streaked with blood, and no doubt looked as jittery and freaked out as she felt, the man had quickly dialed 911. Then he'd pulled a blanket from his trunk and wrapped it around her. When he noticed that his presence made her edgier, he had told her she could sit in the back of his car, then he stood at a safe distance.

Now the cops were coming, and she could hardly dare to believe that she might actually be going home. Wherever home was now.

"Ma'am?" A female cop appeared before her.

Ruby shrank away from the woman.

Yes, she was wearing a cop uniform, and yes, she had a badge. Ruby didn't really think the woman would hurt her, but the cop was a stranger.

Strangers hurt you.

That was her experience of the last four years.

"It's okay, ma'am." The woman smiled reassuringly. "You're safe now."

She nodded slowly, not quite believing it yet.

It seemed too good to be true.

Was she dreaming?

If she was, it wouldn't be the first time since being sold that she had dreamed about being rescued.

Only, this time, she hadn't been rescued.

She had escaped.

She'd done it herself.

"I can see blood on you. Did someone hurt you?" the cop asked, pointing to the blood on her legs. Ruby hadn't even noticed. It wasn't the first time that one of her clients had been so rough, they'd left her bleeding—it wasn't even the hundredth time.

Ruby nodded again.

"I'm Elsie. Can you tell me your name?"

She opened her mouth to answer, but no sound came out.

In four and a half years, she hadn't spoken to anyone but the other girls, and when one of the men she was sent to pleasure demanded that she repeat certain words or sentences.

"It's okay. You really are safe now. There's an ambulance coming. We're going to get you to the hospital, get you checked out, and if you tell me your name, I can call your family ... have them meet you at the hospital."

Family.

Her family.

She could finally find out if her sisters were okay.

"My name is Ruby Hatcher," she said. "My sisters and I were sold by our parents, four and a half years ago. Can you find out what happened to my sisters?"

Compassion flooded the woman's face. "Of course, I can. Where have you been for the last four years?"

"In a mansion outside the city; it's a brothel. There are other girls there too. Usually, the men come out there, but today, I was brought to a house. It's that one over there, behind that house." She pointed to the house in front of the one where she had killed a man.

"Did the man rape you?"

The woman said it gently, but after what she had lived through, she'd become numb to the idea. "He tied me up. He likes to do that ... this isn't the first time I'd seen him." More sirens filled the air, no doubt heralding the arrival of the ambulance, but now she was focused on her sisters. She had to know if they were okay. "My sisters' names are Diamond, Amethyst, Sapphire, and Emerald. It's been four and a half years. I'm so scared they're dead already," she said in a rush. For the second time today, tears brimmed in her eyes, trickling slowly down her cheeks.

"It's okay. I'll ask my partner to find out about your sisters. I'm going to go with you to the hospital if that's okay?"

Ruby nodded eagerly. She didn't care what the woman did as long as someone was looking for her sisters.

"Maybe you can tell me a little more about the men who took you," Elsie suggested.

Again, she nodded. She would tell them whatever they wanted to know because if she didn't, then Igor might come looking for her. She wanted to start talking now, but paramedics came over and started checking her vitals, bandaging the wounds on her wrists, then bundled her into an ambulance.

Elsie, the cop, came with her. When the medics were finished examining her, the events of the last four and a half years came tumbling out in a rush. She wasn't sure how Elsie was keeping up with everything, but the woman was nodding and scribbling notes, stopping her occasionally to ask a question.

By the time they arrived at the hospital, Ruby felt simultaneously exhausted and energized. It felt so good to unburden her soul and let someone know what Igor and his men had done to her.

"Can you stay with me?" she asked Elsie as she was wheeled into the ER.

"Of course." Elsie smiled. "You won't be alone until we have this situation under control. There will be a cop on your door and with you when you're discharged."

"The man I stabbed ... is he dead?"

"No, he was still alive when officers went to the house. He lost a lot of blood, but he's going to be okay."

"Is he here at this hospital?" She bolted upright as panic shot through her.

"It's all right, he can't get to you," Elsie soothed.

Not convinced, she rested back against the mattress and let the doctors check her out. She wasn't surprised to find that she was malnourished and dehydrated. She had numerous old broken bones and scars, as well as a couple of fresh ones, including some bruises on her head and neck, a split lip, welts from the whip, and wounds on her wrists and ankles from the ropes—all from today.

"Did you find my sisters?" she asked once she and Elsie were finally alone. True to her word, the cop had stayed by her side the entire time they'd been here.

"Ruby?"

Her eyes flew to the door of the small ER room she'd been put in.

That wasn't Elsie's voice, but it was a voice she knew.

"Amethyst?"

The door was flung open, and her twin sister came running through it—Diamond and Sapphire right behind her. All three of them rushed the bed, flinging their arms around her. Ruby clung to her sisters and wept.

They were alive.

She was alive.

They were together again.

Wait.

They weren't all together.

One of them was missing.

Littlest sister Emerald wasn't here.

"Where's Emerald?" she asked.

"I'm sorry, Ruby, we don't know. She was never found," Diamond said gently.

Her heart broke at that.

Emerald was still missing, and they might never find her.

"But we have you back." Sapphire grinned, sitting down on the bed beside her.

Ruby wrapped an arm around her little sister. Sapphire was right; despite the hole in their family with Emerald not here, at least she was back. She was so very grateful for that.

"I'll let you guys get reacquainted. I'll be outside your room," Elsie said, but Ruby hardly heard her. She had so much to catch up on.

There was one thing she needed to know—one thing that had played on her mind every single day for the last four and a half years. "What happened to Mom and Dad?"

Sapphire shuddered, and Diamond rested a hand on her shoulder. "They're in prison," Sapphire said quietly, and Ruby assumed that her little sister had been the one to make sure that they were punished for what they had done. Hearing that they were where they belonged gave her a little bit of peace.

There was more she wanted to know. What had happened to each of her sisters? How long had they been back? What were they doing now? Where were they living? How had they readjusted to living in the real world? But she was tired, and she didn't think she had enough energy for those discussions. She knew by the haunted gleam in each of her sisters' eyes that what they had been through had been every bit as horrible as what she had been through, and she knew that those conversations were going to be very emotionally draining.

"You should rest," Amethyst said as though reading her mind.

"Are you leaving?" Ruby asked.

"Are you kidding?" her twin shot back.

Ruby smiled and settled down. She wouldn't say she felt safe, exactly —Igor was still out there—but she felt the best she had since she'd gone to bed that night four and a half years ago, unaware of the nightmare she would wake up to.

As she snuggled under the covers, she enjoyed the soft mattress and the warmth and having her sisters right at her side.

But, as she started to drift off, something occurred to her.

She was safe. She had escaped and saved herself. She was free now and could have her life back. She had her family back, but the emptiness inside her was still there. She still felt disconnected. She still felt dead inside, and she still felt ashamed for not fighting harder to get free. She still felt like a zombie.

She still wished that she could disappear into nothingness.

CHAPTER
Five

Seven Years Later

October 20th
9:49 P.M.

"I think the kids are in bed," Danny Cochrane leaned over his wife's legs, which were sprawled across his lap, to kiss her.

"Hmm?" she said, her attention fixed on her book.

"I said that Terry and Sally have gone up to bed. Maybe we should go to bed too." He winked. With two teenagers in the house, they didn't get a lot of time just the two of them. The kids were always here or had friends over, or they were taking the kids to one of their extracurricular activities. With his work, his wife's work, and the non-stop tornado of activity and family life, they had little time alone together.

"One more chapter," Courtney said, sparing a microsecond glance his way.

"Oh, no," he said. He'd heard that before. One more chapter really meant one more book. "I know how that works." He took the book and set it aside and dragged her into his lap. He kissed her again, while his hands did a little wandering. They may be in their forties now, but he still loved making love to his wife every bit as much as he had when they were teenagers in high school.

Twenty-eight years together, twenty years of marriage, two children —they had built a wonderful life together, and he loved every second of it.

"I guess I can finish my book tomorrow," Courtney said as she curled her hands around the back of his neck and drew him closer.

Success.

"We better go up to our room," Courtney said. "Never know when one of those kiddos of ours will come down for a last-minute snack or something."

That was true.

Their sixteen-year-old daughter and fourteen-year-old son both loved late-night snacks. And often not a sandwich or fruit snacks, but elaborate ones that required the stove and sometimes took at least an hour to cook. Danny had no idea where they got it from—neither he nor Courtney liked midnight snacks.

Reluctantly, he removed his hands from their exploration under his wife's sweater and reached for her hands. Once she was standing, he scooped her up into his arms like he used to do when they were young newlyweds.

"Danny," she giggled as her arms wrapped around his neck. "What are you doing?"

"Carrying my beautiful bride up to our room where we are going to make passionate love like we're characters in those romance books you love."

"Eww, Da-ad," his daughter Sally said as she came jogging down the stairs.

"Your parents are still madly in love with one another. Deal with it," he told her.

Sally rolled her eyes like only a teenager could and passed them in the hall on the way to the kitchen.

"You making a snack?" Courtney asked.

"Yep."

"Don't stay up too late," he warned. His kids might be night owls, but they still had school in the morning, and he wanted them to be well rested and refreshed—ready to learn and do their best. He and Courtney didn't pressure the kids with their schoolwork, but they also made it clear they expected them to work hard and do their best. If they weren't good at something, that was fine, but not trying wasn't.

"Okay, Dad," she called from the kitchen. He could practically hear the eye roll.

"That girl is going to make me go gray before my time," he said as he started up the stairs.

"*Make* you go gray?" his wife teased. "What do you call these then?" She started pointing at various points on his head.

"Character. I call them character," he shot back. They were just reaching the second floor when they heard the sound of shattering glass. "Uh-oh," Danny said. "What did she break now?" This wasn't the first time that one of the kids' nighttime snacks had resulted in broken dishes.

"I'll go check on her," Courtney said.

"No, I'll go. You check on Terry and then go wait for me in the bedroom. Feel free to remove a few items of clothing." He waggled his eyebrows at her.

The sound of her laughter followed him down the stairs. He had such a great wife—a great family—and he loved them so much. Danny knew he was a lucky guy. Not a lot of men had a wife who was as gorgeous today as she was back in high school—who worked hard outside the home and inside the home, a wife who was their partner, their best friend, and their lover. If he could change one thing about his life, he honestly didn't think there was a single thing he would change. Maybe just more time: the years went by so fast. It was already almost Halloween, then Thanksgiving, then Christmas, and then they would be starting a new year. In just a few short years, the kids would be in college, and it would be just him and his wife in the house again. Not long after that, they'd be thinking about retirement and maybe doing a little traveling.

Just as he was about to enter the kitchen, he saw his daughter walk out. He opened his mouth to ask her what she had broken when he froze.

Sally wasn't alone.

There were four other people with her.

One was dressed in a ghost costume, one all in black with a skull mask, one dressed as a witch, and the fourth as a black cat.

All four were armed.

The man—at least he assumed it was a man—dressed as a ghost held a gun pointed at his daughter's head.

His protective fatherly instincts almost had him lunging at the man, even if it got him shot—anything to get that gun away from his daughter. But before he could move, he caught his daughter's eyes. She was crying, begging him without saying a word to save her, and he knew that getting himself shot wouldn't do that.

"Don't do anything crazy, Dad," the one dressed as a witch said in a singsong voice—a female's voice, so at least one of them was a woman. The black cat was small, so he assumed that might be a woman as well.

"Move it," Skull said to Sally, kicking her and almost sending her tripping over.

Danny growled, a deep, primal sound, and he would have thrown caution to the wind, but Witch slammed her gun into his side. She was strong, and he heaved at the sudden shooting pain in his abdomen, and hunched over. Skull took advantage of his momentary weakness and grabbed hold of him, dragging him into the dining room and shoving him into a chair.

"Let my daughter go," he wheezed as Skull produced a roll of rope and began to secure him to the chair.

"No can do, compadre," Skull said.

"Daddy," Sally whimpered as Ghost shoved her down into a chair beside him.

"It's okay, baby," he soothed. It wasn't, but he didn't want to scare her any more than she already was.

"Watch them," Ghost said to Black Cat as the other three left the room, no doubt to search the house for any other occupants.

Danny prayed that Courtney and Terry had heard what was happening and somehow managed to get out of the house to safety.

"Please," he begged, "do whatever you want with me. Just don't hurt my daughter."

Black Cat ignored him, not even bothering to spare a look in his direction.

He strained against his bonds, but he couldn't get free.

Anger and fear battled inside him.

How dare these people break into his home and terrorize his family.

Questions came next.

What did they want?

Were they here to rob them?

Kill them?

Another dose of fury flooded through him when his wife and son were dragged into the room.

"Don't you dare hurt them!" he screamed.

Everyone ignored him.

"Stop it!" he roared as Ghost shoved his wife into a chair beside him, and Skull put Terry in another chair.

These people didn't care about what they were doing.

They didn't even bother to acknowledge him.

"Why are you doing this?" he demanded.

Witch cocked a head. "Because we can and because we want to."

What kind of answer was that?

What kind of people broke into another person's house and tied them up just because they wanted to?

He knew the answer to that question.

Unfortunately.

They did it because they wanted to hurt him and his family because they derived some sort of pleasure from it.

A piece of tape was slapped over his mouth. The same thing was done to each other member of his family.

This was it.

This was how it was going to end.

Just a couple of minutes ago, he was thinking about how lucky he was, and now he was about to die.

He wasn't even going to get a chance to say goodbye.

There would be no last hug, no last kiss, no last I love you spoken.

Ghost stood in front of Sally. Witch stood in front of Terry. Skull stood in front of his wife. After a brief hesitation, Black Cat stood in front of him.

They all had their guns out.

If he was going to die, then he was going to make sure that his killer looked him in the eye while they took his life.

~

10:10 P.M.

"Now, don't say no right away."

Ruby Hatcher arched a brow at her little sister. That statement did not bode well for what was coming next.

Apparently, she wasn't the only one who thought that.

"How bad is it?" her twin sister Amethyst asked.

"It's pretty bad," Sapphire acknowledged, refusing to make eye contact with any of them.

The four of them were sitting around the kitchen table in the house they shared. Ruby loved moments like this when all four of them were together. Especially now.

Soon everything was going to change.

In just over two months, one of her sisters was going to be getting married.

Ruby was one hundred percent happy for Sapphire. They had all been through hell. Sapphire had found someone she loved and who loved her back. Someone who valued her for the amazing woman that she was. It filled Ruby with a hope that hadn't been there before.

If it had happened for Sapphire, maybe it could happen for her too.

She wasn't really sure it ever would, but who knew.

It wasn't that she was jealous of her sister because she wasn't—at all —she was so thrilled that Sapphire had found a chance at a normal life, but she wasn't like Sapphire.

She wasn't like any of her sisters.

She wasn't as strong or as brave as them. Other than her sisters and work, she avoided all other people, spending most of her time in her library here at the house. She preferred paperbacks over ebooks and had three walls of floor-to-ceiling bookshelves crammed full of books, and she was always looking for new authors to read and books to love.

Soon, she would have even more time for books.

Sapphire's absence was going to leave a huge hole in the house and in her life.

In just a few short months, Sapphire would be gone. Sapphire and her fiancé Gideon had already bought a house together. She hadn't completely moved out yet. She still split her time between here and there, but soon she would be gone for good.

Well, not gone for *good*, but once she moved out, things would never be the same.

Ever since she escaped seven years ago, she and her sisters had lived together, and Ruby almost felt like she was losing Sapphire, even though she knew she would still see her sister all the time. Sapphire and Gideon's house was only a ten-minute drive away.

But ten minutes meant Sapphire wouldn't be here every day; it meant she wouldn't see her and talk to her every day. Sapphire had a busy job as a homicide detective, which meant she didn't have a lot of spare time. So, instead of that spare time being spent together as sisters, that time would now be spent with her new husband.

Not wanting to ruin the mood, Ruby pasted on a smile. She knew how much her little sister loved Gideon, and she also knew that Sapphire felt like she was abandoning them by moving out and getting married, and that was the last thing she wanted. "So, tell us how bad it is."

"Okay, but bear in mind that Gideon chose the color. Not me. I would *never* choose this color. I tried to convince him to go with something else, but he wouldn't be dissuaded."

"Just show us already." Diamond laughed.

"Don't say I didn't warn you." With a sheepish sigh, Sapphire turned over a picture of what their bridesmaid dresses would look like.

They were atrocious.

Well, not the style so much. It was just a simple halter neck dress, ankle length, and it looked like it was a beautiful satin, but the color was awful.

"Oh, well," Ruby started, not wanting to dampen her sister's spirits because she knew how excited Sapphire had been about planning the wedding. "They're, um, they're pretty."

"No, they're not," Sapphire shot back. "You guys hate them."

"We don't hate them," Diamond said quickly. Too quickly. A dead giveaway that they did indeed hate the dresses.

"I knew it. I told Gideon that no one wants to wear this hideous mustard color. I don't even know what he was thinking. It's going to clash with your blonde hair," Sapphire said, pointing to her and Amethyst. "I'm going to tell him we're changing the color. I don't know why he's so obsessed with it anyway, but he has this thing for yellow. Yellow and sunflowers. Apparently, we're not having roses or anything pretty and romantic like that. We're having a sunflower bouquet for me to carry, sunflowers on the table, and these horrible yellowy dresses."

"Really, the dresses are fine," Ruby assured her sister, moving her chair closer so she could put an arm around Sapphire's shoulders. "We don't care about what we're wearing. The important thing is we're there celebrating you marrying the man that you love. Right, guys?" she said to Diamond and Amethyst.

"Absolutely," Diamond agreed, also moving her chair closer to Sapphire's.

"I'd go naked just to be there to watch you say your I dos," Amethyst teased, coaxing a small chuckle from Sapphire.

Something was obviously bothering Sapphire. She suddenly didn't seem as excited about her upcoming wedding as she had been the last time they'd talked about it. Ruby knew that her sister loved Gideon, so it wasn't about that. No doubt, it had something to do with their messed-up past. It might have been eleven years since their parents had sold them, but all four of them lived with the scars daily.

"What's going on?" she asked.

Sapphire shrugged.

Even though they all had lived through similar experiences after their parents sold them, and even though they had shared their stories with one another early on, they didn't talk a lot about what that experience had done to them. It was usually enough just to know that they all understood and that they didn't have to explain those wild mess of emotions, but sometimes they needed the words, and now was one of those times.

"No shrugging it off," Ruby reprimanded.

"Are you having second thoughts?" Amethyst asked.

"I still love Gideon," Sapphire replied, which wasn't really much of an answer. They all knew that.

"But?" Diamond prompted.

"But it's hard to leave here," Sapphire said softly. "We're a family, and I don't know how I'm going to cope with not seeing you all every day. We've been there for each other these last eleven years, and I feel like I'm abandoning you all and walking away."

"You're not abandoning us," Diamond told her.

"And you're not walking away," Amethyst added.

Although it felt in a way like Sapphire was, Ruby knew that she wasn't. They would still be a family—just a different family. "You're actually giving us a new member of the family. We all love Gideon, and we love that he loves you and makes you happy." It had been hard for Sapphire to acknowledge her feelings when she and Gideon first met, and Ruby remembered herself and Diamond sitting on the stairs here at the house, counseling Sapphire not to walk away from a chance at happiness. She was so glad that her sister hadn't.

"I'm so glad that you guys love Gideon, too, because if you didn't, I don't think I could marry him," Sapphire said.

"Then you have no reason to be doubting anything. You love him, we all think of him as a brother, and really, you're only moving ten minutes away. We're still going to see you all the time," Ruby assured her little sister.

"I guess it's not so far away, and we'll be over here all the time, and who knows, maybe soon, one of you guys will meet someone, and we'll be planning another wedding." Sapphire shot a pointed look at Diamond, and Ruby wondered what that was about; as far as she knew, her older sister wasn't dating anyone. "Are any of you bringing dates to the wedding?"

"Definitely not," Amethyst said quickly.

Diamond was avoiding Sapphire's gaze and was suddenly very interested in the hem of her sweater. There was obviously someone that Diamond was interested in, and Sapphire knew who it was.

Ruby didn't even know who she would bring even if she wanted to. She didn't know any guys. Well, she knew a couple of Sapphire's colleagues. Ever since her sister had fallen in love, she had mellowed a little and started making a few friends with some of the other cops in her department. They'd come to the house a few times, but Ruby usually got nervous around so many people and hid out in her library.

Part of her wanted to date and fall in love. She wanted to be as happy as Sapphire was now, but part of her felt as though she didn't deserve it.

She had been given a second chance at life, and instead of being grateful and taking hold of it and making the most of it, she had wasted it.

She didn't deserve another chance.

This was the only family she would ever have, and she really shouldn't complain about that. They were a pretty awesome family, and Ruby knew that she was lucky to have them.

～

11:36 P.M.

Quietly, he eased the back door open.

He didn't want to wake anyone who may be inside.

Skull held Black Cat's hand, and he tugged her through the door behind him. He looked over his shoulder, met her eye, and smiled.

Ah, she was stunning.

Every single curve of her body was highlighted by the skintight cat suit that she was wearing. Beneath it, her milky white skin was so soft it was impossible not to touch it. As soon as he got her upstairs, he was going to run his hands and mouth all over every inch of it. While he kissed his way around her body, those pitch-black eyes of hers would watch every move he made. She would pull her bottom lip behind her teeth in that sexy way she did, and the sweet little moans she made would have him rock hard without her even touching him.

Tonight had been exhilarating.

He had never killed anyone before, but he hadn't hesitated once before he pulled the trigger.

He had relished that feeling of being in control. What a rush.

Should he be feeling remorse over the family they'd just killed?

Probably.

But he wasn't.

It had been fun, and now he couldn't wait to get his girl into bed and make her come so hard she screamed his name.

Muffled screams, of course. He didn't want anyone to hear them. That would lead to questions he didn't want to answer.

Together, hand in hand, they crept through the kitchen, into the hall, and up the stairs. They were halfway up when a stair creaked beneath his feet.

The sound seemed amplified in the quiet house, and they both froze.

If someone stumbled upon them, he had no idea how he was going to explain this away.

After a full minute of waiting with no one coming—no lights flicking on, no voices calling out—they resumed their climb. On the second floor, there were four bedrooms to sneak past—three of them occupied—before they reached his room.

Skull hated that he had to tiptoe through his own house. It made him feel like he didn't belong here, and that took the edge off the rush he was still riding out from what they'd done earlier tonight.

It was definitely a relief to reach his bedroom door, and as soon as they walked through it, he locked it behind them.

As soon as the door was locked, he shoved Black Cat up against the wall. He crushed his mouth to hers, pushing his tongue between her teeth and thinking about where he was going to put his tongue once he got her naked.

"Don't stop," Black Cat murmured when he ended the kiss.

"Patience, my little kitty," he laughed, reaching over to switch on the light. He gave his girl an appreciative once-over. She was a goddess, and he loved every single inch of her. "You have a little blood on you," he said as he reached over and touched his fingertips to a spot on her mask. Bringing his fingers to his mouth, he licked it off, and Black Cat's tongue darted out to wet her lips. "You liked that, huh?"

"Mmhmm." She nodded, reaching out to touch his shoulder. She held her hand out, showing the blood that dotted her skin, then seductively put her fingers in her mouth, sucking on them as her eyes met his, watching his reaction.

"That better not be the only thing you put in your mouth tonight," he told her, grabbing her hand and pulling it from her mouth. Picking her up and slinging her over his shoulder, Skull carried her to the bed and tossed her down on it. "Wait right there," he ordered as he left her where he'd put her and walked to the bathroom that adjoined his bedroom. Inside he stripped off his costume and left the clothes where they fell; he'd deal with them later. Naked now, he brushed his teeth, used the toilet, then grabbed a condom. As much as he adored Black Cat, he didn't want a little baby skull cat turning up and ruining the good thing they had going.

When he left the bathroom, he found Black Cat sprawled on his bed, right where he'd left her. He loved a woman who was obedient in the bedroom, and his girl never challenged him. She let him lead things and always let him do whatever he wanted to her.

"Stand up," he ordered.

Black Cat rolled to the side of the bed and stood. Slowly, she reached behind her and undid the zip of her cat costume. Never breaking eye contact, she slowly—excruciatingly slowly—slid her arms free and then shimmied the clingy material over her hips and down her long, lean legs, stepping free of the garment, leaving her naked except for the mask.

"Leave it on," he commanded. He wanted to take it off when he was ready. "Get on the bed."

She complied, stretching herself out like the cats she loved.

When he had her lying down, spread out before him, like the delicious meal that she was, he slunk over to the bed.

"You're so beautiful," he said, running his fingers through her silky black curls. The contrast of her dark hair and eyes with her snow-white skin was stunning, and he could have stood here and stared at her forever.

But there were other things he wanted to do more.

Like climb on top of her and drive her crazy before he gave her what they both wanted.

As soon as his lips touched her skin, zeroing in on the sensitive spot where her neck met her shoulder, she began to purr. He loved that sound; it turned him on like nothing else could, and he was almost tempted to just slide inside her and turn both their worlds into an explosion of ecstasy, but he managed to cling to self-control.

Taking his time, torturing her, wringing purring moan after purring moan from her plump red lips, Skull kissed and licked his way up and down her body, leaving not one patch of skin untouched.

When he was ready to take mercy on her, he reached up and tugged off the mask, pressing his mouth to hers and letting his hands tease her just a little more.

"Skull," she whispered against his lips. "Please."

Please.

She knew just how to manipulate him.

It was such a simple word, and yet, it got him.

He loved this woman.

He loved her as though she were a physical part of him. There was not a single thing that he would not do for her. He would lie, cheat, steal, or kill. He would do anything she wanted, even if that was to throw himself into a fire.

While continuing to kiss her, he grabbed the condom he'd put on the nightstand, ripped it open, and slid it on. Then he was finally entering her. She thrust up to meet him, and the thin thread that was holding his self-control under wraps, snapped, and he began to move with a ferocity that was matched only by hers.

They were two halves of the same person, and they moved as such like this was how they were supposed to be—joined together.

It took only a couple of minutes before they both vibrated with pleasure. He rode it out as long as he could, making it last for both of them. When they were finished, he propped himself up on his elbows, so his weight didn't crush her.

"I love you," Black Cat whispered against his neck, touching her lips to his damp skin.

"I love you more," he said. Skull pulled out of her, disposed of the condom, then spooned her against him. If he could do this every night for the rest of his life, he would consider himself to be the happiest man in the universe.

Exhausted by the night's events, it didn't take long for Black Cat to drift off to sleep. Her breath was warm on his arm, which was tucked under her neck.

This woman.

What could he say about her?

She was gorgeous, smart, tough. She was invincible. She had held a gun to someone's head and killed them, standing strong right beside him.

Without her, he wouldn't just be missing a large piece of himself, he would be missing himself. Black Cat was his life. She was his reason for living. If he lost her, he would be losing his own life as well. He would never let anyone take her away from him. He would kill anyone who tried.

"Sweet dreams, my kitty cat," Skull murmured, as he dragged her closer, enjoying the feel of her warm, naked skin pressed against his. If it were possible, they would stay like this forever. Then, closing his eyes, he let sleep take over, knowing exactly what was going to fill his dreams—Black Cat and everything they had done tonight.

CHAPTER
Six

October 21st
8:48 A.M.

"This is like the picture-perfect neighborhood," Detective Judah Willow said as he looked around. The houses were all well-kept and freshly painted with pretty yards filled with trimmed green lawns and colorful flowerbeds. Fall wreaths donned most of the front doors he could see. Pumpkins and jack-o'-lanterns decorated porches, and there were Halloween displays in several of the yards. The street was lined with huge trees that were currently putting on an epic display of fall beauty, and yellow, orange, and red leaves were piled about everywhere.

This looked like the picture-perfect place to live and raise a family; it looked like something out of a movie.

It was hard to believe that anything bad could happen here.

And yet, it had.

"Hard to believe that something like this happened here," his partner, Detective Zeb Tuck agreed.

It wasn't that it made it easier when the death occurred in a more appropriate location, but in a way, it kind of made sense. As a homicide cop, you expected to find bodies in the woods, dumpsters, or basements. You didn't expect to find them in beautiful suburban family homes.

"We should go in," he said, leaving the safety of the sidewalk to walk into the hell he knew he would find inside the house.

"We should," Zeb agreed, clearly as unenthusiastic about entering the Cochrane house as he was.

Despite their words, they both dawdled up the path and across the porch. With a tightening of his gut, Judah stepped inside. He loved his job. Being a cop was what he had always wanted to do. He wouldn't change a single thing about it, and yet, at the same time, his job made him nervous. Anxious, almost. It was because he took it so seriously. For him, it was more than simply a job. He worked every case as though the victims were his mother or father or older sister.

Making everything that personal had the predictable result of taking an emotional toll on him.

The Cochrane family would be no different. He would work this case with everything he had, and if he couldn't solve it, then it would join the ever-growing pile of cold cases that he worked religiously in between the heavy caseload of current cases he had.

Mentally preparing himself, Judah walked through the house, tapping the fingers of his left hand against his thigh in a repeated pattern of five.

It was eerie in here.

The house almost felt alive. Years of busyness—growing children. Years of arguments, laughter, joy and tears and love, had all left their marks. This had been a family home, a place of safety and security, and yet someone—or multiple someones—had taken that and ripped it away.

"Do we know how they got in?" he asked Zeb. The two of them hadn't been partners for very long—just a few months—but already they were good friends and had developed a good working relationship. They were well matched. He was very intense—he knew that—and Zeb was very laid-back and easygoing, it meant they balanced each other out and made them more productive.

"Kitchen window, I think," Zeb replied.

"Want to start there ... walk it through like it went down last night?"

"Sounds like a plan."

The house was quite large. There was a lounge room to the left of the front door and a study on the right. The hall had a staircase leading to the second floor, then four other doors. Since the doors were all open, he could see that one led to the dining room, one to a den, one to a home theatre room, and the last to the kitchen.

Heading straight there as soon as they entered the room, he saw how the home invaders—and he believed they were looking for at least two, possibly as many as four people—gained entry to the house.

"The family would no doubt have heard that," Zeb said, pointing to the glass that littered the floor around the back door.

"They were cocky, arrogant ... they weren't worried about the family overpowering them. There are four members of the Cochrane family, even though two of them are teenagers, as a group, they could have over-powered one or even two intruders."

"Unless the intruder was armed," Zeb countered.

"Even so, four against one, they could have done something."

"It also depends on the time the intruder broke in. If he breaks in at one or two in the morning when they're all asleep, he could have gone after all of them one at a time, and the others wouldn't have even known anything was going on."

"There's a loaf of bread on the counter." Judah pointed to it. "And a jar of peanut butter and a knife beside it. It looks like someone was making themselves a snack when the intruders broke in."

Zeb nodded. "So at least one person had to be subdued immediately. That could have actually worked to their advantage. They break in, brandishing a gun, get whoever was in here under control, then use them as a hostage to ensure that no one else tries anything."

"We should go upstairs, check the bedrooms and see if we can try to pinpoint an approximate time that this all went down."

His partner nodded, and they bypassed the dining room once again to head upstairs. The first two rooms they entered were obviously guest bedrooms; there were no personal effects—just furniture and a neatly made bed. The next room looked like it belonged to sixteen-year-old

Sally Cochrane. There were textbooks and a notepad spread out over the bed. The lamp on the nightstand was on.

"Looks like she hadn't made it to bed yet," he observed.

"Which means the home invasion probably took place between dark and midnight," Zeb said. "We should check the other rooms though in case Sally was just up late studying for a test or writing a paper."

They headed to the next room. It belonged to fourteen-year-old Terry. The covers on the bed were folded back, and the pillow was smooshed against the bed's headboard. A TV screen was glowing, and a game—he had no idea what the game was because he didn't play video games—was paused in mid action like Terry had stopped it, but never had a chance to come back to it.

"It looks like he heard something and went to investigate, intending to come right back to his game," Zeb said.

"I agree. That's both kids who weren't in bed yet. I don't think the intruders waited until everyone was asleep before breaking in." Which meant that they had *wanted* the family to be awake. They hadn't cared about the risks. They'd wanted the additional adrenalin rush—making the people they were looking for that much more dangerous.

Judah expected more home invasions.

A *lot* more.

This was a game to these people. They were having fun. There was no reason to stop until they got caught.

"We can check out the master bedroom later. I think it's safe to assume that the parents weren't in bed yet either," he said.

"I agree. May as well go downstairs and take a look at the bodies."

Ignoring the anxiety that swelled inside of him, Judah straightened his spine and followed his partner back downstairs. The steady drumming of his fingers on his thigh increased in speed. He paused at the bottom of the stairs, surveying the mess the house was in.

"It looks like they trashed this place before they left," he said. There wasn't a single piece of furniture that was still in one piece—framed photos and paintings that had been on the walls now lay smashed and broken on the floor. Various ornaments and knickknacks also lay in pieces all over the floors, and the walls had been graffitied.

"We'll have to get a friend or relative of the Cochranes' in here to see if they can tell if anything was stolen or if they just trashed the place."

They would add that to the day's to do list.

There was no more delaying. No more procrastinating. It was time to enter the dining room.

When he stepped inside, Judah felt his blood turn to ice.

The scene was one of the worst he had ever witnessed, and he had witnessed a lot of crime scenes in his six years as a cop.

It wasn't that the scene was particularly violent; in fact, it was almost the opposite. There was no gore, no signs of torture, no missing digits or deep gashes, and the only blood was puddled beneath the bodies.

Each member of the Cochrane family had been tied with rope to a chair. There was duct tape covering their mouths but nothing covering their eyes. The killers hadn't cared that their victims had seen their faces because they knew they wouldn't be walking out of here alive.

The Cochrane family had been shot at point-blank range in the middle of their foreheads.

It was cold and calculating.

Almost execution like.

This wasn't about anger. It didn't appear to be about rape or robbery. There was no mania here, no signs of delusions of grandeur. There were no signs that these people were taunting the cops or wanting to make a name for themselves.

They simply found this fun.

These were some of the most dangerous killers he had hunted in a long time.

2:14 P.M.

"We didn't stop for lunch. You hungry?"

Judah looked up from the file he was scanning to answer his partner's question. "I'm not hungry, but you go and get something if you want." Anxiety was a constant part of his life, and one of the ways it affected him was stripping him of appetite. Eating regular meals was supposed to be on his daily to do list, along with two rigorous workouts, but sometimes when his anxiety was particularly high, he wanted to fall back into old patterns.

"I think we should take a short break," Zeb said. "We've been working this nonstop all day. Maybe we need to put it down for a moment and see if we can come back at it with clear heads in an hour."

Zeb was right.

They had been going one hundred percent at the Cochrane home invasion case since they were assigned it, but something about this case said that they didn't have the time to take a break. "What about a compromise ... we grab something to eat and talk through what we know so far while we eat?"

"Deal." Zeb grinned. His partner loved to eat. He didn't think he could remember a day since they'd started working together where they hadn't stopped off on at least half a dozen snack stops.

Except for today.

Because both of them seemed to sense the underlying urgency that filled the Cochrane house. If they didn't hurry up and find who had committed the murders, another family would soon be dead.

Possibly as early as tonight.

"Sandwiches from the vending machine?" Judah asked.

Zeb made a face, scrunching up his nose in distaste, but nodded. "Yeah, those things are terrible, but it'll save us having to go out. I'll go grab some. What do you want?"

"Anything is fine." He wasn't eating for pleasure, but because his body needed fuel. While Zeb went to get them lunch, he took out a notepad and jotted down what they knew about these killers so far.

It wasn't a long list.

They didn't really have a lot of information. What they did have, was mostly supposition based on their years of experience as cops. He was twenty-eight and had been a cop for six years. Zeb was a year older than him and had been a cop for seven years. Between them, they had well over a decade of experience, that was enough for them to be able to figure out the most likely scenario but not enough to give them anything concrete. Hopefully, the crime scene unit would be able to give them something that would help them take their suppositions and turn them into a working theory.

"Ham and cheese okay?" Zeb asked as he sat down at his desk.

"Fine." He took the sandwich, opened it, and took a bite, then set it down beside the neat stack of papers on his desk. "I wrote out a list of everything we know so far. How about we go through that, and you can add in anything I forgot."

"Sounds good," Zeb said, already halfway through his lunch.

"We know that the killers broke in through the kitchen window to get access to the backdoor. We assume this was sometime after dark. Neighbor to the left of the Cochrane house got home from a late shift at eleven and remembers seeing the lights on in the house because she thought that was a little unusual. The neighbor across the street and diagonally to the right remembers that there were no lights on when he went for his early morning run at four. So, we know that they left some-time between eleven and four, meaning that they were there probably anywhere between three and eight hours, assuming they broke into the house sometime after eight last night."

"That fits with what we saw. It probably took them at least an hour to trash the place. Interestingly, nothing was touched upstairs, and while we don't know yet whether anything was stolen, they left behind the TVs, the PlayStation that was upstairs in Terry's room, and Courtney's jewelry appeared to be there."

"Robbery wasn't their primary goal," Judah agreed. "So, we can definitely cross a robbery-gone-wrong off our list."

"Why trash the house, then? Did they do it to upset the family, or were the Cochranes already dead by then? If they were already dead, then why do it at all?"

"For fun," he replied simply. There was no meaningful reason to have done what they did to the house, it was done because they wanted to and derived some sort of pleasure from doing it. "So, we know that they had to get the family under control quickly and that they no doubt used their guns to do that. So, they break in, tie the family up, either trash the house and then kill them, or kill them, then trash the house. We might be able to figure out which depending on the approximate time of deaths. Then, when they're done, they go back out the same way they came in because the front door was locked when the bodies were discovered."

The family had been discovered when the people they carpooled with had shown up ready to collect Terry and Sally for school only to find no one waiting for them. The mother driving for the car pool wondered what was going on and used her key to let herself inside. Thankfully, as soon as she saw the trashed house, she knew something was wrong and immediately called 911, so she wouldn't have to live with the site of the executed Cochrane family embedded in her mind for the rest of her life.

"There's always the possibility that this was personal," Zeb said.

They had spent the day so far speaking with coworkers, family, and friends of the Cochrane family, and no one had a bad word to say about them. To the people in their circle, they were a typical family. Their lives revolved around work, school, and the kids' activities. They were active in their local church. They were good neighbors, good colleagues, good friends. No one could come up with a single reason why someone would want to kill them.

He and Zeb had fared no better when they'd looked into the family's criminal history. There wasn't one. No arrest records for any member of the family. For all intents and purposes, they were the perfect family.

"Just because we haven't found anything yet doesn't mean it isn't there," Zeb continued.

"Agreed." They would continue to work that angle and delve deeper into the family. Maybe if they scratched beneath the surface, they would find something that would lead them directly to their killers. "We know that they didn't come in a car, or that if they did, they parked it at least farther up the street or around the block. The next door neighbor who arrived home around eleven said that she didn't see a car parked in the Cochrane's driveway or on the street outside their house. She said that she didn't see any vehicles that she didn't recognize parked anywhere near her house."

"That means they had to walk. That would be risky, especially if they had blood on them from the shootings."

"It would have been dark out, though, so depending on what they were wearing, any blood might not have been visible, and depending on the time, it wouldn't have been likely they would have seen anyone anyway."

"A couple of the neighbors reported hearing loud music, but none thought enough of it to give it a second thought until questioned. The killers probably turned it on to mask some of the sound from the gunshots and trashing the house," Zeb said. "No one saw anyone coming or going from the house, so we don't have any descriptions or even know for sure how many people we're looking for."

"I might be able to help you with that."

They both looked up as Elsie Mars walked up to their desks. Elsie was a decade older than him and worked for the crime scene unit, her specialty was ballistics.

"I started my preliminary examination of the bullets as soon as they hit my desk, and one thing jumped straight out at me," Elsie told them, her brown eyes twinkling with excitement.

"What did you find?" Judah asked.

"Each of the bullets was a different size," Elsie grinned.

"Meaning that there were four different guns used," he said. He had been sure that there was more than one intruder, and this seemed to be proof of that. Why would one man need four different guns? He wouldn't. The only reason that there would be four guns used in the shootings was if there were four armed intruders in the house last night.

They were looking for a gang.

A gang who broke into unsuspecting family homes to kill whoever lived there and then trashed the place for fun.

They were looking for four people who would strike again as soon as they had the opportunity to do so.

8:50 P.M.

It was quiet here tonight.

Amethyst was on shift at the fire house. Sapphire was spending the night at her and Gideon's new house, and Diamond was out at an art show. Ruby had the house all to herself—which she both enjoyed and hated.

She didn't like being alone in this big empty house; it always creeped her out a little. She felt exposed like the walls weren't enough to keep out anyone who might want to hurt her.

Ruby was so tired of feeling this way.

She had been back in the real world for seven years now, and yet, most days, she felt like she was still living in Igor's basement—living with that constant ball of fiery anxiety in the pit of her stomach. She still got up each morning feeling like she wasn't in control of her own life. Like she was merely a puppet and that someone else was pulling strings making her do things that she didn't want to do.

Okay, so now she wasn't forced to have sex with a myriad of men, but she was still a prisoner. Only now her prison was different. It wasn't a dingy basement full of beds and a bathroom with no walls. Now, it was a beautiful house and the ability to go wherever she wanted and do whatever she wanted, only she didn't know what that was.

She was in a prison of her own making.

A prisoner to her emotions.

Which were usually all over the place.

Like right now. She should be happy. She liked her job; there was no stress involved with being a hairdresser. And she had picked a very low risk place to do it. She worked at a couple of nursing homes in the area, stopping by one day a week to each of the five facilities she worked with and brightening the days of the residents who lived there who suffered from Alzheimer's and dementia. She loved living with her sisters. It was nice to have family close by, and this should be an exciting time, helping Sapphire prepare for her upcoming wedding.

And yet, she didn't feel happy.

Or excited.

Or even okay.

She felt hopeless.

Trapped.

Like she was stuck in a cycle that had no end. She might never get over what happened to her. And not just in a there-would-always-be-scars sense. In a real sense, an everyday sense. Part of her wanted to believe that there would be a fairy tale ending to her own life. That she would meet a man and they'd fall in love. She could let go of the past and look to the future; they'd get married and one day have a family of their own, then they would grow old side by side.

But fairy tales were just that.

Fairy tales.

Stories.

Make believe.

In real life, you didn't always get what you wanted. There wasn't always a prince who came riding in on a white horse to save you. You couldn't always save yourself. She had once before; she had saved herself, and she hadn't relied on anyone to come running to her rescue because no one had. She had spent four years as Igor's prisoner, and no one had saved her. So she had found strength that she hadn't known she possessed and done what she had to, to get free.

Her statement led the cops to Igor's house. Many of the other girls there had been rescued. A lot of her captors were caught, charged, and currently serving out their sentences. Igor himself had been found guilty and had committed suicide in prison a little over a year after her escape.

Suicide.

That one thought had hovered in her brain nearly every single day since she'd come home.

It wasn't always in the forefront, but it was always there—lingering in the background, like some kind of creepy stalker who couldn't let her go.

She had tried it before. About a month after she came home, when she realized that her life wasn't going to magically go back to the way it had been before and that she wasn't going to magically go back to the person she had been before, she had cut her wrists.

An attempt to end her life or a cry for help, she wasn't entirely sure which it had been.

That hadn't been the only time she had tried something like that.

Just before the second anniversary of her escape, she had swallowed an entire bottle of her antidepressants. Then, around eighteen months ago, she had tried slitting her wrists again.

Each time, one of her sisters had found her and rushed her to the hospital, saving her life. She was counseled every time, and the fear and pain on her sisters' faces were enough to stop her from trying again.

For the time being.

It never lasted, though.

In addition to the scars from two of her suicide attempts, there was a myriad of scars where she had toyed with the idea but never actually did it.

What would happen when her sisters all moved on and moved out?

She would be alone here, no one to notice if she tried to kill herself again.

Both Amethyst and Diamond were adamant that they didn't intend to get married and move away, but Sapphire had felt the same way, and now she was head over heels in love. From their wedding planning talk last night, Ruby knew that Diamond liked someone too, so how long before her older sister made a move on the man she liked? Or if she didn't, he might.

Her twin sister was different. She couldn't see Amethyst settling down with a man, or any man being able to handle her, but that didn't mean it couldn't happen.

Then it would just be her.

Alone.

Again.

Ruby lifted her hand and looked at the small razor blade she held in it. It glimmered as it caught the light, and it made her think about what lay beyond this life. Was it bright and sunshiny there? Was it peaceful? Would she finally be happy? Would this heavy weight of fear and guilt finally be lifted away?

She moved the blade to her wrist and held it there, applying no pressure, so the blade didn't cut her skin. It would be so easy. One deep cut and she would bleed out before anyone found her. Amethyst and Sapphire wouldn't be back until sometime tomorrow. Diamond would be home late and would no doubt go right up to bed when she did get home. There would be no reason for her to check the library first.

One move; that was all it would take.

Just one.

The sound of shattering glass jarred her out of her trance, and the blade nicked her skin. Ruby hissed at the sting, but jumped to her feet and headed to the library door to see what had broken.

As soon as she opened the door, she saw them.

Four people.

One was dressed all in black with a skull mask, one dressed as a black cat, one dressed as a ghost, and the last as a witch.

All four held guns.

Ruby froze.

She didn't need to think about why these four people had just broken into her house. She already knew. They were here to hurt her. To kill her.

Her library was at the front of the house, to the right of the front door. They had broken in at the back of the house. If she was quick, she might be able to make it out the door before they got her.

As though reading her mind, Ghost lifted his hand, pointing the gun directly at her, clearly indicating his intentions.

They thought they had her, but she had an ace up her sleeve.

She and her sisters were victims of human trafficking; they had designed this house themselves, and because of their paranoia—or what she liked to think of as smart thinking—they had not only put in a good security system that should have already sent alerts to the police and to Sapphire, but they had also installed safe rooms. There was one in each of their bedrooms, and there was one down here in the living room.

All she had to do was play along, then make her move.

Ruby forced herself to stand still while two of the foursome came toward her. It wasn't all that hard. She had plenty of practice staying still while people hurt her.

"Smart lady," Skull said as he grabbed hold of her arm and began to drag her down toward the living room. Black Cat trailed after him, not really paying attention to what was going on. Ghost and Witch had already walked off as soon as they thought everything was under control.

They thought they were in charge here, but they were wrong.

It was odd. She spent a lot of time thinking about and wanting to end her own life, and yet when she was thrown into a situation where she had to fight for her life, she fought.

There was probably something to that, but she didn't have time to examine the thought right now.

Skull guided her down to the living room where Ghost and Witch were already laying things out on the table, Black Cat was wandering somewhere, so, at the moment, it was one against one. It looked like Skull had the advantage because he had a gun, but she had a weapon too.

The safe room was only about ten feet away, but she was only going to have one chance at this. Mess it up, and she was dead.

Since she hadn't given him any reason not to believe it was true, Skull wasn't acting like she was any sort of threat; he was just pulling her along behind him, heading for the dining table.

It was now or never.

With the small razor blade that just a few minutes ago she was holding to her own skin and contemplating slicing through her arteries, she now swung it up and cut through the man's arm.

He yelped in both pain and surprise and released her.

Ruby didn't hesitate.

She ran.

She heard a commotion but didn't turn around to see what was going on. She just opened the door to the safe room, ran inside, and slammed the door. Then she sagged against the wall, letting it hold her up. Her heart was racing, hammering in her chest like it also wanted to run away.

Breathing hard, she tried to calm down.

She was safe now. There was no way the intruders could get inside, and the cops should already be on their way.

Ruby knew she was lucky to be alive, so why didn't she feel grateful?

∽

9:03 P.M.

It was nine o'clock, but Judah felt like it was much later.

It had been a long and exhausting day, and he didn't feel like he and

Zeb had made enough progress in the home invasion case. Part of him was preparing for a call in the morning to say that another family had been killed. He wished there was something he could do to stop that from happening, but they just didn't have enough information at the moment.

He was stretched out on the couch in his den. He wasn't really a TV watcher; he didn't have a subscription to Netflix or Stan or any of those places. When he was home, he liked to just relax and listen to a little music. He had the tendency to be a workaholic, so he had implemented a no-work-once-he-left-the-station policy; otherwise, he probably wouldn't do anything but pour over cases.

Tonight, he had hit the gym on the way home, cooked a risotto, then collapsed onto the couch. His cat had curled up on his lap, and that was basically an order to not move for the foreseeable future. He loved cats, but he'd been thinking about getting another dog. It had been almost two years since his last dog died, and he thought he was finally ready to let a new one into his heart. Punkin, the cat, had loved the dog, and they had grieved Domino the Dalmatian together. He hoped that Punkin would be willing to let a puppy into their home.

Risking the wrath that only a cat who had been disturbed while sleeping could deliver, Judah scooped him up and stood. Punkin blinked, yawned, glared at him, and hissed his displeasure. Before he could get caught with the cat's claws, he set Punkin down on the floor, and the cat meowed irritably at him as he headed for the bathroom. By the time he took a shower and ran through his evening routine, it would be late enough to go to bed.

He'd just turned on the shower when his phone rang. For a moment, he debated leaving it; it was probably his mom. She was a night owl and often called around this time, but at the last minute, he snatched it up. What if it was another home invasion?

His boss's name was on the screen when he pulled his phone out of his pocket. Immediately, he felt nervous energy buzzing through him. "Debra, what's up?"

"The alarm was just triggered at Sapphire's house," Debra said. "I tried calling her, but she's not picking up. Dispatch has sent officers, but you're only a couple of minutes away. Can you head over there, see what's up?"

Relief that there wasn't another home invasion was quickly replaced with fear for Sapphire's sisters. He wasn't sure who was home, but Sapphire lived there with three sisters—Diamond, Amethyst, and Ruby.

He may or may not have a crush on Ruby.

Okay, he did have a crush on her.

"I'm leaving right now."

"I'll keep trying, Sapphire," Debra said, then hung up.

He grabbed his gun and his keys. He didn't bother changing out of the shorts and tank top that he'd put on at the gym. It was cold out, but he doubted he was going to be worrying about that.

The Hatcher house was about five streets over from his, and the streets were quiet. It was after nine, and the fall weather had come. Most people were tucked inside their houses by now. He was there in about three minutes. The house was dark and quiet, and he parked out front and didn't pause to lock his car, heading straight for the front door.

Judah found it locked, and since he didn't know what he was going to walk into, he circled the house to the back and froze at what he saw.

The window beside the back door was broken.

The back door was standing wide open.

Déjà vu flushed through him.

This was exactly the same as the scene at the Cochrane house. Had the Hatcher house been the next one the gang of home invaders had decided to hit?

Were they still in there?

Cautiously, he stepped inside. He didn't see anything moving, but that didn't mean that there wasn't anyone there. Carefully and thoroughly, he cleared the living room, library, gym, office, and the art studio before heading upstairs and clearing all five of the bedrooms.

There was no one here, but was that because the intruders had abducted whichever of the Hatcher sisters were here at the time of the break-in or killed them? Or were they hiding out here, squirreled away some place? Or maybe they had managed to get away and go into a neighbor's house?

Having seen how easily the four intruders had controlled things at the Cochrane house, that someone had managed to evade them here seemed unlikely.

Judah went back downstairs and surveyed the room.

The place hadn't been trashed, but there were a few broken chairs all lying in one corner of the room. He walked closer, looking at the wall.

No.

Not a wall.

A door.

He knew that Sapphire and her sisters had all been sold to human traffickers by their parents when they were teenagers; it would make sense that they had put a safe room in here. If whoever was here when the intruders had broken in had gotten inside the safe room, then it would make sense that the intruders had been frustrated and thrown the chairs at the door, trying to break through.

If there was someone in there, there was no way he was getting it open except if they opened it for him.

He looked up at the ceiling, searching for a camera. If someone locked themselves in the safe room, then there had to be a way for them to know that it was safe to come out.

Locating what he thought was a camera, Judah ran over to the light switch and switched it on. For a moment, the bright light was too much for his eyes, and he had to squint as he ran back to the safe room door, holding up his badge. "It's Judah," he called out in case there was a microphone in there as well. "They're gone; it's safe to come out."

He'd done what he could. Now, he needed to wait.

There was no way to know if whoever was in there was injured. They were no doubt traumatized, but maybe they weren't capable of opening the door. Cops would soon be arriving, and he had to assume that Sapphire wasn't here because if she had been, they would no doubt now have the home invaders in custody, so hopefully, Debra could contact her, and she'd know another way into the room.

Judah was just about to give up hope that the door was going to be answered by whoever was inside when suddenly the wall swung open.

A pale face cautiously peeked out.

Ruby.

It was Ruby who had been in there.

His heart jumped into his throat. He had been trying for the last couple of months to be alone with her long enough to ask her out. Whenever they were in the same vicinity, she avoided him. He couldn't tell if she did it on purpose or if it was just her habit to avoid everyone.

"Ruby, it's Judah. You're okay now. They're gone." He tried not to let his fear show in his voice; he didn't want to upset her any more than she already was.

As though she didn't quite believe him, she slowly took one step out of the safe room and then another, her head swiveling from side to side as she scanned the room, searching for the people who had broken into her home. Then, when she was seemingly convinced that he was right and no one else was here, she gave a small sob and ran to him, throwing her arms around his neck and clinging to him.

Judah wrapped his own arms around her and held her close for as long as she needed to be held. He hoped that she didn't notice how his heart was racing in his chest. The very idea of her in danger was enough to get his pulse hammering and his anxiety jumping.

After a couple of minutes, she heaved a sigh and then gently extricated herself from his grip. He gave her a scrutinizing once-over, trying to see if she was hurt. He didn't see any blood, which was definitely a good sign.

"Are you okay?"

"Yes," she whispered so quietly he could hardly hear her.

How had she managed to get away from four armed men, assuming that it was the same intruders as the home invasion at the Cochrane house? "What happened?"

"I heard breaking glass ... there were four people ... in costumes ... they had guns," she relayed haltingly.

So, there was a good chance that it was the same men who had killed the Cochrane family. "How did you get in the safe room?"

"One of them was dragging me through the house. I cut him and ran in there," she said, nodding at the safe room.

She had saved herself.

She had done the near impossible.

He had never been prouder of anyone in his life than he was of her at this moment.

Ruby was shaking and paper pale. She was in shock, and whether she had been intentionally avoiding him or not, he was the only one here right now to offer comfort.

"Come here," he said, reaching for her and drawing her back into his arms. She stiffened and resisted, then with a small sigh, she relented and allowed him to hold her.

She might not believe it, but she was one strong woman. He wished he could help her see it. Unfortunately, he knew all too well what it was like to not realize your own strength and resilience. He wouldn't wish that on anyone, especially this beautiful, sweet, tough woman he held in his arms.

~

9:24 P.M.

Sapphire sucked in a breath as Gideon slid inside her.

She was already teetering on the edge, and from his moan, he was close too. He began to move, and somehow, he worked her higher and higher when she had thought that she was ready to come in seconds.

Water rained down on them. Steam filled the air, but it couldn't even come close to matching the steam that she and Gideon created when they made love. He dipped his head and kissed her. The second their lips touched, the world burst into a mass of starry diamonds. Gideon came moments after her and continued to move, drawing out both of their pleasure.

When she finally started to fall back to earth, her legs turned to Jell-O, and she wobbled. If Gideon wasn't holding her up against the shower wall, she would have slid to the floor.

"That good, huh?" Gideon whispered in her ear, a satisfied smile on his face.

She couldn't help but laugh.

Her fiancé had such an ego, and he never missed an opportunity to tease her. When they'd first met, it had driven her crazy, but the attraction had been instantaneous—even though she had denied it and fought against it—and it had quickly grown into something much more serious. Now, they were in love, and in just a couple of months, they would be getting married.

It still didn't seem real.

A year ago, if someone had told her that this was where she would be twelve months later, she would have laughed in their face. She had never seen herself as someone who would fall in love and get married. She hadn't wanted to; it hadn't been on her radar. It wasn't like she was walking around trying to meet guys.

In fact, just the opposite.

She avoided any situations where she might grow close to anyone—not just romantic partners, but friends as well. It had been her and her sisters, and that was the way she'd liked it.

But Gideon had changed that.

He had changed her.

What her parents had done to her and her sisters had understandably changed her. It had left scars so deep she hadn't thought that they would ever heal. She had been angry and was still hurting, and she just pushed everyone away because it was so much easier than letting them get close and then being hurt all over again.

Gideon hadn't taken no for an answer.

He had plowed through all of her defenses until he defeated them, and she was so glad that he had. Now she wished that Diamond, Amethyst, and Ruby could find the same happiness she had. If it had happened for her, then it could happen for them too.

"Want to continue this in the bedroom?" Gideon asked.

She had a thing for the shower. As a teenager, she'd thought it was so romantic to make love in the shower, and the second time—by then she knew there was something real between them—that she and Gideon had made love had been in the shower, and she still had dreams about that night. But they'd just done the shower, and she was exhausted after wrapping up a major case that she and her partner Elijah had been working hard to break for nearly nine weeks. Making out with the man she loved, then falling asleep in his arms sounded like a pretty awesome way to end the day.

"I do," she said and immediately thought about how she would be saying those same words in a couple of months at her wedding as she committed to sharing her life with Gideon.

Not needing to be told twice, Gideon turned off the water, opened the glass door to the huge shower in what would soon be their master bedroom en suite, and grabbed a fluffy towel from the rail, and wrapped it around her. Once he'd dried her off a little, he patted off most of the water from his skin, then scooped her into his arms and carried her to the bedroom. Although she was splitting her time between the home she shared with her sisters and this house that would soon be her home with Gideon, he had already moved in.

Just as he was laying her down on the bed, her phone rang.

"Leave it," Gideon begged.

But he knew that she couldn't. She was a cop. She didn't work a nine-to-five job, and calls sometimes came in the middle of the night. "You know I can't do that," she said, kneeling up and leaning over to kiss the tip of his nose before picking up her phone.

Immediately, she knew that something was wrong.

Really wrong.

"There are a dozen missed calls," she said, already running scenarios in her head.

"It's probably just a new case," Gideon reassured her, coming up behind her and kneading her shoulders. "Just answer and find out what's going on; don't stress yourself out until you have some facts."

Her fiancé was a criminal psychiatrist, and even when he wasn't working, he was in psychiatrist mode. Sapphire both loved and hated that about him.

Pressing answer, she lifted the phone to her ear. "Debra, what's going on? Why have you called me so many times?"

"Didn't you get the alerts from the security system at your house?"

Alerts.

The security system.

Something must have set it off.

Amethyst was working tonight, and Diamond had an art show that she wouldn't be home from until closer to midnight.

That meant Ruby was home alone.

Her hands were shaking so badly that she nearly dropped the phone.

"What happened?" she asked, her voice trembling as badly as her hands.

"There was a break-in at your house. We think it might be related to a home invasion the night before," her boss explained.

That must be the case that Zeb and Judah were working.

Four people had died in that home invasion.

"Ruby?" she had to force the word out.

"I don't know. Judah was closest to your house. When I couldn't reach you, I called him and asked him to go there."

Without saying goodbye, Sapphire ended the call and ran to the door only to be snatched back.

"Honey, you're naked," Gideon reminded her.

She just nodded at him.

She couldn't think, couldn't function, couldn't do anything right now.

Her fear seemed to be a living being, consuming her molecule by molecule. If something had happened to Ruby, this was all her fault. She shouldn't have left. She shouldn't have moved out, even if she hadn't completed the move yet. She had been selfish; she'd put her own needs and desires before her family, and now her sister might have paid the ultimate price.

Without any help from her, Gideon somehow managed to put yoga pants and a sweatshirt on her, then slip her feet into a pair of sneakers. Then he took her hand and led her downstairs and into the garage. In the car, he had to fasten her seat belt for her because her hands just wouldn't stop shaking.

Sapphire remembered nothing about the ten-minute drive to her house.

If Ruby was dead, she would never forgive herself.

Never.

It felt like an eternity before they were pulling into her street.

The first thing she saw was a couple of cop cars.

Her eyes frantically scanned the street, but she didn't see her sister.

The second Gideon stopped the car, she rocketed out of it, getting tangled in her seat belt and almost falling flat on her face.

Again, Gideon was there, undoing her seat belt, and holding her hand as they hurried toward the house.

She was just at the front door when she was suddenly blocked from entering.

Zeb.

It was Zeb standing there, his hands on her shoulders.

This was it.

She was about to learn that Ruby had been killed.

Why hadn't she been here tonight?

She was a cop. It was her job to protect her sisters, keep them safe, make sure that nothing bad ever happened to them again.

Sapphire fought to get past Zeb. If her sister was dead, she needed to see it with her own eyes. "Let me go," she ordered.

"Listen to me," he said, shaking her until she stopped struggling, earning him a glare from her protective fiancé. "Ruby is okay. All right? She was able to get into the safe room, and she's not hurt. She's just shaken up. Judah was the first one here, and at the moment, she's a little scared to let anyone else get too close. I know she's going to be so relieved to see you, but you have to calm down. If you go in there all hysterical like you are right now, you're only going to upset her."

Ruby was okay.

She'd basically stopped listening after she'd heard that.

Relief had her knees buckling, and Gideon wrapped an arm around her waist before she hit the ground.

"Sapphire, you have to calm down before you go in there. I know this has been a shock, and I can't even imagine how scared you are right now, but if you go in there like this, you're going to freak Ruby out," Zeb warned.

Calm down.

Right.

She didn't want to upset her sister more than Ruby already was.

She just didn't know how she was going to do that.

Gideon seemed to know, though. He turned her around and very gently tilted her face up and kissed her. Not a passionate kiss, not a kiss like the one in the shower earlier tonight that had pushed her over the edge into indescribable pleasure. This kiss was different. This kiss was one of love and support, and it was just what she needed.

"Thank you," she whispered when he broke the kiss.

"I love you," Gideon told her, his fingertips brushing lightly over her cheek.

"I love you too."

"This wasn't your fault. You aren't responsible for all the bad things that happen in the world, not even the ones that happen to the people you love."

She knew that was true, and yet a little voice screamed in her head that he was only saying that because he loved her. Being with Gideon had changed her, but it wasn't a magical pill, and it didn't erase her past; she still lived daily with those scars.

"I'm ready to go in," she said.

Gideon nodded, and hand in hand, they walked inside the house. The lights were on in the living room down the back, so they headed straight there.

It wasn't until she finally saw her sister that she actually believed that Ruby was okay.

Their eyes met. Ruby stood from where she'd been sitting on the couch with Judah. Sapphire tugged her hand free from Gideon's grip and ran to her sister, flinging her arms around her. She never used to be very demonstrative with her emotions—not even with her sisters—but Gideon had taught her that it was okay to show that you were vulnerable sometimes. This was one of those times. She and her sister held each other, comforting one another, and she was so very grateful that she hadn't lost someone she loved so much.

9:39 P.M.

Ruby was so glad that Sapphire was here, and yet ...

She couldn't deny that it was *Judah's* arms that had made her feel safe and secure—not her sister's.

Maybe it was just because Judah's had been the first face she knew that appeared on the screen inside the safe room, or that his was the first voice that she had heard, telling her that she was safe and that it was okay to come out.

Or maybe it was because she knew that he had a crush on her.

She'd known for a couple of months now. Whenever Sapphire had a few of her work friends over to the house for dinner or a BBQ or just to hang out and talk and watch movies or play board games, he was always trying to get her alone. She was pretty sure that it was because he wanted to ask her out. She might not have dated since she was used as one of Igor's prostitutes, but she hadn't forgotten that look a guy got in his eyes when he found you attractive.

Although, what, exactly, Judah could possibly find attractive in her, she had no idea.

Nor did she care to find out.

She wasn't interested, and rather than have to have the embarrassing conversation of turning him down and telling him she wasn't interested, she just avoided him.

Because she wasn't interested.

She could barely handle herself, let alone a relationship. And even if she did want a relationship, she really wasn't sure that she would be any good at it. She was a prostitute. She'd had sex with more men than she cared to count, and although she'd had her blood work done when she escaped and she was now clean of all STDs, she was still dirty inside, and she didn't want that dirtiness to infect another person. Especially a person who was as sweet and kind as Judah Willow.

So, she would stay alone for the rest of her life. That way, she wouldn't hurt anyone else.

"Are you okay?" Sapphire asked, holding her at arm's length and scanning her from head to toe in search of blood or broken bones or whatever she had been imagining had happened to her.

"I'm fine. Really," she added when her little sister didn't look convinced. "They didn't hurt me, and it was over really quickly. I'm just a little shocked."

Okay, so she was way more than a little shocked.

She was still shaking, and she felt like someone had dumped a bucket of ice water over her. She just couldn't seem to get warm, but considering how things could have turned out tonight, she didn't really think that was anything to complain about.

"I should have been here," Sapphire murmured, more to herself than to anyone else Ruby assumed, but still, she shook her head.

"No, you were with Gideon at your new house. That's where you wanted to be, so that's where I wanted you to be." She didn't want her sister to give herself a guilt trip. There was no way they could have known this would happen; it was just one of those random things. Sapphire couldn't give up her whole life to become her and Diamond's and Amethyst's bodyguards—nor did Ruby want her to.

Sapphire didn't look convinced, and she knew that the new living arrangements were making all of them nervous. It would take a while for them to get used to things this way, but that was the way life was. It moved forward, not backward, and it never stayed the same for long.

"You up to giving your statement?" Judah asked. He was still on the couch where he'd been sitting, his arm around her shoulders, while they waited for more cops to arrive.

When she looked at him, she could still almost feel his arm resting heavily against her shoulders. It was a big, strong arm, well-muscled, and practically screamed safety. The weight of it had been reassuring, and she'd known that if those four people came back that Judah would never let them hurt her. If she wasn't so messed up inside, she would definitely have found him attractive. He had brown hair, which he wore shorter on the sides and a little longer on top, and gorgeous big blue eyes. He had a great smile, and he just oozed a steady, reliable, in-control composure.

She should be flattered that a guy like him wanted to ask her out.

She *was* a little flattered.

But she was also way too scared to do anything about it.

"I'm up to doing it," she said, trying to decide where she would sit. She wanted to go back and sit where she had been before, beside Judah, but sitting next to him with their thighs touching would just remind her how safe and secure he made her feel, and she wasn't sure she should be letting herself get used to that feeling. But if she went and took another seat, it would be like a deliberate snub. He would know that she didn't want to be too close to him, and that felt mean after he had just saved her tonight.

Full of uncertainty, she resumed the seat she'd had before because she would rather feel uncomfortable than hurt someone else's feelings.

Zeb came to join them and started the interview. "Why don't you run through what happened, and Judah and I will stop you if we have a specific question."

That seemed doable. "I was in my library. I wasn't really reading, just kind of curled up in my armchair, thinking." There was no need to add in what she'd been thinking about. It wasn't really relevant to the break-in, so she left out that little piece of information. "I heard glass shattering," she continued, "so I went out to see what it was—"

"You went to see what it was?" Sapphire interrupted. She and Gideon were sitting side by side on the other sofa, but her sister leapt to her feet as she spoke. "Why would you go to see what it was? Why wouldn't you just climb out a window and run?"

Ruby didn't really have an answer to that.

To be honest, she'd been too preoccupied with her thoughts to really give any thought to what caused the glass to break and hadn't considered what she was doing.

"Maybe you should head home," Zeb suggested to Sapphire.

"I'm not going home," her sister shot back. "And this *is* my home."

"Then why don't you go and see if crime scene is here yet," Judah said.

"I'm staying here," Sapphire said stubbornly, crossing her arms across her chest, and Ruby had to smile. She loved that her sister was so protective of her; it meant she knew that she mattered to someone, and that was such an important thing.

"Then, you need to keep your mouth shut." Gideon grabbed Sapphire's arm and pulled her back down onto the sofa. "You're here as Ruby's sister, not as a cop," he reminded her.

"Fine," Sapphire snapped, but from the fear shining out of her sister's green eyes, Ruby knew that she wasn't trying to be difficult, she was just afraid.

"What did you find when you left the library?" Judah asked, refocusing her.

"There were four people holding guns. They were dressed in costumes." Sapphire sucked in a distressed breath, and Ruby shot her a reassuring smile. She didn't want Sapphire to doubt her decision to move out and move on with her life.

"Costumes?" Zeb repeated.

"Like Halloween costumes. One was dressed in black with a skull mask; one was a black cat; one was a ghost; and, one was a witch."

"So, you weren't able to see their faces?" Judah asked.

"No. One of them spoke, but it was only a couple of words. I'm not sure I'd be able to pick out his voice if I heard it again." Everything had happened so quickly, and she had been busy planning her escape. She hadn't paid too much attention to what the four intruders looked like.

"Did you notice anything about them? Were you able to see skin color? Were they short or tall, big or small?" Zeb asked.

She thought for a moment. "Two of them were smaller than the other two. The black cat and the witch—they were shorter—had more of a woman's build."

"Which one spoke to you?" Zeb asked.

"Skull; he definitely had a man's voice, and he was tall—over six feet."

"How did you get away from them and into the safe room?" Judah asked.

"I had a blade with me," she replied, hoping no one asked why. "When we got to the living room, Ghost and Witch were unpacking things onto the table, and Black Cat was distracted, so it was really just Skull and me. He was holding my arm, and he'd been pulling me through the hall down to here, but he wasn't really paying much attention to me. I cut him ... he was caught by surprise, and I was able to run into the safe room," she explained.

"You were lucky," Judah said quietly.

He was right.

Four against one—the odds were not in her favor—and yet, somehow, she had managed to make it through the night alive.

"Is there anything else you remember?" Zeb asked.

"Not really. When I got into the safe room, they were angry—screaming at one another and throwing things at the door, trying to break through it. I don't know what they were saying; it looked like they were just blaming one another. When they realized they weren't going to be able to get to me, they packed up their stuff and left. About five minutes after that, I saw Judah come through the back door."

"You said that they had guns," Judah said.

Ruby nodded.

"Do you remember if the guns looked the same or different?"

"They were different, I think. Black Cat had a really small gun, but Skull's was pretty big. I think the other two had different ones, too, but I'm sorry, I don't know enough about guns to know what kinds they all were." She had seen plenty of guns in her life, but she had never been interested in learning anything about them. If she had her way, she would never lay eyes on another one as long as she lived.

"Okay, that's great, Ruby. You've told us a lot that will hopefully help us find these people before they hurt anyone else," Judah told her.

"Can I stay here tonight? I'm tired, and I just want to go to bed."

"You can't stay here tonight," Sapphire objected. "You can spend the night at Gideon's and my house."

While she appreciated the offer, Ruby just wanted to be in her own bed tonight with the security of being in her bedroom with her things around her. "I'd rather stay here. If I can." She looked to Judah and Zeb to get their permission.

"Crime scene will be working down here for a while, but you can stay upstairs in your room," Judah told her.

"Then Gideon and I are staying here too," Sapphire said, her face set. She wouldn't be persuaded otherwise, and Ruby wasn't complaining. She would feel much safer with her sister here.

"Thank you for coming here tonight," she said to Judah as she stood. She was eternally grateful for him just being here and holding her when she had been scared out of her mind.

"Anytime," he said, smiling at her, and she had a feeling he meant it. Like *really* meant it, and she had to wonder why she had convinced her sister that it was okay to move on with her life, and she shouldn't let the past hold her back, and yet, she didn't take her own advice.

"Gideon and I will check in on you before we go to bed," Sapphire said.

"Okay. Goodnight everyone, and thank you."

As she walked upstairs to go to bed, Ruby felt lucky to be alive, but at the back of her mind, right where it always lurked, was the lingering thought that maybe she would be better off dead.

It was beginning to feel like she would never be rid of the thought of suicide.

~

10:13 P.M.

"I can't believe what that woman did to you," Black Cat complained as she gently eased up Skull's sleeve so she could see the wound. "It looks deep," she said when she saw the gash. It was still oozing blood, and the sight of the wound fueled her anger.

How dare that woman hurt the man she loved!

She wished they'd been able to get into the safe room. If they had, she'd have made sure that the woman knew that *no one* messed with her man and got away with it.

"Does it need stitches?" Skull asked.

"I don't think so." She calmed herself because she knew that Skull would only get more upset if he knew how upset she was, and she didn't want him to do anything stupid like go back to the house to find the woman and punish her for upsetting her. By now, the house would be crawling with cops, and going back there was only going to lead to one thing.

Arrest.

And she didn't want to see her man behind bars.

"Come into the bathroom," she said, standing and taking Skull's hand, leading him into her bathroom. "Sit," she ordered, pushing him down to perch on the edge of the bath. She grabbed a washcloth and ran it under the hot water and began to clean his wound. The gash was jagged, and it would definitely form a scar as it healed. She found scars so sexy on a guy, and every time she looked at it, she would remember tonight.

Black Cat washed Skull's arm until she'd cleaned away all the blood, and then she collected her first aid kit from the bathroom cabinet. She pulled out some antibiotic cream and applied it to the wound, letting her fingertips glide up and down Skull's arm, enjoying the feel of his torn skin because it reminded her of how fierce he was. How ferocious. Once the cream was applied, she wrapped a bandage around his arm and then closed the lid of the kit and set it aside.

"Playing doctor was kind of sexy," she whispered in his ear, nibbling on his neck.

Skull groaned, and she knew he was no longer thinking about the botched home invasion—at least, for now.

For now, he was thinking about her and only her.

"Strip," he ordered.

She obeyed.

Black Cat straightened and reached behind her to unzip the one-piece costume. Because she knew it drove him wild—and she would do *anything* to drive her guy wild—she took her time pulling the black material down, exposing her bare breasts, then sliding out first one arm and then the other.

With more self-control than she would have if their positions were reversed, Skull's breathing quickened, and his eyes glittered with desire, but he didn't move from his spot on the edge of the bath.

He watched her every move as she pushed the costume down one leg, then let her fingers trail up her skin, pausing when they reached the V between her legs, before sliding the material down her other leg. She stepped out of the costume, leaving it on the floor where it fell and stood before him wearing nothing but a pair of black silk panties.

Skull's eyes set on fire every place on her body that they looked at, and by the time they worked their way up to meet her own eyes, she felt like she was about to explode.

"Turn around," he ordered.

She complied.

She felt him come up behind her. He dipped his head, and she felt his hot breath on the back of her neck, but he didn't touch her.

"Walk into the bedroom," he commanded.

Black Cat started walking.

She thought he would tell her to go and lie down on the bed, but he didn't. He pressed a hand to the small of her back, telling her without words that he wanted her to stop.

"Remove your panties and get down on your knees."

Again, she did exactly as she was told.

Skull wrapped her long dark curls around his hand and shoved her head down so that it rested on the carpet.

Then he knelt beside her.

She was dying for him to enter her.

She wanted to beg, but begging would only ensure that he tortured her, working her right to the edge, but not allowing her to fall over it.

Instead, she kept her mouth shut and waited.

And waited.

Then finally, she felt him move behind her, but instead of entering her body, he reached around her and very lightly ran his fingertips over her breasts.

She couldn't help it.

She purred her pleasure, and she could feel him smiling smugly even though she couldn't see him.

He ran his fingers down her stomach, circling her belly button, before dipping lower. With excruciating slowness, he brought his hand between her legs and gently brushed his fingers across the part of her that ached for him.

It wasn't enough.

Her body tried to move.

To force him to do more.

To give her what she needed.

"Uh, uh, uh," he said, delivering a swift whack to her bare backside. "Don't be impatient."

"Sorry," she whispered.

"That's better," he said. He touched her again—firmer, this time—but not enough to bring her any pleasure.

She could feel he was already hard and growing harder by the second as he got off on dominating her. Black Cat pressed backward a little so that her bottom brushed against him, and she heard him gasp. She had a few tricks of her own, and although he liked to think he was the one who was always in control, she knew how to get what she wanted.

"Please," she purred. "Please, Skull."

That was enough.

With a grunt, she heard him shove down his jeans, and then he was entering her from behind. One hand wrapped around her hair, his other was still between her legs, touching her as he moved inside her, working them both into a crazy state of anticipation.

Then with a moan, he came. She followed a few seconds later, riding the wave for as long as she could before she finally sank down against the rough carpet, completely spent.

Satisfied that he had given her what no one else could, Skull pulled out of her, then scooped her into his arms. She immediately curled into him—nuzzling his neck and purring—as he carried her to the bed. He laid her down and tucked the covers around her, before stripping off his clothes and joining her.

"We weren't successful tonight," she said as he spooned her against him and began to stroke her hair.

"No, we weren't."

"What are we going to do about that?" She had no idea what Skull was planning on doing. Did he just want to accept tonight had been a failure, or did he want to try again, get things right this time?

"I don't know yet," he said thoughtfully, and she could practically hear the wheels in his brain spinning madly.

"There was no way we could have known that she would have a safe room. I mean, who actually has one of those? I thought they were just something for the movies."

"I don't like leaving loose ends, but I don't know how we'd get a chance to finish what we started tonight," Skull said.

She wanted a second chance. She wanted to punish the woman for what she had done. Part of her felt guilty too. She hadn't been paying proper attention. She hadn't noticed that the woman was armed. If she had, then they would have killed their fifth person.

"We need to meet with Ghost and Witch in the morning, decide what our next plan of action is. We never intended to leave a witness, but now the police have her, which means that they might be on to us.

First thing in the morning, we need to decide how to minimize the damage done tonight and how we should proceed. That's tomorrow, though," he said, licking the side of her neck and then blowing on it, making her shiver.

"Oh?" she purred. "And what about tonight?"

"Tonight is about us." He palmed her breast and then began to tease her nipple, making her shiver again. "You ready for round two?"

"Are you?"

"Baby, with you, I'm *always* ready."

Skull grabbed her wrist and flipped her over onto her back, then threw the covers aside and moved down the bed, settling himself between her legs. Black Cat loved what his hands could do to her, but she loved even more what his mouth could do. How could one tongue drive her so wild?

As his mouth began to work its magic, her fingers curled into the sheet, and she started to purr. The ability to think left her. All she could do was feel the amazing things he was doing to her.

CHAPTER
Seven

October 22nd
8:29 A.M.

Judah stifled a yawn as he walked into the precinct. It had been close to two in the morning by the time he got home and into bed. He and Zeb had waited until the crime scene unit finished up before they left. They weren't optimistic about finding any forensics. From what Ruby had told them, the four home invaders were wearing costumes, including gloves, so there would be no fingerprints. Although Ruby had cut one of them, the wound obviously hadn't been deep enough to drip blood onto the floor because they hadn't found any. There hadn't been any guns fired at the Hatcher house, so there was no way to positively prove that it was the same people who had broken into both the Hatcher and Cochrane houses.

But Judah knew that it was the same gang.

Two home invasions. Both by a gang of four. Both broke into the houses by breaking back windows, and both had been armed with guns. What was the chance that they weren't the same groups of people?

Zero.

As far as he was concerned, the crimes were related, and what they had learned from Ruby changed things. They weren't looking for a gang of four men; they were likely looking for two couples. He was sure that was important information; he just wasn't sure why.

Yet.

But he would figure it out.

He had to because if he didn't, there was no way to keep Ruby safe. She had survived, but the gang hadn't intended to leave any witnesses behind. There was a chance that they would try to go back and finish what they had started.

He could not allow that to happen.

When he reached the homicide floor, he saw that he was the last to arrive. Zeb was there, and Debra, as well as Sapphire, Gideon, and Sapphire's partner, Elijah. Hopefully, between the six of them, they could figure this out before the gang hit another house. Two days, two houses. There was every chance they would continue with that pattern and hit another house tonight.

"Morning," he said as he approached the group.

"What are we doing to keep Ruby safe?" Sapphire asked without preamble, as though she couldn't contain the question any longer. Judah could sympathize. He was out of his mind worrying about Ruby, and he only had a crush on her. Sapphire was her sister, and he knew that they were close. He didn't even want to think about how afraid she must be right now.

"There's no way to know that they'll try anything," Zeb said.

That didn't appear to be good enough for Sapphire. "There is no way to know that they won't."

Judah had spent half the night thinking about just that. "I had an idea," he said.

Sapphire arched a brow. "What is it?" she asked suspiciously. If he was ever able to convince Ruby to give him a chance, then he suspected cracking Sapphire and getting her to support the relationship might be quite the challenge, she was extremely protective of her family.

"I thought it might make sense for me to stay at the Hatcher house until this is sorted out, and we have suspects in custody," he suggested.

He'd spoken with his mom and asked her to take Punkin for a couple of days so that he could stay with the Hatchers, so everything was sorted on his end.

"No," Sapphire said immediately.

"They're only hitting houses after dark," he reasoned. "She should be safe enough during the day, and if I'm there at night and they *do* come back, she'll stay safe, and we'll have our gang behind bars."

"No," Sapphire said again. "I think that *I* should be the one to stay at home, I mean, I live there anyway, so it makes perfect sense."

"When are you going to sleep?" Gideon asked his fiancée.

"I don't need sleep." Sapphire said it so straight faced that Judah couldn't help but laugh, and he wasn't the only one.

"You don't need sleep?" Gideon echoed. "Do you know what happens when someone is sleep deprived? They become moody, irritable, depressed, forgetful, are unable to concentrate, and they can become uncoordinated. Does that sound like a good idea when you're trying to protect someone from potential danger?"

"Why are you not just agreeing with me? We're getting married; you're supposed to agree with me," Sapphire snapped.

"Because I love you." Gideon leaned over and kissed Sapphire's cheek, seemingly unperturbed by her outburst. "There is more evidence about how people actually need to sleep if you're not convinced."

"Fine," she huffed. "But if I need sleep, then Judah does too. I suppose since we're talking about Ruby's safety—and Diamond and Amethyst's too—that he can stay at our place, and you and I will stay too."

"Deal," Gideon said, holding out his hand. Sapphire rolled her eyes, but quirked up one side of her mouth in a smile and shook his hand.

"Judah?" she said, looking to him.

"I'm fine with that plan," he said. He just wanted to keep Ruby safe. He didn't care if Sapphire wanted to be there. *He* just wanted to be there. He needed to know that she was safe so he could focus on finding the people who had terrorized her. And he was man enough to admit—at least to himself—that having an excuse to spend time around her where she couldn't avoid him was also a reason he wanted to stay at the Hatcher house.

"Now that we have that sorted," Debra said, "let's get down to business."

"Elsie is still running the bullets from the Cochrane house to see if she can match them to any other crimes. That might give us a direction to move in," Zeb said.

"As soon as we're done here, we're going to go and interview the neighbors; maybe someone saw something. Since they were interrupted, they left earlier than they had planned, which means there were probably people still up and out jogging or walking dogs; someone might have seen them," Judah said.

"Now we know that they were dressed in costumes, we know exactly what to be asking people about," Zeb added.

Since it was almost Halloween, the killers had found a great way to blend in and hide their identities. Had this been any other time of year, four people walking around dressed as a skull, a cat, a ghost, and a witch would have stood out like a sore thumb, but now people would have just assumed they were going to or coming from a costume party. While people might have seen them, no one would be able to give them a description of what they looked like, save from the fact that they were dressed up.

They had their work cut out for them with this case, but he wasn't giving up. He couldn't. Every time he thought of Ruby's terrified blue eyes as she crept out of the safe room, he felt a rush of protective anger flush through him. Your home was supposed to be your sanctuary— your safe place. These people had ripped that safety away from Ruby. She'd already been through so much—lost so much. She didn't deserve this. Once those four people were in prison, maybe she'd be able to feel safe in her home again.

"Gideon, I know you don't know all the details of the case, but how would you profile the gang we're looking for?" Debra asked.

"Young," Gideon said immediately. "College kids, maybe, judging by the costumes they chose, the way they trashed the house, and the way they were so brazen in how they broke in—knowing that whoever was inside would hear the breaking glass. And, the temper tantrum they had when Ruby got into the safe room, they aren't very old—not more than early twenties. They're enjoying it, and they were annoyed when they were deprived of what they wanted at Sapphire's house last night. Two couples, but they're probably all friends. One ringleader; this is someone's plan, and the others are all going along with it."

"Willingly, though. There were four people there, and they each shot someone at the Cochrane house," he countered.

"An initiation," Gideon said. "To prove that they're all in. Now someone can't turn on the others without implicating themselves."

"Which one do you think the ringleader is?" Judah asked.

"I don't know enough yet to make that kind of decision, possibly the man who Ruby cut. He seemed to be the one in control, but again, right now, we don't know enough to figure that out."

It would have been helpful if the security system at the Hatcher house had had recording cameras, but the only camera was the one outside the safe room, and it only live streamed; it didn't record. For now, unless ballistics got a hit, the only thing they could do was keep trying to gather information, which, unfortunately, meant waiting for another family to die. That was one of the things Judah hated the most about his job. To solve a case, you needed evidence, but a lot of the time, the only way to get that evidence was for more crimes to be committed. This gang would mess up eventually, but how many more people would die before then?

Selfish or not, Judah was eternally grateful that Ruby had survived. Whether he stood a chance with her or not, he would never want anything to happen to her. She was too special.

9:35 A.M.

Ruby wandered aimlessly around the house.

She felt kind of out of place here now.

The crime scene people had been gone before she got up this morning, and Sapphire and Gideon had left early. While she was alone in the house, she knew that her sister had made sure officers were sitting in a patrol car outside so she wouldn't be alone should the intruders come back.

It wasn't that she felt unsafe, exactly. It didn't seem like anyone really thought that the people who had broken in here last night would return—more like they wanted to play things safe rather than be sorry later. Ruby just felt unsettled. It was kind of hard to explain; she wasn't even sure she could properly explain it to herself.

It was kind of like she didn't really know her place in the world.

Amethyst had the job that she adored, a job that she was good at, and that was contributing to society. Diamond had her art. It brought her happiness and joy, and she made beautiful paintings that were hanging in houses and businesses around the city, bringing happiness and joy to others as well. Sapphire also had the job that she adored—a job where she saved people's lives—and now she had a man who loved her and wanted to share his life with her.

What did she have?

She did people's hair.

That was it.

She enjoyed it, and she liked chatting away with the elderly people in the nursing homes—listening to them reminisce about the past. In a way, she was almost like them. She was only twenty-eight, but she felt like she was eighty-eight, and her reminiscing was about the first seventeen years of her life.

It felt like she had been robbed.

She'd been young and pretty and smart, and she had her whole life ahead of her. A life where she should have been able to do anything she wanted, to have anything she wanted. Now, "what could have been" was gone.

If she hadn't been sold and spent four years as a sex slave, she would have all those things that everyone else had—all those things that Sapphire was about to have.

When she was honest with herself, Ruby admitted that she was jealous of her little sister. It wasn't that she wished that Sapphire *didn't* have those things; it was more that she wished that she *did*.

But that was just human nature.

Right?

It didn't make her a bad person.

So why did she feel like one?

All morning, she'd been replaying the events of last night in her mind. Sitting in the study contemplating killing herself, the glass breaking, finding four strangers in her home, getting into the safe room, Judah arriving ...

And that's where she usually got stuck.

Judah.

He was a great guy; his arms around her last night had made her feel warm even while her body was shaking. He had been like a rock in her crazy, spinning world.

She didn't want to give that up.

So, the logical thing to do was stop avoiding him and let him ask her out, and then say yes.

Simple, right?

On the surface, it sounded like it was simple, and for most people, it probably was. If a guy liked you and you liked them, you dated and found out if you were compatible, and if you were, you took the relationship to the next level.

Easy.

Only she wasn't a normal person.

Far from it.

Her ordeal had irrevocably changed her. She was a woman in her late twenties who was starting to feel like the clock was not on her side and life was ticking by, and she wasn't doing anything to stop it. She had the same needs, wants, and desires. She wanted to be loved. She wanted to belong. She wanted to be something special to someone. She wanted someone to look at her the same way that Gideon looked at Sapphire.

If she liked Judah—and she *did* like him—she should just say yes if he asked her out. He was gorgeous, sweet, and really nice, and she definitely considered him sexy, even though she had mixed feelings about sex.

What was the worst that could happen?

She could get hurt.

Judah could end up betraying like her parents had—not in the same way exactly, but he could definitely earn her trust and then end up using it against her.

Was it worth the risk?

She was giving herself a headache.

Ruby paused in her aimless wandering when she heard what sounded like a key sliding into a lock.

Someone was here.

It had to be one of her sisters because they were using a key.

Still, she stood rigid—on edge—ready to run to the safe room if she didn't recognize whoever came through the door.

"It's only me," a voice called out a second after the door swung open.

She relaxed. It was only Diamond. Her sister had arrived home a little after she had gone up to bed last night and had been up early, saying she wanted to go for a run before they had breakfast. She'd been gone ever since. Ruby didn't know what was going on with her older sister; she seemed skittery and on edge and even withdrawn the last couple of days.

"Look who's with me," Diamond said as she came through the front door.

"I can't believe someone didn't tell me what was going on!" Amethyst raged as she stormed through the house.

"You were at work," she reminded her twin. "According to Sapphire's boss, you were on the scene of an apartment fire, battling to put it out and walking through the flames rescuing people who were trapped. You were saving lives, and there wasn't anything you could do here anyway."

"Are you trying to butter me up?" Amethyst demanded with a glare.

"Of course not." Ruby managed a smile despite the mess of confusing emotions and thoughts that were swirling around inside her head.

"I would have come here if I'd known," Amethyst said, her blue eyes shooting daggers.

"I think that's why Sapphire didn't want anyone to tell you until you got back to the firehouse," Diamond told her.

"Well, Sapphire isn't the boss of this family. I wish someone had told me ... I wish I had been here." She stopped, closed her eyes, dragged in a breath, and Ruby could see her mouth move as she counted to ten. When Amethyst opened her eyes again, it was clear she had calmed herself down a little. "Are you okay?"

"I'm fine," she said. She felt like she had said those words so many times in the last twelve or so hours, and she wasn't sure if they were true. So far, she hadn't really given herself a chance to think too much about what might have happened. She knew she couldn't do that indefinitely, but for now, avoidance was working for her.

"You look okay, and you even sound okay, but for some reason, I don't buy it," her twin sister said shrewdly.

Fighting her natural instinct, which was just to continue to say that she was fine, Ruby went and sank down into the couch cushions. They were soft and cozy and reminded her of Judah's arms. These were her sisters, and they deserved honesty. They were all each other had in the world, but more and more that was starting to change. She was afraid of being left behind and alone, and it was spurring her on to maybe do something about it, but she was so afraid. That annoyed her; there was nothing to be afraid of when it came to dating a nice man that she and her family knew.

"What's going on?" Diamond asked as she and Amethyst joined her on the couch.

"I just feel so mixed up," she said, knowing that was being vague but feeling too confused to try to explain it better.

"That seems pretty normal. For anyone. Having people break into your home and threaten your life is bound to leave you a whole lot more than mixed up. And given our past and what we lived through, I think that just adds to those feelings," Amethyst said.

It wasn't that her sister was wrong; in fact, she was right, but it wasn't her feelings about the break-in that were confusing her the most right now. It was her feelings for Judah. She wanted to tell her sisters. But for some reason, she was embarrassed—which was stupid. When they were teenagers, they would talk about boys all the time. As kids, it had been her and Amethyst and Diamond, and then Sapphire and Emerald. There were only four years between the oldest and youngest, but they'd broken up into those two groups, and she and

Amethyst and Diamond would often stay up late discussing boys they liked.

They could do that again.

"It's Judah," she said in a rush before she could back out.

Immediately, grins broke out on her sisters' faces. "You like him," Diamond said delightedly.

"I guess I do."

"There's no guessing," Amethyst laughed. "Has he asked you out?"

"I think he's tried, but I usually avoid him. Until last night. He was the first one here, and he was great—so comforting and reassuring—and it made me wonder if I'm making a mistake by not giving him a chance."

"Judah is a good guy ... you know him. Sapphire knows him and likes him. He's a cop, and he seems to like you; I don't think you could ask for a better guy to try dating," Amethyst said.

"I know everything you said is right, but in my head, I keep running through all the pros and cons and making a mental list to try to help me make a decision."

"Then let's make an actual list," Diamond said, already standing and grabbing a notepad and pen from the desk in the corner. "If it's going to help you see that you should go for it, then let's do this."

Ruby smiled. She loved her sisters so much. Her future would change from how she'd lived for the last seven years. As scary as that thought was, maybe things didn't have to change *too* much. They would always be sisters—a family—and they would always be there for each other. No matter what.

Maybe she really didn't have anything to lose by giving Judah a chance.

～

11:57 A.M.

As much as he was happy to be at work trying to find evidence that would lead them to the identities of the home invaders, Judah was also looking forward to tonight. It would be weird spending the night—or the next few nights—in the same house as the woman that he liked. He didn't want to use this as an opportunity to try to get close to her. He would never take advantage of Ruby when she was vulnerable, but at the same time, he couldn't deny that it would be nice to have an excuse to hang out with her.

Right now, though, he had to focus on work.

He and Zeb worked their way up and down the Hatchers' block, speaking to residents to see if they witnessed anything unusual. So far, there'd been two home invasions. They weren't specifically looking at the people who lived there. They assumed the killers had chosen the houses at random. There didn't appear to be much point wasting time trying to see if the families had secrets that might have led to them being targeted.

This was definitely the harder way to work a case.

Looking through a victim's life to find something that got them killed gave you something tangible to do. But knowing that the killers likely just picked a house and killed whoever was inside didn't help find them. It didn't give them a direction to move in either, which meant they had to look in every direction at once.

His gaze fell on the Hatcher house. They were currently about four houses down on the opposite side of the street, so he had a good view of the house. It looked quiet. There were cars in the driveway, and the patrol car that Sapphire had requested was there too. It was reassuring to know that, should the home invaders try something crazy and come back to finish what they'd started last night, they wouldn't be able to get to her.

The door in front of them opened, and Judah snapped his attention back to it. He'd be seeing Ruby in a few hours. He should be able to set all thoughts of her aside until tonight.

Probably.

Maybe.

Or not.

"Hi, sir." Judah greeted the elderly man who had opened his front door. The busier he kept, the less likely his mind would wander off to thoughts of Ruby. "I'm Detective Willow, and this is my partner, Detective Tuck."

"Why are you here?" the man asked, bluntly. He was mostly bald with a few tufts of pure white hair sticking out. He had brown eyes that were magnified by his thick-rimmed glasses, and he was dressed in sweatpants, a shirt, and vest. Despite the mass of wrinkles that spoke of his age, the man stood straight, and his gaze was clear and piercing.

"We're here about what happened at the Hatcher house last night," he replied.

"What happened at the Hatcher house?" the man asked, looking over their shoulders at the house in question.

"There was a break-in there last night." Judah didn't think it was likely they'd get anything from this man when he didn't even know that something had happened. "Ruby Hatcher was home alone when four armed people broke in. Did you see anything?"

"Son, I'm ninety-six years old. I'm in bed before the sun goes down and up well after it's risen. I didn't see anything ... I didn't hear anything, but Ruby Hatcher is a sweet girl, and I hope you find whoever terrorized her."

"We're doing everything we can, sir," Zeb said.

"Sorry I couldn't have been more help," the man said, looking and sounding sincere. "Now, if you'll excuse me, I have a lady friend waiting for me to return." He wiggled his bushy white eyebrows at them.

"Okay, thank you for your time," Judah said. There was no point in dragging things out since the man didn't have anything to offer them.

"Good luck," the old man said as he closed the door.

"If I live to be ninety-six, I want to be that guy," Zeb said as they walked back down to the sidewalk. "All that sleep, and still getting the ladies."

Judah laughed; he couldn't argue with that. The guy was certainly making the most of his twilight years. "He looked in pretty good shape, too," he added.

"Some definite life goals in that house," Zeb joked.

"Excuse me."

They both turned around at the small, timid voice that popped up behind them. A young girl who looked to be seventeen or eighteen was standing there. She had short blonde hair in pigtails and nervous brown eyes. Her entire demeanor was anxious—it was practically coming off her in waves.

"Can we help you?" Judah asked, wondering what she wanted and why she had approached them.

"Are you the cops?" the girl asked.

"We are."

"Are you here because of the break-in last night?"

"We are. Do you know something about it?" he asked.

Her eyes darted about nervously, and when she answered, her voice was quiet like she was worried someone would overhear them. "My parents don't like me to go out running at night when it's dark, but I want to run a marathon next month. It's raising money for cancer research and my brother suffered from cancer when he was younger, and …"

"Did you sneak out of the house last night?" Zeb asked.

The girl nodded. "I pretended I was studying, but then I climbed out of the window and started running."

"Did you see something?" Judah asked. He assumed she had, and it was why she had tracked them down. But, so far, she hadn't said much of anything.

The girl nodded again. "I didn't want to get in trouble, but I wanted you to know what I saw. I pretended that I was sick and stayed home, then as soon as my parents left for work, I came and waited here because I was sure you would show up eventually."

"What's your name?" Judah asked.

"Julie Johnstone."

"How old are you, Julie?"

"Seventeen. Almost eighteen," she added.

"Where do you live?"

"Behind the Hatcher house and one over," Julie said, pointing over her shoulder.

"What time did you go running last night?"

"Around eight."

"How long were you out?" he asked. They knew that the break-in at Ruby's house had been a little after nine.

"About an hour?"

"Are you asking us?" Zeb asked.

"No, it was about an hour," she repeated, but she still looked and sounded uncertain. "I wasn't really paying attention; I was just running." From the way she responded, it sounded like running meant something to her, something beyond just running to train for marathons, and he wondered whether running was her happy place. Growing up with a seriously ill sibling would be rough. A lot of time and attention would have to be devoted to the sick child, leaving the other children to fend for themselves.

"Where were you when you saw something?" he asked.

"I was just at the end of the block, just down there." She pointed behind her.

"And what did you see?"

"I saw four people. They were dressed in Halloween costumes. When I first saw them, I thought they must be going to a party. It's only ten days till Halloween, and there are lots of costume parties at the moment."

"What made you realize there was more to it than that?" he asked. Four people in costumes was enough to convince him that she had indeed seen the people who had broken into the Hatcher house, but once they knew what she had seen, he would confirm what the costumes were.

"I heard arguing. Loud arguing. Something told me that I should hide, so I did. I ducked behind a hedge on the Dettman property ... the one on the corner," Julie added.

"Could you hear what they were arguing about?" Zeb asked.

"One guy was angry. He was dressed in black with a skull mask; it kind of glowed freakishly white when it caught the light from the street-lights. He was yelling at some of the others, saying it was their fault that things hadn't worked out. I didn't know what that meant at the time. It wasn't until this morning when my mom told me about the break-in that I realized I had probably seen them. And also, uh, the guy who was yelling, he, uh, he had a gun. I saw him waving it around."

"You said that he was yelling at *some* of the others," Judah said. "Which ones?"

"The one dressed like a witch and one in a ghost costume."

So, he hadn't argued with Black Cat. That was interesting. They thought they were dealing with two couples. What Julie had seen implied that Skull and Black Cat were a couple, and Ghost and Witch were a couple. It also implied that Skull was the ringleader. That was what Gideon had suggested earlier today—that the man Ruby had cut was the one in control. It looked like maybe he was right. Now, how did that help them find the four people they were looking for?

5:28 P.M.

"So, what's the plan tonight?"

Ghost looked over to where Witch was lounging on his couch. She was stretched out, her head propped up on a pile of pillows, red hair fanned out around her face, her legs were crossed at the ankles, and she was filing her already perfectly manicured nails.

How could she be so calm?

Last night had been a disaster, and he wasn't just talking about the safe room fiasco.

Skull had lost it last night—shown his true colors. He'd been waving his gun around at them, threatening them, like it was their fault that he had messed up. He was the one in charge of getting the woman tied up; that was the way he had wanted it. How was it his and Witch's fault that she'd cut him and run? They'd been getting out the rope and duct tape, as well as the cans of spray paint. They'd done what they were supposed to. It was Skull who'd messed up and then thrown a temper tantrum when he couldn't break through the safe room door to get to the woman who had just shown him up.

"Aren't you angry?" he asked.

"At who?" Witch glanced up from her nails for a brief second and then went right back to filing them.

"At Skull," he replied.

"Because he threw a fit last night?"

"Of course, because he threw a fit last night," he growled. *What on earth else would he be angry at Skull for?*

"It's over and done with. No point getting yourself all twisted out of shape," Witch told him.

Why was she so calm?

She'd had a gun waved in her face just like he had.

She'd been threatened with bodily injury just like he had.

She should be hopping mad like he was.

Instead, she was all relaxed and acting like she didn't have a care in the world.

This girl.

She both drove him crazy and drove him wild. As much as he sometimes wanted to throw her out of his life, he equally as badly wanted to throw her down on the bed and make her scream his name as she came. Their relationship was complicated. They fought a lot, and most days, he wondered why they stayed together. Things between them were fiery and hot and passionate, and while that led to explosive arguments, it also led to explosive sex.

Ghost knew he couldn't leave her, even if he tried. Witch somehow seemed to cast a spell over him, and even when he wanted to scream at her and leave, he couldn't.

He guessed he was okay with that. When it boiled down to it, he didn't really want to leave her anyway.

"I don't like Skull thinking that he has all of us under his thumb," he said, stalking over to the couch and lifting Witch's legs. He sat and then rested her legs on his lap, gently stroking the bare skin.

"So, what are you going to do about it?" Witch asked.

"I'm not sure yet," he replied. He wasn't quite sure how he wanted to go about upsetting the balance of power in their group, but he was sure he was going to come up with something. He had to. There was no way he was playing second fiddle to some other guy. No way. "There wasn't supposed to be a leader; we're all supposed to be equal partners in this venture. That was the whole point of the first kill. We each took a life; we're all in this one hundred percent. Why does he get to think that he's the one in charge?"

"Well, if you don't like it, then change it," Witch said simply. "You're right; we did all take a life that first night—a blood bond, a blood oath—binding us all together forever. You can't turn him into the cops without incriminating yourself ... without incriminating me."

"I would never incriminate you," he promised. "Ever." For better or for worse, he loved this woman. No matter how many times she drove him crazy or how many times they argued, they were in this together. Not just in the gang, but life as well. He couldn't imagine his life without Witch in it.

"Well, if you're not planning on turning him into the cops, what are you planning on doing?"

Maybe there was a way to pin all of this on Skull and then kill him, letting the cops think that they had their man without allowing him to turn them in as well. But he wasn't sure that he could kill the other man. Like it or not, they were friends, and you didn't kill a friend.

Maybe he could hit Skull where it really hurt.

His girl.

If he found a way to get to Black Cat, that would effectively destroy Skull without him ever having to lay a hand on the man.

"No."

"No, what?" he asked, looking over at Witch.

"You can't hurt Black Cat. She's my best friend. I don't want you to hurt her. Promise me." Her gray eyes were serious, and he knew she wasn't going to let it go until he told her what she wanted to hear.

"Fine," he snapped. He was running out of ideas. He didn't know how he was going to show Skull that he wasn't the boss, that he wasn't in charge, that they could all do whatever they wanted.

Wait.

Maybe that was it.

Maybe he could just show Skull that he was going to do whatever he wanted, and there wasn't a single thing the other man could do about it.

"You thought of something," Witch said, finally setting down the nail file to give him her full attention.

"I did," he acknowledged.

"Well, what is it?"

"Tonight," he replied. "You'll find out tonight when we hit the next house. I promised you I wouldn't do anything to Black Cat. Now you promise me that you have my back. Tonight, when I make my move, you'll back me up, right?"

She pulled her legs off his lap and knelt up, so she was right beside him, her hands splayed on his chest. "You know I'm with you all the way. Whatever little scheme you're cooking up, you know I'm in."

Ghost put his hands on her hips and lifted her over so that she was straddling his lap. He held her in place as his lips claimed hers, kissing her until his lungs burned and begged him to take a breath.

Tonight, Skull was going to realize what a mistake he had made.

He was going to realize that threatening him and Witch and waving a gun at them—blaming them for something that clearly wasn't their fault—was the biggest mistake of his life.

Ghost had always prided himself on being the biggest, strongest, and smartest in any and every situation that he found himself in.

Nothing was going to change that.

Certainly not some guy who thought he could break the pact that they had made to put himself in charge.

He couldn't wait.

But there was certainly something he could do to pass away the time.

Lifting Witch up, he stood her in front of him and shoved her jeans and panties down her legs, then he pulled her back onto his lap, her legs on either side of his so he had perfect access to the part of her he wanted.

His lips found hers again as his fingertips began to brush up and down the inside of her thighs.

He was in no hurry. They had a couple of hours to fill in, and they had to wait until it was dark before they could make their move. He liked to make Witch squirm. Usually, she was the one who liked to tease him, but today he was going to drive her wild.

At least, that's what he'd thought.

But his girl was never one to be predictable.

Never breaking the kiss, Witch leaned down and grabbed his hand, stilling the lazy trails his fingers were making on her sensitive skin. She took one of his fingers and pushed it inside her, then reached out and with one hand, snapped open his jeans and shoved her hand inside, wrapping her fingers around him.

They kissed, they touched each other, they teased each other—going slow and then faster, then slowing back down, increasing the pressure, then decreasing it. When neither of them could hold out a second longer, he freed himself from his jeans and lifted her, lowering her down, so she took him inside her. He dug his fingers into her thighs as he pumped into her, then he reached between them and touched her, rolling her most sensitive spot between his thumb and forefinger and pushing her over the edge. Her interior muscles clamped around him, sending him spiraling over the edge as well. He didn't stop moving until he had wrung out every last drop of pleasure for both of them.

While he was itching to get things moving tonight, he couldn't deny that there wasn't a better way to pass away the time than doing this.

∿

7:37 P.M.

Ruby stirred the spaghetti sauce, then checked the pasta. It was almost ready. She hummed as she opened the fridge and took out a bottle of sparkling water. Despite everything that had happened in the last twenty-four hours, she felt like she was handling things pretty well.

The day had been uneventful; she hadn't gone to work. Sapphire had insisted that she stay here until they had a handle on the situation, so she had obliged. She and Diamond and Amethyst had chatted for a couple of hours—about Judah and a whole lot of other things. Then she'd curled up in her armchair in her library and lost herself in a book.

Now, she was cooking dinner and looking forward to spending the evening with her sisters. She was sure that Sapphire and Gideon were going to be staying here until the people who had broken in had been apprehended, and she was kind of looking forward to it. It was nice to have all four of them together again. Not that they had really been apart, but with a change in the air—for Sapphire and who knows, maybe for her too—it was nice to just enjoy each other and not take life for granted.

Life could change in an instant.

She and her sisters knew that better than most. Not only had their lives turned upside down when their parents sold them, but one of them had never come home.

Emerald was still out there somewhere.

It was hard knowing that because they knew what was happening to her—if she was still alive. Every day, Ruby felt torn because she didn't want to think that her baby sister was dead, but the alternative was that she was stuck in hell.

What choice was that?

When the four of them had decided they wanted to move out of their aunt's house and get a place of their own, they'd designed this house. When they had designed this house, they'd included a bedroom for Emerald in the hope that one day she would come back to them.

That was six years ago.

Eleven years now since they'd been sold.

How could Emerald still be alive?

Even though there was a hole in their family as long as Emerald wasn't with them, their family was growing. Gideon would soon become a part of the family, and it was kind of fun to think that soon she would have a brother. Growing up, she had always wanted a brother; with five sisters in the same house, sometimes things got kind of crazy. There had been times when she and Amethyst had liked the same boy. They'd fought over clothes and makeup, and although they'd always been there for one another, she'd thought it would be nice to have a boy in the house to break up all the estrogen.

Now when Sapphire married Gideon, she'd have a brother, and if Judah ever asked her out, maybe they'd be adding another male to the family.

After her talk with Diamond and Amethyst, she had decided that if Judah made the first move, then she could take a leap of faith. He would have to make the first move, though. She wasn't in a place yet where she could do something like that on her own. It was like, for her to make her move, she had to know for sure, one hundred percent, that he wanted to be with her, that he saw something in her that made her worthy of his time and attention. Four years being told that you were nothing but an object to be used to bring pleasure to others was a hard thing to overcome.

But if Judah could look past that and see through her pain and scars to the person beneath them, then who knows, maybe she could too.

"Hello," a voice called out as the front door opened. Sapphire was home, and she could hear Diamond emerging from her art studio and Amethyst from her gym.

Her family.

She loved them so much.

They were everything to her, and no matter how things ended up working out with Judah, she was eternally grateful that she was no longer all alone in the world.

"Dinner will be on the table in just a few minutes," she called out as everyone made their way down to the living room.

"Spaghetti!" Sapphire broke out into a huge grin as soon as she walked into the kitchen. "I'm starving."

"You're always starving." Amethyst rolled her eyes.

"Starving for me," Gideon said, so straight faced that all of them laughed.

"You have such an ego." Sapphire swatted him playfully on the arm.

Ruby still wasn't quite used to seeing Sapphire so calm and relaxed and easygoing. Of all of them, Sapphire had been perhaps the angriest. Trauma often displayed itself in different ways, and while hers had zeroed in on depression, Sapphire's had picked fury. But Gideon had changed all of that. He had given her permission to be angry, and that had validated her feelings and taken away the power they had over her. She was glad that her sister had found someone to help her carry around her burden, and she hoped that maybe she might find it too.

"You love that about me," Gideon told Sapphire, putting his hand on her hip and pulling her closer, so their bodies touched. He kissed her cheek and then just held her close.

"I suppose," Sapphire said, but her love for Gideon was written all over her face. She adored him.

"You two are adorable," Diamond told the happy couple.

"Thank you," Gideon said with a grin.

"Now, let's eat," Sapphire said, a little uncomfortable with all the attention.

"Salad is in the fridge, and there's garlic bread in the oven," Ruby said as she drained the pasta and started spooning it into bowls.

"I got the salad," Amethyst said.

"I'll grab the garlic bread," Diamond said.

"I'll get drinks. Gideon, can you get glasses, please?" Sapphire asked.

"Sure thing." Gideon released her and went to the cupboard.

For the next minute, they set the table and collected the food and drinks, and then they all sat down and started eating.

"So," Sapphire said slowly, once she'd taken her first mouthful of spaghetti.

The way she said it implied that whatever was coming next might be something that Ruby didn't want to hear, so she raised a suspicious brow. No one else looked confused, and all of a sudden, everyone was very interested in their meal, so she knew that this was all about her. She had to assume that it had something to do with the break-in last night, because what else could it be?

"So?" Ruby prompted when her little sister didn't say anything else.

"Well, this isn't really my fault because I thought that there was another option, but they all ganged up on me, and I ended up getting out voted—"

"Stop rambling, and just tell me. You're making me nervous," she interrupted.

"It's really nothing to be nervous about. It's just that Judah and Zeb found a witness who saw the intruders leaving here last night, and apparently, the one you cut was pretty angry. We were already wondering if there was a chance they might come back and try to finish what they came here for, so Gideon and I are going to stay here until this case is wrapped up."

"Oh." She let out a relieved breath. "That's all? I thought that you two would be staying here."

Gideon nudged Sapphire. "Stop stalling."

"Well, Gideon, Debra, Elijah, Zeb, and Judah all thought that I need to sleep sometime, so there should be someone else here too," Sapphire admitted.

So she was going to have to have a stranger stay here for a while. That wasn't ideal; she didn't really like meeting new people, but it was what it was. She could deal with it, considering the alternative. "Who's going to be staying here? Is it one person, or will it be someone different every day?"

"Actually, it's someone you know," Sapphire answered.

Ruby assumed that meant Elijah would be staying with them since he was Sapphire's partner. She knew him, and he was a nice guy. It wouldn't be so bad having him staying here, and hopefully, it wouldn't be for long anyway. "Who is it?" she asked again, just as the doorbell rang.

"That's him," Sapphire said, standing and walking down the hall to open the front door.

She wondered who it was and why Sapphire was so weird about it. What was the worst it could be?

"Hi," a voice said.

She froze.

There was her answer as to how bad it could be.

And it wasn't bad.

But it wasn't good either.

It was Judah.

Judah was going to be staying here in her house for the next few days.

That filled her with a weird mixture of nervous excitement. Would he ask her out? Would he keep things professional? Did he even still want to ask her out after she had avoided him every other time he'd been here?

Ruby turned at the table to see that Judah was watching her. Their eyes met, and she felt her stomach fill with butterflies. "Hi."

~

9:44 P.M.

. . .

"Can't you just close your eyes and go to sleep, my sweet little baby?" Tiffany Kendrick said as she rocked her four-month-old son in her arms.

It had been a *long* day.

One of those tear-your-hair-out, bawl-your-eyes-out, collapse-in-a-heap kind of days.

She loved being a mom. Even more than that, she loved that she worked from home, so she was able to spend each and every day with her little boy whom she loved more than life itself. But as much as she loved her baby and wouldn't change a single thing about her life even if she could, there were days when being a mom was just plain hard.

It was hard breastfeeding.

It was hard starting her son on solids.

It was hard not getting enough sleep and spending most days in a fog.

It was hard when her baby cried for hours on end.

It was hard feeling like she was on a never-ending circle of changing diapers, doing laundry, and cleaning messes.

And yet, as hard as it was, she loved this tiny little human being and felt so lucky to be his mom.

But still, it would be nice if he just went to sleep this one time.

"Come on, honey, just close your eyes, you've been crying on and off all day," she said as she rocked him in her arms and walked up and down the nursery. Usually, Marcus was such a happy little thing. He loved to be cuddled, but he also liked to lie on his play mat and play with his toys. He laughed a lot, and the look on his chubby little face every time he saw her warmed her heart, even on the coldest of days.

"Daddy to the rescue."

Tiffany turned toward the door as her husband came into the room. "I thought you went to bed already. You have to be up early in the morning to get to your conference on time."

"The little guy is having a tough day ... you must be too. Why don't you go grab a shower, and I'll stay with him, put him to bed and then meet you in bed. Maybe we can even have a little grown-up time before we go to sleep." He winked at her, and she couldn't help but smile. They hadn't been intimate since the baby had been born. She'd been too tired and too embarrassed about the extra pregnancy weight she hadn't lost yet, so she'd kind of hinted that he should keep his distance, but today the idea of making love to her husband actually made her feel good.

"Sounds like a plan," she agreed.

"Hashtag winning," Ace joked as he reached out to take the baby.

Tiffany kissed Marcus's head and passed him over to Ace, then kissed her husband's cheek as she headed for their bathroom. The prospect of a long, hot, uninterrupted shower was delightful. Usually, she squeezed in a shower while the baby was napping—in between chores and work; she'd gotten her system down to a solid three minutes —but tonight she was going to take her time and just relax.

She stripped off her clothes, leaving them in a pile on the bedroom floor and walked into the en suite. She turned the shower on and got it as hot as she could stand, and when the room was filled with steam, she stepped under the spray.

It was heaven.

Tiffany soaped up her hair, then conditioned, and then lathered herself up, scrubbing every inch of her skin until she felt cleaner than she had in four months. When she was all clean, she just stood there, letting the hot water pour down on her, drumming at her skin like a gentle massage.

By the time she turned the tap off and stepped out of the shower, she grabbed a fluffy towel and wrapped it around herself. She heard footsteps in the bedroom.

"I'll be right there," she called out, wondering how Ace had managed to get Marcus to sleep. Sometimes her husband was a miracle worker. He worked hard, spending long hours at a job he tolerated but didn't love, then coming home and spending time with the baby and with her. She loved him so much, and she loved their little family. One day, when they had recovered from baby number one, they might add a couple more kids to their family. It had to get easier the older they got, right?

Not bothering to put her clothes back on or stay wrapped up in the towel—baby body or not, her husband loved her and thought she was beautiful, so she should stop being ashamed to be naked around him— Tiffany sauntered into the bedroom.

Then froze.

It wasn't Ace lounging on the bed. It was a man dressed in a ghost costume holding a gun and standing in the middle of her bedroom.

Her first thought was her family.

Had this man hurt her son and her husband?

Without thinking about what she was doing or the consequences of her actions, she started for the door. She had to know if Ace and Marcus were okay.

She made it only halfway when something hard slammed into the back of her head, and she dropped to the carpet. The world was spinning around her, but she was spurred on by fear for the people she loved. She tried to get to her feet, staggered, and was roughly grabbed from behind. The ghost man bound her wrists with rope, and although she fought against him, he was much stronger than her and began to drag her toward the stairs.

"Did you hurt them?" she asked. "Did you hurt my family?"

"Relax, lady, no one is dead," Ghost replied.

That didn't reassure her.

The word *yet* hovered in the air.

Death was coming.

For all of them.

"I see blood, did you hurt her?" A man dressed in black with a skull mask stalked toward them as Ghost walked her into the dining room.

"She was trying to run," Ghost said, sounding a little like a petulant child.

"If we don't stick to the plan, that's when the cops are going to find us. Don't do anything that might end up leaving forensics behind," Skull snapped. He was obviously the one in charge, but from the feel of things, Ghost wanted to change that. She did *not* want herself, and her family caught up in some power struggle between two deranged men.

"This isn't a one-man show. You're not the boss here. We're all in this together. If I want to do things a little differently this time, nothing is going to stop me," Ghost said, walking her into the middle of the room.

As she moved forward, Skull no longer blocked her view of the room, and she saw her husband sitting tied to a chair, duct tape over his mouth. His terrified eyes found hers, and she locked onto them, seeking his strength and reassurance. She didn't know what he could do to save them, but just having him there was reassuring.

"Get down on your knees and lick the floor," Ghost said, jabbing her shoulder and trying to push her down.

Lick the floor?

What possible reason could he have for wanting her to do that?

"No?" Ghost said to her. "Maybe this will change your mind." He nodded to a third person, a smaller one who was probably a woman. She was dressed as a witch, and she had a knife in her hand. She walked over, so she was standing behind Ace and slashed the knife across his chest.

"No, don't!" she shrieked as pain flared across her husband's face. "Don't hurt him."

"Then do what I said," Ghost said smugly.

Tears streamed down her face as she awkwardly got onto her knees. With her hands bound behind her back, it was hard to balance, and her face smashed into the hardwood floors as she leaned down to lick it.

"Smart lady." Ghost laughed delightedly as she complied with his demands. "Now, lie down on your back, legs spread wide," he ordered. It wasn't until he said that that Tiffany realized she was still naked. The terror over her family's fate had shoved everything else out of her mind.

Apparently, she didn't move quickly enough because Ghost nodded at Witch, who pushed the knife into Ace's shoulder, making him grunt in pain—the sound muffled through duct tape.

"I'm sorry," she sobbed, rolling sideways, so she was lying down on her side, then wriggling over onto her back, she spread her legs wide as she had been instructed so that her husband wasn't hurt again.

"This is ridiculous," Skull huffed, and Tiffany prayed for a reprieve. *If they were going to kill them, then just do it. Why were they intent on humiliating her first?*

"What, you're not finding this fun?" Ghost asked. Crouching between her legs, he curled his fingers into a fist, then shoved it inside her. She'd given birth, but that was nothing compared to the ripping pain that spread throughout her body.

So, it wasn't just death that was going to find them tonight; they were also going to be tortured.

Where was Marcus?

She hadn't seen him in the dining room. Did that mean he was already dead?

Tiffany would gladly endure the most excruciating agony if it meant that her son could live.

~

10:12 P.M.

He felt both uncomfortable and completely at home here.

Judah had been at the Hatcher house for a whole two and a half hours, and already he didn't want to leave. He liked being here surrounded by people, and something with Ruby felt different. It wasn't that she had said anything, she'd sat quietly—as was her way—while they ate dinner, and then watched and kept to herself while they'd moved to the couches, but he could just feel that something was different. Maybe she'd had second thoughts about always avoiding him.

She couldn't avoid him now.

He was living here for the foreseeable future, so they were going to have to get along.

Not that they didn't. Ruby just ignored him. Not in a mean, rude way, just in a way that made it clear she wasn't up to conversations with men she didn't know. Now that they were living in the same house, he was going to try to find a time to get her alone so they could talk. Maybe once she realized that she didn't have to be afraid of him, then they could be friends, and once they were friends, she might be more likely to say yes when he asked her out.

Because he *was* going to ask her out.

He'd wait until the time was right. He didn't want her to feel like he was using this situation to his advantage. He would wait until he knew that she felt comfortable around him, and then he'd ask her out to dinner. Nothing fancy—no pressure—just dinner, the two of them, and maybe a movie. They wouldn't have to talk much at a movie, so it shouldn't make Ruby feel awkward.

Judah glanced over at her and found that she was watching him.

As soon as their eyes met, her gaze jumped away, her porcelain skin turned bright red, and he knew that she was embarrassed. He just didn't know why. Of course, he knew about her past, and he understood why she might be apprehensive about dating, but it wasn't like he was just some random stranger. He worked with one of her sisters. He was over here probably once every two weeks, at least, and she knew him. She knew that he wouldn't hurt her, and she knew that he knew about what happened to her when she was younger. She also knew that she was safe with him.

Which meant there was something else making her hold back and hide away.

Something he was determined to get to the bottom of.

Now he had the perfect opportunity to do just that.

Sooner or later, it had to be just the two of them. One of her sisters couldn't hover around them all the time, although he was sure Sapphire would give it a pretty good shot. But Gideon was a great guy, and being a psychiatrist, he was observant enough to know that this was something both he and Ruby needed and would, no doubt, make sure Sapphire gave them some space.

"I think I'm going to head to bed," Diamond announced, standing and stretching. "I have an art class before work in the morning, and I was out late last night. I'll see you guys in the morning."

"I might head up too," Amethyst said, also standing. "I just might be exhausted enough to fall into a deep enough sleep that I won't dream."

He knew about the fire that Amethyst and her fellow firefighters had fought the day before, and how they had walked through the flames and smoke several times rescuing both people and pets who hadn't been able to make it out in time. He couldn't imagine what that was like, but surely it must feel like walking through the very fires of Hell. He respected Amethyst and what she did every day.

"We'll go up too," Gideon said, taking Sapphire's hand and trying to pull her up.

"We're supposed to—well, *I'm* supposed to—be here to make sure that no one tries to break in here tonight. I'm not going to bed this early," Sapphire argued.

"That's why Judah is here to help keep watch," Gideon reminded her.

"Yes, to *help*," Sapphire said with exaggerated patience.

"I could stand here and argue with you until the cows come home, but instead, I'm just going to do this." Gideon leaned down and picked Sapphire up, draping her across his shoulder and started walking for the stairs.

"Put me down!" Sapphire shrieked, her hands curling into the back of Gideon's sweater.

"Night, ladies," Gideon said, ignoring his fiancée's insistence that he put her down.

"Why am I marrying you?" Sapphire demanded.

"Because you love me," Gideon laughed.

"You're lucky that I do," Sapphire huffed.

"Those two are crazy," Amethyst said when the couple had disappeared up the stairs.

"Crazy in love," Diamond added, a slight bit of wistfulness in her tone. He wondered if there was someone that she was interested in but had yet to do anything about it.

He could commiserate. He'd been interested in Ruby since the first time he saw her. It had been months, and he hadn't made a single move yet.

Until now.

Now he was going to stop hiding in the shadows and do something that would make himself happy. No more living in his own dark past. Now he was ready to leave it behind and walk into the light.

"If you change your mind and want to go and stay in the other bedroom upstairs, you can," Diamond told him.

He felt both Amethyst and Ruby tense.

It wasn't really the *other* bedroom.

Judah knew it was the one that would be Emerald's if she was ever found. There was no way he was going to upset them by sleeping in the room that was a beacon of hope to them.

"I'm good down here on the couch," he assured her.

"Well, you know the offer is still there. Night."

"Night," Amethyst echoed.

The two disappeared up the stairs, and then it was just him and Ruby.

Alone.

"If everyone else is going to go to bed, then I may as well, too," Ruby said. Her blue eyes skittered across him before darting away to look at something else.

"Night," he said. He wasn't going to push her tonight. Everything that had happened the night before was too fresh. He'd let her get used to him being here over the next couple of days, and then he'd ask her out.

Ruby stood, took a couple of steps toward the stairs, then stopped. "You really can use the fifth bedroom if you want to. We don't mind."

Since he knew how hard it was for her to say that, he was touched. That bedroom was more than just a room with a bed in it to the Hatcher sisters. It was hope that one day they would all be reunited again. While he prayed that happened, he wasn't holding out much hope that it would. The odds were Emerald was long since dead. But the odds had been against *all* the sisters. One by one, however, they'd been rescued or escaped and came home. Maybe one day, Emerald really would be found.

"Thank you, I'm going to stay down here though. That way, if anyone does try to break in, they won't even make it up the stairs. I don't want them anywhere near you."

She turned around to face him. "Do you really think they might come back?"

"I don't think we know enough about them yet to determine that, but since we're talking about your safety, there is no way that I'd risk it." He meant that one hundred percent. There was nothing that he wouldn't do to make sure she wasn't in danger.

She smiled at him, and this time, even though her cheeks pinked, she didn't break eye contact.

"Ruby," he began.

"Not tonight," she interrupted. "I know that you want to ask me out—at least, I think that you do." She looked at him, awaiting confirmation. When he nodded, she continued, "And I'm not saying that when you do ask, I'll say no, but tonight, I just need this to be over first before we can look to the future. Once this is all over, then maybe ..." She didn't need to finish her sentence.

"Sweet dreams, Ruby," he said, and she smiled again before turning and hurrying upstairs.

That smile.

He could look at that smile for the rest of his life.

If he played his cards right and everything worked out the way he hoped, maybe he would be looking at that smile for the rest of his life.

Unable to wipe the smile off his own face, he tidied up downstairs, put the last of the dishes in the dishwasher, checked that both the front and back door were locked, as well as all the windows, then he switched off the lights and settled down onto the couch. It might not be the most comfortable night of his life, but he couldn't be any happier.

CHAPTER
Eight

October 23rd
12:42 A.M.

Ruby set her e-reader down.

Tears were blurring her eyes, but the good kind. *Dark Side of Chemistry* by Ryleigh Sloan had been a roller coaster ride. At times, it had her fuming and made her want to throw her e-reader across the room; at other times, it had made her cry, and it certainly had her staying up till nearly one in the morning because she just couldn't put it down until she knew how it was going to end.

Books were her happy place.

As a child, she had loved to read, but when she came back home following her ordeal, it had become her lifeline. When she couldn't face her own life, she had escaped into someone else's. She'd lived a million lives in the last seven years and visited a million worlds, and she loved every one of them.

She yawned and leaned over to switch off the light on her nightstand. She snuggled down under her covers. As soon as her eyes closed, the darkness in the room began to seep inside her.

It was like this every night, which was why she usually read until the early hours of the morning. That way, she could at least keep the bad thoughts that creeped into her mind at bay for as long as possible.

Ruby had hoped tonight might be different. She had made real progress in moving forward with her life. She'd told her sisters about the feelings she'd been harboring for Judah, and she had even gone as far as to tell Judah. Once this was over and the people who had broken in here had been caught and were safely in prison, then she was ready to see if things would work out with her and Judah. She wasn't sure whether they would, but she was willing to take that risk.

It was a huge step forward.

And one she hadn't been sure she would ever be in a place to take.

Maybe she should go and see Judah. He was downstairs in the living room—maybe still awake. They could talk for a while, get to know each other a little better.

She almost threw back the covers and climbed out of bed, but at the last minute, she changed her mind. It was late, and he was probably asleep anyway. They had plenty of time to get to know each other. There was no rush, no pressure—she just wanted to take this slowly.

Instead, she cleared her mind, imagining a black, empty room. She kept the room black and empty; if she let even one tiny little thought get in there, she would never sleep.

This was how she went to sleep every night, and having perfected her system over seven long years, it didn't take long for her to drift off.

In her dreams, the blackness faded away. Her quiet, peaceful place was replaced by the house of the man she had stabbed to escape her life of hell.

Her minder was there. He opened the car door, escorted her to the front door, and delivered her on a platter to a man he knew was going to beat and rape her.

He didn't care because she was nothing.

She didn't matter.

She was just a toy he loaned out to make money.

The man in the house grabbed her arm and pulled her inside.

She tried to fight him, but she couldn't seem to remember how.

It was like her arms and legs belonged to someone else, and she had no control over them.

Against her will, he pulled her up the stairs and threw her onto a bed.

Metal handcuffs were snapped around her wrists and her ankles, binding her to the bed.

Then he stood above her.

Snarling.

He held a whip in his hands, and he began to strike her with it.

Over and over again.

Ruby tried to hold her sobs in.

She wasn't really a person; she shouldn't be crying and fussing.

Some of her clients didn't like it when the girls cried or fussed.

Clients.

She hated that Igor and the others called them that.

They weren't her clients.

They were evil men who paid money to abuse girls.

Girls like her.

She was a girl, she wasn't nothing, she was a person who mattered.

"Scream," the man with the whip ordered. "Struggle."

On autopilot, she did as she was told.

It was *always* easier to do as she was told.

Ruby struggled.

Ruby screamed.

1:19 A.M.

Judah made another round of checking doors and windows.

Everything was still locked. Nothing was moving outside. It was after one, and there had been no signs of the killers. Hopefully, that meant that they weren't stupid, and they weren't going to try to make a second attempt at coming back here, but who knew. They might have thought they'd wait a day or two before trying it, maybe assuming that cops would be watching the house but would sooner or later become complacent.

That was never going to happen.

So long as Ruby was in this house, he was going to stay here to make sure that she was safe.

Especially now.

He knew now that his feelings for her were reciprocated and that she was willing to trust him and see if they made a good couple. Just how hard that was for her to do wasn't lost on him. She had trusted her parents, and they had smashed that trust into smithereens. To try trusting again was terrifying for her, but she was willing to do it.

For him.

He would never do anything to make her regret her decision.

The two of them were more alike than she realized.

There was a lot about him that no one knew—only a few people from his past and his family. But no one here. It was part of the reason he'd moved here. He wanted to be where no one knew about him, where no one would judge him, where no one would use his weaknesses against him.

When he moved here, he hadn't intended to ever tell anyone, certainly not his colleagues who were quickly becoming his friends, but then he had met Ruby. Something inside her called out to something inside him. They were similar in so many ways, and he sensed that she needed to know that she wasn't alone, that she wasn't the only one who struggled with certain things. He knew that probably sooner, rather than later, he was going to wind up telling her about his past.

Finished with his eighth check for the night, he went back to the couch and opened up his laptop. In between taking a couple of power naps, he'd been working the case. As much as he was enjoying staying here, he wanted Ruby to be able to let go of the fear that the people who had broken into her home and intended to kill her might come back.

Settling into his work zone, he didn't know how much time had passed, but the next thing he knew, an ear-piercing scream shattered the quiet night.

His head darted up.

Ruby.

Taking the stairs three at a time, he was just reaching the second floor by the time Diamond, Amethyst, Sapphire, and Gideon, were coming out of their rooms.

"Is that Ruby?" he asked.

"She has nightmares often," Amethyst told him.

He hated that.

He hated that even in her sleep, she couldn't get any relief from the trauma her parents had thrown her into.

What kind of people did that?

What kind of people sold their own children to human traffickers?

It was so unbelievable to him that he could barely believe that it was true. Except he knew that it was. He was so grateful that Sapphire had been able to testify against her parents and send them straight to prison where they belonged.

Sapphire was opening the door to her sister's room when he stopped her. "Let me go in," he said.

"Why?" Sapphire demanded. "She doesn't really know you; she'll probably be startled waking up from a nightmare to find a stranger in her bedroom."

"I'm hardly a stranger," he reminded her.

"Maybe it would be a good idea," Gideon told his fiancée.

"Is that how our marriage is going to be? You always taking everyone else's side against mine?" Sapphire shot arrows at Gideon.

"Only when you're wrong," Gideon answered smoothly. He never seemed to get worked up by her outbursts. He seemed to be able to see through Sapphire's barriers and know that her anger was just a coping mechanism.

"I think it would be a good idea," Diamond ventured.

"Fine," Sapphire huffed. "All of you gang up against me then. Let Judah go in there; do whatever you want." With that, she turned and stomped off back into her bedroom.

"She's just scared," Gideon explained. "She blames herself for not being here when those people broke in."

"It's fine," he assured the others. He wasn't offended by Sapphire's protectiveness of her sisters; in fact, he loved it. He loved that Ruby wasn't alone and that she had such fiercely loyal people in her corner.

"Good luck," Amethyst said as she, Diamond, and Gideon all returned to their respective bedrooms.

Alone, he turned to Ruby's room and eased the door open. Although she hadn't screamed again, he suspected that she wasn't awake, and from the whimpering moans falling from her lips as he stepped into her bedroom, he knew he was right. Ruby was lying in the middle of a huge four poster bed. She was tangled in the bed clothes and thrashing frantically against them.

He quietly crossed the room. The last thing he wanted to do was startle her. Standing beside the bed, he reached out and lightly touched her shoulder. Her skin was ice cold but covered in a thin sheen of sweat.

She continued to fight the sheets, and he gave her a firm shake. "Ruby. Wake up."

She whimpered, trapped in her dreams.

"Ruby, it's Judah. You're dreaming ... it's just a dream ... wake up now." He shook her again, firmer this time.

She didn't wake up.

The look of pure unadulterated terror on her face hit him directly in the gut. Where was she trapped right now? He hated seeing her suffering like this. He wanted to take away her pain and sorrow and make it his own so that she never had to deal with it again.

"Ruby, wake up." He placed his hands on her shoulders and dragged her up and out of bed, ripping another scream from her lips as her eyes popped open, filled with terror and wildly scanning the room.

1:35 A.M.

She was ripped off the bed. The handcuffs that had bound her seemed to disappear. Ruby wasn't sure where they'd gone.

She hadn't done what he wanted.

He was angry with her.

She searched wildly for something to use as a weapon.

Last time she'd stabbed him and run, but this time, she didn't have a knife.

She didn't have anything.

Ruby screamed and swung her fist.

If he was going to kill her, she wasn't going down without a fight.

Her fist connected with something. She wasn't sure what, but she heard someone grunt in pain.

Good.

She'd hurt him.

"You have a wicked right hook," a voice said.

A voice.

A familiar voice.

Judah.

It was Judah.

She blinked, and her vision cleared.

She wasn't in that bedroom with that man. She was in her own bedroom, and the man who was here with her was Judah—someone she liked and respected, someone she knew would never hurt her.

Only she might have hurt him.

Judah was rubbing the side of his face, and she could see a red mark where her fist had connected.

"Oops, sorry about that. Are you okay?" she asked, reaching out to run her fingers over his cheek. She wasn't particularly strong—she didn't spend hours working our every day like Amethyst and Sapphire —but she had been hyped up on adrenalin and trapped in a dream where she was fighting for her life, and she hoped she hadn't seriously injured him.

"I'm fine," he assured her, catching hold of her fingers and bringing her hand to clasp between his. "But you're not ... you're like ice." He began to vigorously rub her hand, sharing his warmth with her.

Ruby watched him. None of this was new to her; she had night-mares at least once a week and was used to waking up freezing cold and drenched in sweat—disoriented and confused and embarrassed—always embarrassed. Usually, it was one of her sisters who would come in here, shaking her until she was finally dislodged from the dream world and was brought back to the real one.

It wasn't that she liked living her life like this. She hated the nightmares, but for her, they were just a part of life, and she had to make the best of it and deal with them as best as she could. Usually, after being woken by one of her sisters after a nightmare, she would flick on the light, pick up her e-reader, and read another book, but tonight she wouldn't be doing that. Tonight, Judah was here, in her room, and she had a sense that he wouldn't be leaving any time soon.

"You're shaking," Judah said, looking concerned. He reached over and pulled the blanket free from the tangled mess she'd twisted it into as she'd fought her dream demons. Then he wrapped the blanket around her shoulders, picked her up, and carried her over to the armchair in the corner of her room where she loved to curl up and read, where he sat down with her on his lap.

She had never been held like this before.

When she was a very small child, she'd sat on her parents' laps, but then she'd grown up, and while she'd had a boyfriend, one she'd slept with, they'd never been intimate like this. At the time, she'd thought that she was in love. Looking back now, she knew that at seventeen, she hadn't even known what love was.

But now ...

Now, she thought she might have come to understand it. At least enough to know that the man who was holding her so gently on his lap, cocooned in his arms, was someone whom she might be able to fall in love with.

"Are you sure I didn't hurt you too badly?" she asked. She felt horrible knowing she'd hurt him when he was just trying to help her, even if it had been an accident.

"I'll be fine, but whoever taught you to hook like that did an excellent job."

"It was Sapphire, and she'll be happy to hear that."

"I bet she would. I bet she wishes she was the one who'd hit me," he said lightly.

Ruby couldn't help but smile at that. Her sister wasn't actually violent, but she was protective, and she did like to always be in control.

She was surprised that Sapphire hadn't insisted on coming in here. "I'm shocked she let you come and wake me up."

"She got out voted."

"Gideon has been so good for her. He pushes her and challenges her. He drives her crazy, but he loves her so much, and she knows it. She was lucky to find him." Had she also been lucky? Had she also found someone who would end up loving her the same way Gideon loved Sapphire? It was too early to know that, but she could certainly hope. "I'm glad you're here," she admitted.

"I'm glad too," he said, adjusting her on his lap so that she was pressed right up against his chest.

For a moment, a teeny thread of panic took hold inside her.

Being this close to a man for the first time since she had escaped reminded her of those four long years she had spent as a sex slave.

Her breathing quickened a little, and an involuntary shudder rippled through her even though she was no longer cold.

That relaxed and hopeful spirit that had been growing inside her immediately went out. What was the point of thinking about the future and maybe having the same things everyone else had—the same things Sapphire had—if she was always going to be afraid of men?

Of course, Judah noticed her mood change, and because he was a good guy and one she knew she never needed to be afraid of—she really did know that even if her body tried to tell her differently—he quickly moved her farther away from his body, so she was perched on the edge of his lap.

That wasn't what she wanted.

She didn't want to push him away.

The reaction she'd had to being so close to a man wasn't a conscious one. It was just a conditioned response. Igor and his men had conditioned her to be afraid and to doubt everyone, to try to fade into the background, so you didn't get hurt—or, at least, you minimized it.

But it wasn't the way she wanted to be.

She didn't want to keep reliving her past. She didn't want to be afraid anymore. She didn't want to keep thinking about ending her life. She didn't want to be the person that she was.

She wanted to be free.

"You don't have to do that," she said, wanting to move closer again but not knowing whether or not she should. She had no idea what to do when it came to having a healthy and successful adult relationship.

"I don't want to pressure you," Judah replied.

Which was what she liked the most about him.

He had tried to get her alone to ask her out for months now, and when she made an excuse and avoided him, he never kept coming after her; he had given her space. Even now, when he was going to be staying here for a while, he had been clear about what he wanted without making her feel uncomfortable.

In fact, he made her feel the opposite.

"I don't feel pressured, I just feel ..." She trailed off, unsure of how to explain. "Confused," she finally settled on. It was the only word that completely summed up her life.

"That, I understand," he said, drawing her close again.

The way he said it told her that he really did understand what it meant to be confused about everything, including yourself. Ruby realized that she didn't really know anything about Judah. She knew that he was a cop and a good one, and she knew that she trusted him and felt safe around him, but that was it. She wanted to know more about him, his childhood, what had led him to become a cop, what were his hobbies and his interests and his favorite food.

Before she could ask him, a gigantic yawn nearly split her head in two. She was tired, and she didn't usually have two lots of nightmares on the same night, so the idea of going back to bed wasn't a terrible one. There was plenty of time to get to know Judah. There was no rush, and that was what made this so much easier. She didn't have to make any decisions right now. She could just go slow and wait to see where things went.

"You should get some more sleep," Judah said, noticing the sudden wave of tiredness that had washed over her. He carried her over to the bed, laying her down and tucking her in.

Tucking her in.

Could this guy get any better?

He was sweet, made her feel safe, held her in his arms, and he tucked her into bed when she was tired.

Ruby really could see something developing between them.

"Judah?" she said as he switched off the light.

"Yeah?"

"Do you mind spending the night in here?" It wasn't that she was afraid of more bad dreams, she was just tired of being alone, and falling asleep with Judah in the room just felt right.

"Of course not. I'll sleep in the armchair."

He came and stood beside the bed, looking down at her. It was dark, and she couldn't see him properly, but she could feel his eyes on her. They were like a warm caress, touching every inch of her body and making her feel something she had never experienced before.

"Goodnight, Ruby. Sweet dreams." Judah stooped and pressed a tender kiss to her forehead.

"Night, Judah." As he walked over to the armchair and she rolled onto her side and snuggled the blankets up to her chin, Ruby wondered whether maybe she should have asked him to spend the night sleeping beside her in her bed.

7:47 A.M.

This was not how Judah wanted to start his day.

It was never how he wanted to start his day, but after spending the night holding Ruby in his arms and then watching her sleep, he particularly didn't want to be out here first thing in the morning walking into a new crime scene. He wanted to be back at the Hatcher house, cooking breakfast for Ruby, getting to know her better, letting her get to know him better.

But he wasn't.

Because this was his job, and this was where he had to be right now.

The home invaders had struck again. Another innocent family killed because some kids—assuming Gideon was right and they were college kids—were bored and wanted to have some fun.

"Are we sure this is the same gang?" Zeb asked as they walked through the house and into the dining room. "The MO is completely different than the other break-ins."

"Not completely different," he said. "They broke a back window to gain entry to the house."

"That's true."

"And since they got distracted at Ruby's house, we don't really know what they would have done if she hadn't gotten into the safe room." Every time Judah thought about that night, it felt like his heart wanted to make a quick exit from his body. If she had been just a little slower getting inside the safe room, if the other gang members hadn't been distracted, or if she hadn't had a weapon on her, then he wouldn't have walked into her house to find her hiding and afraid. He would have walked into her house and found her dead body lying on the ground or tied to a chair.

He would have lost her before he even had a chance to have her—before he had a chance to see if the two of them could have been happy together—see if maybe they could fall in love.

Who was he kidding?

He was already in love with her—or very close to it, at least.

Whenever they were together, everything just felt right. It felt like that was where he was supposed to be. No other person had ever made him feel that way, and he wanted to spend the rest of his life with that feeling and the woman who gave it to him.

Okay, realistically, he knew it was too soon to be thinking the L word. Yes, they'd known each other for months, but they didn't really know each other. All he knew was that he thought she was beautiful, sweet, and stronger than he could ever hope to be. That was a pretty good foundation to build on. Plus, he knew that she liked him and that she wanted to find out what could grow between them.

Judah never thought he would say this, but he was glad that the Hatcher sisters had such a dark past because if they didn't, they'd have never put a safe room in their living room. He hadn't lost Ruby, and they had the whole rest of their lives to get to know one another, and for that, he was so very grateful.

"Still, this is a huge jump from breaking into the Cochrane house, tying everyone up, and shooting them, to this ..." Zeb waved his hand at the scene before him.

He couldn't argue with that.

While the scene at the Cochrane house had been simple—not graphic—this one was the complete opposite.

"They're devolving, already," he added. If the gang had gotten to this point this quickly, then what were they going to be like when they hit another house tonight? So far, they'd been breaking into a house every night. That meant that in less than twenty-four hours, another family would be dead. And they wouldn't stop there. They'd gotten a taste for blood, and it was going to take more and more to satiate it.

"I can't even imagine what they're going to do next," Zeb said. "What could they do that is worse than this?"

Judah didn't have an answer for that.

He honestly couldn't think of what anyone could do to another person that was worse than what these people had done to the Kendrick family.

Ace Kendrick was sitting, tied to one of the dining room chairs, just like the Cochrane family had been left. But, unlike the other family, Ace didn't just have a bullet hole in his head. There were at least four other wounds that Judah could see, and from the amount of blood streaking his clothes, he was sure there were more.

As bad as Ace looked, his wife looked worse.

Tiffany lay on the floor a couple of feet away from her husband. There were four bullet holes in her head, and although there didn't appear to be any other wounds, there was blood between her legs.

Even without hearing the medical examiner say it, Judah already knew that she had been raped.

A stone settled in his stomach.

This could have been Ruby.

This is what they could have done to her.

Anger took the place of fear. He wanted these people in prison more than he had ever wanted any other criminal behind bars. They *would* pay for what they'd done, and if any of them even so much as attempted to put up a fight to resist arrest, he wouldn't hesitate to serve up a different form of justice.

"Do you think they came here intending to do this or was it spur-of-the-moment when they found her naked?" Zeb asked. They already knew that the gang had found Tiffany Kendrick naked because they'd walked the house and found her clothes and a towel lying on the floor of the master bathroom, along with a small amount of blood on the carpet in the master bedroom.

"I think we have a power struggle going on between two of the gang," Judah said thoughtfully, walking over to the other side of the room where there were a couple of bullet holes in the wall. "I think one of them doesn't want to follow the rules of the other anymore. He wants to change up the script, do things his way."

Thinking about what Julie Johnstone had told them, it looked like Skull and Black Cat were a pair, and Ghost and Witch were a pair. It also looked like Skull was the one in charge because he'd been the one who was angry and threatening Ghost and Witch. What if Ghost wanted to shake things up, what if he wanted to take over?

"I think you could be right," Zeb agreed. "At least two of them were into this. They hurt Ace to manipulate Tiffany into doing what they wanted."

"I'd agree with that."

They both looked over to medical examiner Luke Dunkin who was crouching beside Tiffany Kendrick's body.

"What did you find?" Judah asked, positive he didn't really want to hear the answer to that question.

"I'll finish my examination back at the morgue, but just from looking at her, there's extensive internal damage. She was raped with something big. I'm talking fist size. Internal damage on the other side too. She was raped anally, and I see what I think is semen on her chin and neck. I'd guess that they forced her to perform oral sex on at least one of them."

These guys were a piece of work.

And stupid.

They had just left a piece of themselves behind.

Again, images of Ruby floated before his eyes.

This time, it fueled his anger.

These men weren't getting away with this.

"Judah, look."

He walked over to where his partner was crouched down by the dining room table. "What did you find?"

"This probably fell out from their bags when they put them on the table." With a gloved hand, Zeb picked up a metal tag hanging from a chain.

"Dog tags?" he asked. Were they looking for someone in the military?

"Nope. There's a logo on here. Judah, it's the local high school logo."

High school?

They were looking for high school kids?

Kids.

How could it have been kids who did all of this?

His eyes roved over Ace and Tiffany Kendrick's tortured bodies. The level of disregard for other human beings that was displayed in this room was off the charts. How could they be looking for teenagers?

He couldn't comprehend that.

He didn't *want* to comprehend that.

Thinking they were looking for college kids was bad enough, but that they could be looking for minors seemed to make this so much worse.

And yet, the complete lack of care they were taking with the crimes definitely hinted that they were looking for someone young. Leaving behind semen was an unbelievably stupid move. Even if the kid wasn't in the system, they could still find him, especially since they now had a link to the school.

"They're not making smart choices, but the thing that confuses me the most," Judah said, "is why they didn't kill the baby. Compassion? A shred of humanity? Were they all in on it, or was it just one of them that wanted to save the baby?" Whatever the reason that four-month-old Marcus Kendrick had been spared, it gave him at least a small ray of hope. If one of them had saved the baby, then it meant that the bond between them wasn't unbreakable. It meant that at least one of them had a conscience, and that might become the difference between finding these four teenagers and sending them to prison or not.

❧

9:03 A.M.

Judah hung up his phone and sighed with relief.

At least one thing had gone right with this case.

Zeb was looking at him expectantly, so he said, "That was the hospital. The Kendrick baby was given a clean bill of health. Whoever wrapped him up in the blankets and left him hidden in the backyard kept him warm enough that he wasn't hypothermic." Whoever had snuck the baby out of the house obviously hadn't wanted the others to know, and they had also wanted to make sure that the baby would be all right until someone found him.

Marcus Kendrick had been found by the neighbor when she'd gone to walk her dog early before leaving for work. She had heard crying and gone looking for the source, expecting to find a homeless family who was sleeping in someone's yard or an abandoned baby. She had not been expecting to find her neighbors' baby swaddled in three blankets and tucked away under a bush.

Knowing that something was wrong, the woman had picked up the baby and taken him inside her house then immediately called 911. The first cops to respond had gone into the Kendrick house, found the bodies, and the case had been assigned to them on the assumption that it was the same gang of home invaders who had committed the murders.

At this point, it was still an assumption.

As if reading his mind, Zeb said, "We don't even know yet that these are the same people who killed the Cochranes and broke into the Hatcher house. Yes, the back window was broken in, but that's about the only similarity."

"Tiffany Kendrick was shot four times. We know that we're looking for a group of four perpetrators. When ballistics compares the bullets to the ones from the Cochrane house, then we'll get our answer," Judah said.

"Until then, we should keep our options open," Zeb said. "For all we know, Tiffany had been having an affair, and her husband wasn't the baby's father. Maybe the father decided to get his revenge."

"Then why leave the baby? If he wanted revenge, it would be from Tiffany keeping the baby away from him."

"Maybe he doesn't want the baby—he just wanted Tiffany to suffer for trying to make decisions for him."

"How would the school dog tag play into that? Are we thinking that the woman was having an affair with a teenager?"

"Doesn't have to be a kid from the school. Maybe it was a teacher or a parent or even a sibling."

"I suppose," he agreed, not really feeling the theory. "I agree we should keep our minds open until we get confirmation, but I'm not sold on the affair idea yet. Once we finish up here, we can speak with the Kendricks' family and friends, see if anyone knows anything about an affair. We should hear from Elsie within the next couple of hours; she said she would get to comparing the bullets as soon as she could."

Whether or not the Kendrick murders were the next in the killers' spree wasn't what was weighing on his mind the most. What was bothering him was motive. It was what always got him. Like most people, he wanted the world to be a place that made sense.

Only, murder didn't make sense.

As far as he—and most of the population—were concerned, there were very few acceptable reasons for taking the life of another human being. Self-defense was about the only one that most people understood. But the majority of his cases had nothing to do with self-defense. Most of his cases were selfish people doing whatever they wanted to satisfy their own needs and desires.

So, what were these killers' needs and desires?

It was unusual for four people to work together like this. In a way, they appeared to be a little cult of sorts, following out the game plan of their leader. The leader appeared to be the man who dressed in the skull costume, only it looked like someone wanted to challenge that leadership. Which implied that they had all been on the same page at some point but that things were spinning out of control, and they were no longer a cohesive team.

So, how had they become a team?

How did four people decide to come together and start breaking into people's homes and murdering them? It wasn't like you got the urge to kill and then walked up to friends—or strangers—and asked them if they wanted to join in.

The whole thing was baffling.

Which was worrying.

Just because they hadn't made an attempt to come back and finish what they started with Ruby so far didn't mean they wouldn't come at some point. He didn't want the woman he was falling for in danger, but so far, he couldn't see any way to end this case. "We should make sure that we have a cop on Marcus Kendrick's grandparents' house," he said to his partner. "Just in case they decide to start coming back and tying up loose ends."

"I'll text Debra and ask her to set something up," Zeb said, just as the door to Principal Barone's office opened.

"Detectives, come on in," the woman said, ushering them into her office. She led them over to her desk, and he and Zeb took seats facing her. "What's going on? I was told this was urgent."

"It is," he told the woman. "This was found at a crime scene this morning." He handed over a photograph of the dog tag with the school's logo to the principal. "Can you confirm that this is the school's logo?"

The woman took the picture and studied it for a brief second or so before nodding, her eyes grave. "This is ours. It's the senior class's. They chose the dog tags specifically because a couple of the kids have lost loved ones who were in the military."

Well, at least that was one step forward. "Who would have one? Just the kids in the senior class?" he asked.

"Yes and no. Yes, they are for the kids in the senior class, but other staff sometimes collect the things that the seniors have made up. It's not the same things every year, and some of the teachers who teach them like to buy them, kind of like mementos of that year's class."

"What about students' families?" Zeb asked. "Would they have access to them?"

"Only through their kids. May I ask what the crime scene was?" Principal Barone asked.

"It was the scene of a double murder," Judah informed her.

The principal's eyes grew wide. "You think that one of our kids committed a murder?"

He did.

Gideon had profiled their killers as young, and although at the time they'd been thinking college age, high school seniors weren't that much younger and were certainly old enough to have pulled this off.

"Are there any of the students that you can think of who might be capable of murder?" he asked. It was a long shot. He thought that these kids were probably smart enough not to let their hidden dark inner selves be seen.

"Murder? No," Principal Barone said emphatically. "This is a high school. We have an abundance of testosterone, and there are fights from time to time. And teenage girls can be catty sometimes. There have been a few fights between them as well—usually over a guy. Although we have a zero tolerance for bullying, there are still instances of that as well. We jump on those immediately, and we have very strict punishments for those found to be bullying as well as offering support to victims, but there is nothing and no one that I can think of who would be capable of killing two people. Are you sure that you're looking for one of these kids?" Her eyes moved from his face to his partner's, seeking the answer she wanted, which was no, they didn't think they were really looking for one of these kids.

"All we know right now is that one of the dog tags that your senior class had made up was found at a crime scene. It could be one of the kids. It could be a parent or sibling who had it in their possession, or it could be a teacher. Have you had any problems with any of the staff? Anyone you think might be capable of murder?" Zeb asked.

"I wish that I could tell you that there was, especially if you're right and a killer is walking these halls, but there isn't. I'm sorry."

Sorry didn't help them right now.

Not that it was the principal's fault that she couldn't identify the killer.

Walking in here, Judah had hoped to at least get a direction to move in, but instead, they didn't really have anything. Elsie would hopefully get them proof that it was the same home invaders that killed the

Cochranes and the Kendricks, and he and Zeb would start going through staff and students of the high school looking for anything that could point to one of them being the killer.

It was a long shot, but it was the best they had.

The dog tag said the killers were in some way associated with the school, so if they looked closely enough, they would find them.

No one could hide forever.

He knew. He'd spent half of his life hiding parts of himself, but sooner or later, they came out.

The same would be true for the killers.

~

11:50 A.M.

Witch was nervous today.

Anxious.

She couldn't settle to anything.

In fact, she had already given up trying to focus and had gone home sick, so she could just be alone.

She didn't want to be around people right now because she was sure that one look at her face was going to give away everything that was going on inside her head, and then she would be in even more trouble.

And she was already in pretty big trouble.

She touched a finger to her sore chest and tried to draw in a full breath. Ever since Skull had hit her last night, she hadn't been able to breathe properly. He had probably broken her ribs, but she was pretty sure that those healed on their own and you didn't really need to go and see a doctor.

They better, because how would she explain the bruises to a doctor?

Walking over to the mirror, she carefully eased up her sweater and examined the bruises. They were darker than they had been this morning, a mottled mix of black and blue that looked like she had taken one hell of a beating.

And she had.

When Skull had realized that the baby was no longer in the house and he wasn't going to be able to kill the entire family like he wanted to, he'd lost it. She had never seen someone get so angry. And over killing a tiny little baby. Who cared if the infant lived; it wasn't like it was going to tell on them.

She had known the risks when she'd decided to get the baby out of the house. She had known that Ghost had already been intending to mix things up, do his own thing, stop blindly following orders, and do what he wanted to do. And she had known that if she also decided to break the rules, then she was only asking to have a punishment rained down upon her.

And that was exactly what she'd gotten.

Witch ran her fingertips over the marks. They would fade in time. She was lucky that he hadn't hurt her worse.

Or killed her.

The look in his eyes had said he'd wanted to kill her.

It was worth it, though. There was no way she could have stood by and watched Skull kill that sweet little baby. He was innocent. He hadn't done anything wrong, and he didn't deserve to be killed.

Okay, she got that she was a hypocrite about that.

All of the people who lived in the houses they had broken into were innocent and didn't deserve to be killed, but that little baby ...

Her hand dropped from her bruised and battered chest to her stomach.

No one knew it yet, but she had her own little baby growing in there.

It still didn't feel real, which was part of the reason she hadn't told anyone.

Being pregnant changed everything.

Everything.

She was still trying to think through all the ramifications and how they impacted what happened next, but it was hard—especially trying to do it alone.

Witch knew that she had to tell someone.

Specifically, Ghost.

He was the baby's father, after all, so he had a say in what was going to happen next. It was a whole lot more complicated than simply was she or wasn't she going to keep the baby. She almost wished things *were* that simple.

But her life was never simple.

The door to her bedroom suddenly swung open, and she quickly dropped her sweater down. It wasn't like she was showing already. She was only a month or so along in her pregnancy, but finding her standing there with her hand on her stomach was going to look odd and lead to questions she wasn't sure she wanted to answer yet.

"Hey." She mustered a smile and turned to face Ghost.

"Hey, yourself. I heard you were sick ... you okay?"

"Oh, yeah, sure," she said, spinning around and beginning to pick up the clothes scattered around the room. She wasn't a very good liar, and she knew that if she kept looking at him, he was going to be able to read in her face that something was going on, and she was trying to keep secrets from him.

Apparently, he knew anyway.

Ghost stalked across the room and grabbed her shoulder. He turned her around to face him and stared into her eyes so deeply it was like he was looking all the way into her brain.

"You're lying to me. What's going on?"

"It's nothing," she said, once again averting her gaze, this time to stare at the floor.

"Liar. Did Skull hurt you worse than you said last night?" Without waiting for an answer—or perhaps assuming he wouldn't get an honest one—he pushed her backward and down onto the bed, shoving her sweater up so he could examine her bruised chest.

Usually, when her man looked at her naked breasts like a switch had been flipped, she would get this warm and fluttery feeling in her stomach.

But not today.

Today, sex was the last thing on her mind.

Ghost muttered a curse as he ran a hand over her bruises. "Skull is going to pay for this."

There was no point in reminding him that he was part of the reason she had been beaten up. If he hadn't decided that it was no longer

Skull's way or no way, and started humiliating and hurting the woman at the house last night, then Skull would never have been in such a bad mood and wouldn't have gone off the deep end when he realized she had hidden the baby.

"I'm really okay," she assured him, ignoring the pain in her chest to reach up and touch a kiss to his lips.

"Well, if it isn't your injuries, something else is bothering you. What is it?" he demanded.

"Nothing, really," she muttered.

"You forget, I have ways of making you talk," he warned. "Last chance, what is bothering you?"

She should probably tell him.

He had a right to know.

And it wasn't like she could keep this secret indefinitely.

Still, she stubbornly pressed her lips into a line.

"Fine," he snapped. Grabbing hold of both her wrists with one hand, he pinned them above her head, while his free hand slid down below her waistband and settled between her legs. With practiced ease, he slipped a finger inside her and began to stroke her while his thumb rubbed circles on the spot that drove her wild.

Okay, so maybe sex *wasn't* the last thing on her mind today.

She tried to fight against it, think unsexy thoughts, but Ghost knew her body inside and out, and he knew just how to work her quickly right to the very edge of pleasure.

And then he stopped.

She whimpered and pressed her pelvis up toward him, begging him to keep going.

But he didn't.

He left her hanging.

"Got anything to tell me?" he asked, his eyes glittering wickedly, enjoying torturing her like this.

Stubbornness got the better of her again, and she kept her mouth shut.

"Fine." He reached down and picked up a pair of discarded stockings and used them to tie her wrists together behind her back. Then he pulled her sweatpants down her legs and threw them onto the floor. Her panties quickly joined them, and then his tongue was touching her. He touched her with a feather softness that had her squirming and moaning and whimpering, that kept her stuck on the edge but wouldn't allow her to fall over.

"Okay, okay," she finally cracked. "I'll tell you, just please, let me come."

"If I take mercy on you and you don't follow through, I'm going to be angry," he warned. She wasn't stupid. She knew she was involved with a dangerous man. A man who had viciously tortured a woman last night. A man who killed without remorse. A man who *would* punish her if she tried to trick him.

But she was helplessly in love with him and powerless to resist.

"I promise, just please, please let me come," she begged.

His head buried itself between her legs again, and this time when his mouth touched her, the strokes were firmer, faster, and in less than a minute, he had her spiraling into another world. A world filled with nothing but pleasure.

His hands pressed her hips down when they greedily tried to seek more, and he sucked and nipped every last drop of pleasure out of her, leaving her completely and utterly spent.

It took her a full couple of minutes before she was even able to hold a coherent thought.

When her vision finally cleared, and she saw him looking down at her expectantly, she knew that she had no other choice.

She had to tell him.

Despite her stubbornness, part of her wanted to do it anyway.

Even if he was angry about it, it was what it was. She was pregnant. He was the father, and nothing was going to change that.

4:21 P.M.

If she could have just one wish, it would be that she didn't have to live inside her own head anymore.

Ruby had woken up this morning excited and positive. She had felt like not only did she have a future but that it could be anything she wanted.

She had been so exhilarated.

She felt like she could so anything.

She felt so strong.

And now ...

Now, she was staring out the kitchen window with a razor in her hand.

The constant up and down of her moods was exhausting. Sometimes it left her feeling physically dizzy. It was depression—she knew that. It was also part of her post traumatic stress disorder; she knew that too. But knowing that didn't help her. It didn't take away the thoughts of ending her life, and it didn't help her hold on to the good moments and make them last longer.

It didn't help her at all.

Some days she hated her life. Some days she wished she had never found the strength to fight for her freedom and escape. At times, she wished she had died in that basement or at the hands of one of the men she was forced to pleasure.

Then, there were good days.

Like yesterday.

Days where she took a stand and reached for what she wanted. Yesterday, she had admitted to her sisters that she liked a guy. She had told Judah that when this case was over and he was no longer here on assignment to keep her safe, that she would say yes when he asked her out. Yesterday, she had felt safe and happy when she'd been held in the arms of the man whom she had feelings for. She'd felt like a normal woman, the same as everyone else.

Yesterday, she had been falling in love, and today, she was right back to wondering if she should slit her own wrists.

Why?

Why did she have to be like this?

Why couldn't she pull it together?

Why did she still feel like she wanted to commit suicide when she had felt happy about her future when she had climbed out of bed this morning?

It wasn't like anything bad had happened.

No one she loved had been hurt—which, when you had two sisters with dangerous jobs, could be a daily concern—and there had been no attempts by the home invasion gang to return. No one had said or done anything mean to her; her sisters and Gideon had all kissed her goodbye this morning and wished her a good day as they headed off to work. Judah had kissed her cheek and promised that he would make progress on this case, then wished her a good day. The cop guarding her door had checked in and told her she had nothing to worry about and wished her a good day.

You would think with so many wishes for a good day that she would be bound to have one no matter how hard her emotions tried to tell her otherwise.

But no, that wasn't the way her brain worked.

Slowly, she moved the razor, pressing it hard enough into her skin to draw blood.

One move ... that was all it would take.

Then she would be free.

She wouldn't be stuck here anymore, suffering her own personal and never-ending hell.

Part of her wanted to do it so badly. It would be so nice not to have to feel this way anymore. She was so tired of it.

She was just so tired.

Ruby pressed deeper, watching the blood bubble and then flow out.

"Hey."

The voice startled her. She spun around so quickly that the razor— now slick with blood—slipped from her fingers and clattered to the floor.

Judah was standing there.

He had to have seen what she'd just done. He was only two feet away.

Still, she quickly tried to bend down and retrieve the razor before he saw it.

She managed to snatch it up, curling her fingers around it, so it was hidden in the palm of her hand.

"What are you doing?" he asked, his hand moving from the blood on her forearm to her fist.

"Nothing," she muttered, trying to get past him so she could escape into the downstairs bathroom where she could wash away the blood, stick a Band-Aid over it and hide the razor.

"Hold on," he said. His large hand circled her small wrist and held it still while he pried her fingers open one by one.

Ruby wished the floor would open, and she could disappear.

This was a man whom she'd dreamed about having a future with. What was he going to think of her when he realized that she spent half her life thinking about ending it?

Without saying a word, he pushed the sleeve of her blouse up, revealing not only the bloody cut but her scars as well.

"You were thinking about killing yourself," he said, his voice gone strange. She couldn't decipher the tone, and that scared her.

Had she lost him already?

If she had, it wouldn't be like she had anyone to blame but herself.

"Is that why you had the razor with you the night of the break-in?"

She could lie, but what would be the point?

Ruby nodded.

"I thought it might have been, but I hoped that I was wrong."

So far, no one seemed to have thought to ask her why she'd been holding a razor when four people had broken into the house. They were so glad that she had been able to get into the safe room and that she hadn't been hurt that that little detail had escaped them all.

"Come and sit down." He took the razor off her palm and set it on the counter, then took her hand and led her over to the table. He pushed lightly on her shoulders, so she sat down in the chair he'd pulled out, and then he disappeared off into the bathroom, leaving her staring after him.

She couldn't get a read on him.

He didn't sound angry; he didn't sound scared; he didn't sound anything.

She needed him to tell her what was going on inside his head.

Judah returned, first aid kid in hand, and came and sat in a chair beside her, where he picked up her arm, cleaned the wound with calm, confident strokes, then his long fingers spread a little antibiotic cream over the cut and put on a Band-Aid.

Returning everything to the first aid kit, he snapped it closed, then sat there and stared at it.

Ruby didn't know what to say.

Did he want an assurance she wouldn't try it again?

Did he want an explanation?

Did he want her to just sit here and not say anything?

Her mouth started moving all on its own, having bypassed her head in the decision-making process. "I think about it a lot. And it's not the first time I tried it. About two months after I escaped was the first time, then again nearly two years after I was back home, and again nearly eighteen months ago."

He lifted his head and looked at her, those piercing blue eyes cutting right through her. "I would think for someone who went through something as traumatic as you did that it's a fairly normal reaction."

Immediately, she shook her head in disagreement. "My sisters all went through the same sort of traumatic experience, and none of them have ever tried to kill themselves."

That had always eaten away at her. It wasn't what had happened to her that made her want to end her own life because if it was, then all of her sisters would have tried suicide as well. It was her. *She* was the difference and weaker than her sisters.

"Different people react differently," he said.

She'd heard that before.

Actually, more than once.

From several of the shrinks she'd seen.

She didn't believe it any more coming from Judah's lips than she had from theirs.

"No, it's me. I'm not strong." She began to cry quietly. She didn't want to, Judah had already seen her thrashing and screaming, trapped in a nightmare, and now he had seen her contemplating killing herself. He certainly didn't need another reason to walk away before he got in too deep.

"Stop it," he said fiercely, grabbing her shoulders and dragging her to her feet. "Stop it," he repeated when tears continued to tumble down her cheeks. When she couldn't do as he asked, he curled a hand around the back of her neck and dipped his head, crushing his mouth to hers and kissing her.

Startled for a moment, she froze.

That was not the reaction she'd been expecting.

Then, like magic, his lips began to calm her, and she lifted an arm and wrapped it around his shoulders and began to kiss him back.

They were kissing.

Normal kissing.

Not some psycho who paid to play with her kissing her, but the two of them kissing each other.

Because they wanted to.

This was nice.

Too soon, he ended the kiss, but he didn't release his hold on her. That was a good thing, right?

"Thinking about suicide doesn't mean you're weak. It just means you're hurting," he murmured against her lips. "Even though you're hurting, you have to try to remember that you're not alone. You have a lot of people who care about you. You have your sisters and Gideon, and you have me. I care. I don't want to lose you. I care about you, and I am here for you. Any time you need someone to talk to, someone to remind you that you're special and that you would be missed, you call me, okay? I mean it. Any time that you feel overwhelmed and you want to end your life, you call me, and I'll be here. Promise me, Ruby, please." He reached out and brushed the back of his knuckles across her cheek, his cornflower blue eyes catching hers and refusing to let them go until she promised.

It wasn't that she didn't know that she couldn't do that exact same thing with her sisters. If they knew that she was having suicidal thoughts, they would want her to reach out to them and let them help, but somehow, it was different with Judah. Maybe it was because he wasn't related to her. He didn't have to be saying this; he didn't owe her anything. He was asking her this and offering her himself just because he wanted to.

"Okay," she agreed, and immediately saw his shoulders sag with relief. She got it. He had lost someone he loved to suicide. He'd wanted to build something special with her that they could cherish the rest of their lives, and he didn't want to lose her before they got a chance to do that. She probably didn't have any right to ask this, but she was going to anyway. "Who did you lose? Someone you loved committed suicide, didn't they? Who was it?"

Abruptly, he released her and snatched up the first aid kid, stalking over to the bathroom door.

She'd blown it.

She had gotten nosey, and it had made him angry.

"I'm sorry," she said quickly before he could walk away. She hadn't meant to upset him, she just wanted to understand him better, to date him and see if they could build something that would weather the storms of a lifetime.

"I didn't lose anyone," he said softly. "It was me. I attempted suicide."

With that, he opened the bathroom door, stepped inside, and slammed it behind him.

Ruby just stood there—shocked. That was the last thing she had expected him to say.

~

9:46 P.M.

"Did you hear about the home invasions in the neighborhood?"

He glanced up at his fiancée. "No. What home invasions?"

"Apparently, there have been three of them, all within about ten minutes from here. Someone managed to escape one of them, but in the other two, everyone in the house was killed except for a baby," his fiancée explained, her eyes wide as she joined him on the bed.

"What, so you think that they're going to come here next?" he asked, setting his book down and taking off his glasses. Dan Lanely pinched his nose. He was really going to need new glasses soon. These always left him aching by the end of the day, but he had three kids, and his fiancée, Judy, had two. They were planning a wedding, and had just bought a new house—one big enough to fit their joined families—and things like new glasses were at the bottom of the list.

"Well, no," Judy said, getting under the covers. "The odds of them coming to our house next are pretty slim, but still, three home invasions in our neighborhood all within the last three nights ... that's scary stuff."

"It is," he agreed. He was usually too busy to spend time watching the news. Between work and raising five kids—aged between six and fifteen—he didn't really have time for anything else. He didn't use social media, preferring to spend his time either with his friends and family in person, or squeezing in a little reading when he found the occasional spare moment, so unless someone told him, he didn't usually catch the news.

"I'm kind of glad that all the kids aren't here tonight," she said. "I mean, I know that the chances of them coming here are slim, but still, what if they did?"

Dan had to admit that he was glad the kids weren't here tonight as well. Judy was right; it wasn't likely that the home invaders would choose their house to break into, but he couldn't stand the thought of his kids in danger. His six, nine, and twelve-year-old children were at their mother's house this week. They shared custody and did a week on, week off rotation. His fiancée's ten-year-old was at school camp, and the fifteen-year-old hadn't wanted to be the only kid in the house and was having a sleepover at a friend's house.

"Well, the kids are all out, and we're perfectly safe here. We have a security system, and the doors are all locked. No one is breaking in here," he assured Judy as he draped an arm around her shoulders. They did have the house to themselves tonight—a rare occurrence. He was divorced, so his kids spent half their time at their mother's. But Judy was a widow, so her kids lived here full time. There weren't many nights where it was just the two of them. They could make the most of it, have a little romantic time before bed, but he was exhausted, and he knew that Judy was too. A full night of uninterrupted sleep sounded wonderful.

Judy rested her head on his shoulders. "Grown-up time is nice, but sleep sounds so much better tonight. And you're right, I guess I got a little freaked out about those murders, but we're safe here."

"Absolutely," he said, sensing she needed to hear it one last time. Leaning over, he gave her a quick kiss and then switched off the lamp on his nightstand. They both lay down, and Judy rested her head on his chest. He began to stroke her hair as he closed his eyes. "Night."

"Night. I love you."

"Love you too." He was really lucky to have been given a second chance at love. He hadn't done so well the first time. The pressure of raising three kids—one with special needs—and working full-time jobs had eroded their love until all they did was fight. It wasn't until they realized the effect it was having on their kids when the oldest began to act out in school that they realized they were better off as co-parents than partners, so they'd divorced. He met Judy, and now they were getting ready to share their lives. This time around, he was determined that nothing was going to come between him and the woman he loved.

Dan was just drifting off when he heard the sound of breaking glass.

From the way she bolted upright, he knew that Judy had heard it too.

"Hide," he said, already climbing out of bed. What were the chances the breaking glass was the home invaders breaking in? He had no idea, but it seemed greater than he had originally thought.

"Dan," Judy whimpered, clinging to him.

"Go, on, hide," he hissed. If someone really was in here, he didn't want them getting to his fiancée. They didn't own a gun, but his twelve-year-old son played baseball and owned a bat. It couldn't compete with a gun, but it was better than nothing.

Leaving Judy in the bedroom, he crept out into the hall where he froze and stood still as he listened for any sounds.

Footsteps.

And voices.

Someone was definitely inside his home.

As silently as he could, he ran down the hall to his son's room and grabbed the baseball bat. He didn't think it was going to help him, but it was better than confronting the intruder—or intruders—unarmed.

He was just approaching the top of the stairs when he saw them.

There were four of them all dressed in costumes—a skull, ghost, witch, and black cat.

They were all armed.

Fear sliced through him. Fear that he couldn't protect his fiancée and that she was going to wind up dead because of it. Fear that while his children wouldn't be physically harmed, they would be scarred for life growing up without their dad. Fear for Judy's kids that he loved like his own who would now be orphans.

"Hello," Ghost singsonged up at him when they caught sight of him standing there.

For once, he wished that he didn't have a no cell phone in the bedroom policy. His phone and Judy's were sitting uselessly downstairs on the kitchen counter. He might only have a baseball bat to their four guns, but he wasn't going down without a fight.

"Get out of my house," he growled.

"Um, yeah ... no," Ghost said.

They were advancing, and he had nowhere to go.

So, he stood his ground.

As they approached, he swung the bat at them. Skull, who was leading the group, dodged backward, and then, without a word of warning, he fired his gun, aiming it at his knee and hitting his target perfectly.

Pain shot through him, and he yelped as he dropped the bat—which clattered down the stairs—and he fell to the floor, clutching at his shattered joint.

"I'm not in the mood for games tonight," Skull snapped, standing above him and glaring at him, then turning that glare on his comrades.

"Oh, lighten up," Ghost laughed. "I'm going to go search for the Missus."

"Take your girl with you. I don't want a repeat of last time," Skull ordered.

"You better not put your hands on her again," Ghost said, getting all up in Skull's face, but the other man stood his ground.

"Go find the woman ... bring her to the bedroom. I'm not dragging him down to the dining room," Skull ordered.

"Yes, sir," Ghost mocked, saluting. It was clear the two were engaged in a battle for control, but he wasn't sure how that helped him and Judy.

He wasn't sure it did.

Ghost and Witch went off, and Skull grabbed hold of him and began to drag him toward the bedroom. Dan prayed Judy had hidden away someplace she would never be found, but he wasn't optimistic.

They were both going to die.

That much was clear.

In the bedroom, Skull draped him on the bed and then dragged him up, so he was lying flat on his back, securing his wrists and ankles to the bedposts.

He was trapped.

Helpless.

If he wasn't in unimaginable agony, he would have been furious.

"You want to do the honors?" Skull asked Black Cat, holding up a knife.

So, it was over already.

They were going to kill him here and now.

"It would be my pleasure," Black Cat purred, taking the knife and kneeling on the bed beside him. Instead of stabbing him, she used the knife to cut the T-shirt and sweatpants he slept in off his body, leaving him stark naked.

"Looky what we found," Ghost sang as he dragged Judy into the room by her hair.

"Let go of her," Dan growled.

They ignored him.

"How about a last ride on your stallion," Ghost said, shoving Judy toward the bed.

She shook her head wildly. Tears streamed down her face, and her eyes locked onto his and begged him to save her.

But he couldn't.

That hurt worse than the bullet through his kneecap.

"We talked about no more games," Skull told Ghost.

"Relax, man, you'll get your kills, but what harm is there in having a little fun first?" Ghost suggested.

"Fine, but you only have twenty minutes," Skull said.

Ghost nodded his agreement of the terms, and Skull strode over to the rocking chair in the corner and sat. Black Cat went and curled up on his lap.

"You heard Skull," Witch said to Judy, speaking for the first time. "Go take one last ride on your man."

"Or we can take out his other knee," Skull added, pointing the gun at him.

Judy whimpered but walked on shaky legs over to the bed. "I'm sorry," she whispered as she removed her underwear.

"No, I'm sorry," he whispered back. He was the man of the house. It was his job to protect his soon-to-be wife and kids, and he'd failed.

He had failed so very badly.

11:13 P.M.

He had been avoiding Ruby all evening.

It was a little immature, Judah acknowledged, but every time he thought he should just go and talk to her, he backed out.

He hadn't meant to tell her like that. It had just kind of slipped out. She'd been beating herself up like there was something wrong with her because she suffered from a medical condition.

Because that was all it was.

She had been through something horrific; she suffered from post-traumatic stress disorder and depression. That she had attempted suicide and still had suicidal thoughts was nothing for her to be ashamed about. He just hoped that she was getting herself the medical treatment that she needed.

Judah didn't want to lose her.

Maybe if she realized that she wasn't alone and that other people suffered from the exact same thoughts and feelings that she did, she wouldn't feel so bad.

And maybe if *he* remembered that he wasn't alone and that other people suffered from the same thoughts and feelings he had, then *he* wouldn't feel so bad either.

Maybe they could help each other.

But only if he actually went and talked to her.

With a last look at the starry night sky, he opened the back door and stepped inside the Hatcher house.

"Finally stopped hiding."

He turned at the voice and saw Sapphire and Gideon curled up together in front of the TV. Their dog—a Border Collie, called Luna—was curled up beside them, and Sapphire was absently stroking the dog's head. He should have checked to see if anyone was still in here before coming in, but he'd thought it was late enough that everyone else would be in bed.

"What happened with you and Ruby? Last night you were so chummy, and today she's hiding out in her room, and you're hiding out in the backyard. What's going on?"

"Sapphire," Gideon chided, but she just shrugged and awaited an answer.

Judah didn't want to break Ruby's confidence in confessing the dark thoughts that she had to her sisters, but more than that, he didn't want anything to happen to her. They were only just at the beginning of a relationship—assuming she still wanted one. Things might not work out between them, but she would always have Sapphire and her sisters.

"We talked earlier, and she let me know that the night of the break-in, she'd been thinking about hurting herself. That was why she had the razor she used to escape into the safe room," he told them.

Sapphire jumped off Gideon's lap where she'd been sitting. "I should have known that. I was too busy beating myself up for not being here that I didn't even think about why she had a razor with her."

"You can't know everything," Gideon said, standing and resting his hands on her shoulders. Sapphire leaned into him for a moment, drawing strength from him, and Judah couldn't help a stab of jealousy that the two of them had found love.

"So, she trusted you and told you that, and then you avoided her?" Sapphire's green eyes shot daggers at him.

"No, I told her something about myself, and that's why I've been avoiding her all night." There was no way he was telling them what; telling Ruby had been hard enough.

"Oh." The fire seemed to dim in Sapphire's eyes. "Well, that I understand. Advice?"

"Sure." It wasn't like he had anything to lose.

"Go to her ... don't leave it any longer."

He was surprised to hear that coming from her. Not because it was good advice, but because she was encouraging him to actually go to Ruby.

Judah smiled at her, and she smiled back. He could read in her face that Sapphire didn't have a problem with him, specifically. She was just protective of her sister and battling her own demons.

Taking her advice, he headed up the stairs but paused at Ruby's bedroom door.

Talking about his past wasn't easy, and it wasn't something he liked doing. He knew that if he and Ruby were going to have a future that, at some point, he would have to tell her, but he hadn't expected to do it so early.

Taking a deep breath, he knocked on the door.

"Come in," she called out. So, she *was* awake. As much as he would like to put this off, it would be better just to get the conversation over and done with.

He opened the door and found her lying in bed, her e-reader in her hand. When she saw it was him and not one of her sisters, she put the e-reader down and got out of bed, wincing and stretching as she did as though her muscles were aching.

Unsure where to start, Judah just stood and looked at her, and she stood there staring right back at him.

"You told them, didn't you? That I still think about suicide?"

He wasn't going to lie to her. "I did."

Ruby sighed. "Part of me wishes you hadn't done that, but the other half is relieved. I wanted them to know; I just didn't want them to be disappointed in me."

"They could never be disappointed in you," he reminded her. "They love you. For better or for worse, they're never walking away from you."

"Just like your family," she said, watching him carefully to see if he was going to bail on her again. She needn't worry. He wasn't.

"You look stiff," he said, needing to stall for just a few more minutes.

She arched a blonde brow at him, telling him she knew that he was stalling but would play along for the moment. "It's the nightmares. I get so tense that I sometimes get stiff and achy all over."

"I might be able to help a little with that."

"Oh?" Although Ruby and her twin sister were blue-eyed blondes, and Sapphire and Diamond were green-eyed brunettes, she looked just like Sapphire when she said that and gave him a suspicious look.

"Go lie down on the bed ... on your stomach," he instructed.

"What?"

The look on her face made him laugh. "I'm just going to give you a massage." Two birds with one stone. He could help with her stiff muscles, and he wouldn't have to look her in the eye when he told her about his past.

"Okay," Ruby said slowly, still sounding a little suspicious, but she went and lay down on her bed.

Judah walked over and climbed onto the bed beside her. She was wearing only an oversized T-shirt and a pair of plain white panties that he could see because when she lay down, the T-shirt moved up enough to show her long legs.

He deliberately averted his gaze. Tonight wasn't about making out; it was about growing closer emotionally. There would be time to take their relationship to the physical level when they were both ready.

Starting with her shoulders, he began to knead her sore muscles. Almost immediately, she sighed delightedly, relaxed, and settled down farther into the soft mattress.

"You know how you told me earlier how if I needed someone to talk to, that you were there?" Ruby asked.

"Yeah."

"Well, you know the same goes for you. You can tell me anything. No judgment. The only thing I'll give you is my support."

That meant a lot to him.

More than he could ever express.

Ruby had more than enough on her plate, and there she was offering her support to someone else.

"I was eleven," he started. "I was different than the other kids, I had —have—OCD, obsessive compulsive disorder. For as long as I can remember, I had to have everything just a certain way, and if for some reason I couldn't, then I would freak out. These days I have my obsessions and compulsions mostly under control, but back then, I didn't. Back then, I would have meltdowns at school when I couldn't do things the way I wanted to, and there were several compulsions that I had to complete throughout the day. There was a group of other boys in my class who used to bully me."

They had been relentless.

Torturing him every chance they got.

Every day.

Every class.

They never gave him a break.

As his hands moved from Ruby's shoulders to her back, he couldn't help but flash back to those times—broken bones, black eyes, teasing, mocking, exclusion, threats. In the end, he just couldn't take it anymore.

"They never stopped. They would find me on my way to school and follow me home. The whole day they would laugh at me, tease me, beat me up. I didn't fill out until my late teens. Back then, I was a short, scrawny little thing, and it was always a few of them against me at a time. Then they started telling me I should kill myself, that I was worthless, that I would be better off dead, that my family would be better off if I was dead, that the world would be a better place without me in it. They said it so often that I started to believe it. So, one night I came home and swallowed every pill I could find in the house."

"Oh, Judah." Ruby scrambled up onto her knees to face him and took his hands in hers.

"It all worked out okay," he said, his thumbs brushing absently back and forth across her knuckles. "My mom came home, found me, and got me to the hospital in time. I got help for my depression and my OCD. Things got better, and I was able to move on with my life."

"But you never forget," she said softly.

"No, you don't."

"When I was being held prisoner, and I thought about being rescued and going home, everything was so perfect, it was like life just went back to normal. But reality wasn't anything like that. I think that was the worst part of it all. It never completely goes away. Those memories are always there—lurking at the back of my mind—and sometimes it feels like the only way to make them stop is if *I'm* not here anymore."

Judah lifted her hands and pressed a light kiss to the back of one of them. "The world wouldn't be a better place without you in it. It would be a much worse place."

"The world wouldn't be a better place without you in it, either," she told him. "You're such a good guy. You're sweet and kind, and you chose a job where you spend all your time saving people. I'm really lucky to have you in my life." Her gaze moved from his eyes to his lips and back again; her tongue darted out to wet her own lips.

Releasing his hold on her hands, he cupped her cheeks and gently drew her closer, then leaning down, he kissed her.

There were no fireworks or stars.

There was something better.

There was a sense of completeness.

Like all his life, there had been a piece of him missing, and now he had found it.

CHAPTER
Nine

October 24th
9:50 A.M.

Another day, another family dead.

Judah was getting sick of this.

Three families destroyed in four days. This group was relentless, and he didn't see an end in sight. So far, all they had were suppositions and a bit of flimsy evidence that gave them literally over a thousand suspects. They knew they were looking for four people—two men and two women—but between students and teachers and families of the students and teachers, there were more suspects than they could ever hope to work their way through.

It was starting to feel like they were never going to catch a break.

All they needed was one small thing to point them in the right direction. They had the connection to the school, but that was too broad. They needed something to narrow it down.

At least things with Ruby were looking good. Last night they had talked for a couple of hours before he'd finally gone back downstairs to spend the night on the couch. They'd done a little more kissing too.

It actually felt liberating in a way to have told her about his past. He didn't want secrets between them, and knowing that she understood—and for her knowing that he understood—only strengthened their bond.

The bond that was growing between them only furthered his resolve to close this case. Judah took all his cases seriously, but he'd never worked a case before where one of the victims was someone that he knew. And not just someone that he knew, but someone whom he cared a great deal about.

"They've completely changed the script," he said to Zeb as the two of them walked slowly down the stairs at the Lanely house. His fingers drummed their usual pattern on his thigh. The controlled movement not only helped keep his anxiety under control, it was also a small compulsion to focus on that others at bay.

"Other than breaking in through a broken back window, nothing else was the same," his partner agreed.

"Except that they shot them," he added. Ballistics needed to link this case to the others because when they did find this gang, he wanted to make sure they got punished for every single thing they'd done.

"Elsie will confirm for us that the cases are linked," Zeb said, his mind obviously going in the same direction of his.

"They're devolving, and it doesn't seem like this was in the original script. I think it's the power play between the two men. This gang of four is split right down the middle—two couples—but which one is going to end up on top? And what does that mean for us?" There were so many different ways that this could end up playing out, and it was hard to know which one was going to give them the best chance at finding them—and quickly.

"I'm still not getting a sense of motive," Zeb said as they stepped out into the cool fall morning. "They start by tying people up and shooting them. Nothing more. Then things get messed up with Ruby, and that seems to change things. We know that the skull man was angry with the others, and then all of a sudden, the next break-in involves torture, and in this one, they tortured the couple again before killing them."

"We assumed that the random bullet holes in the wall at the Kendrick house meant that skull didn't like the torture and wanted to put a stop to it, but we don't really know that. Maybe this was always the plan to escalate things each time. If they are doing it on purpose, then what can we expect next?"

Zeb didn't answer.

He couldn't.

Neither of them knew where this was going to end.

Which was every bit as frustrating as it sounded.

Judah was about to say that at least the kids who lived in the Lanely house hadn't been there last night, so none of them had been hurt when he noticed something moving across the street.

It wasn't uncommon for a killer to return to the scene of their crime. Blend into the crowd of people who had gathered to watch. See the police scramble to figure things out, and keep tabs on what the cops were doing and the investigation, or just soak up what they saw as their good work.

"Zeb, over there," he said to his partner, nudging his head in the direction of the movement he had seen because if the killer was watching them, he didn't want to alert them and give them a chance to run. "There's someone over there, behind the hedge in the house right across the street. We should go check it out."

"You think it could be the killer?" his partner asked, discreetly looking over at the hedge.

"The only way to find out is to go over there."

Zeb nodded, and they both strolled across the street. Although it was ten in the morning and most people should be at work or at school, quite a few people were standing in the street, gathered in small groups and whispering and pointing at the Lanely house.

Judah had never gotten the fascination with evil.

He had chosen this job because he wanted to save people, and he thought that he would make a good police officer and would be able to accomplish that goal. To him, this job was about looking at a scene and collecting the pieces of evidence then putting them together like a puzzle to find the person they were looking for. That was it. He didn't take any secret pleasure in the gory crime scenes, and he didn't enjoy getting inside the head of a psychopath. He loved this job, though, and he couldn't imagine doing anything else with his life. There was nothing like the satisfaction he got when a case was closed and a criminal was locked away. The only thing that rivaled it was the look of relief on a victim's face when they learned the person who had hurt them was behind bars, and they were safe.

He wanted to see that look on Ruby's face, and he would do whatever it took to make it happen.

As they approached the house, he saw movement again. This time it was someone heading toward the front door.

"Hey, stop," he called out. "Police."

The person froze.

"Turn around," he ordered. This guy was big, and he didn't want to risk having to take him down physically if he decided to ignore them and make a run for it.

Ever so slowly, the person turned around, and he saw that it was just a kid. The boy looked about seventeen, and he shot them a defiant stare. They had been looking at someone who attended the high school. This kid, no doubt went there; this could be their guy. He was dressed all in black, and he immediately thought of the costumes that Ruby and Julie Johnstone had described. Was this Skull or Ghost? From their working theory, Skull was the current leader of their little gang, and Ghost was intent on challenging that leadership.

"What's your name, son?" Zeb asked.

The kid pouted, looking more like a spoiled brat than a cold-blooded killer, but there was one thing that stood out to Judah. They had identified themselves as cops, and the kid didn't look afraid. Was that because he didn't have anything to hide or because he was cocky enough to believe that they could never pin the murders on him? Even if he hadn't done anything wrong and he was just a kid who was supposed to be in school but was home for whatever reason, most people were at least a little nervous when they were approached by the police. But not this kid, he looked more annoyed than anything else.

"What's your name?" Zeb repeated.

"Wilson," the kid muttered. "Wilson MacAvoy."

"Is this your house, Wilson?" Judah asked.

"Yes."

"Why aren't you in school?" he asked.

Wilson shrugged.

"Do you attend Van Nielson High?" Zeb asked.

"Yeah."

"You a senior?" his partner asked.

"Yeah."

So, he would have had one of the dog tags. This could definitely be one of the kids they were looking for.

He was about to ask the kid if his mom or dad were home because he wanted to bring him down to the station for questioning when he saw something. Something white. Fluttering in the breeze. It looked like sheets hanging on a washing line in the corner of the yard around the side of the house. But something was interesting about the sheets. It looked like someone had cut two holes in them, right where your eyes would be if you put the sheet over your head. It looked like a ghost costume.

All the pieces of the puzzle were falling into place.

This kid was Ghost from the home invasion gang.

"Wilson MacAvoy, you're under arrest for the murders of the Cochrane, Kendrick, and Lanely families," he announced, snapping cuffs onto the kid, whose face had gone from irritated to shocked to furious.

All Judah felt was relief. That was one down, and now that they had one of them, the rest would fall like dominos.

10:29 A.M.

"There you go, Mrs. Manthey, how do you like that?" Ruby asked as she set the blow dryer and comb down and turned to survey her work.

"I love it," Mrs. Manthey grinned. "Very hip."

Ruby couldn't help but smile along with the other woman. Mrs. Manthey was one of her favorite residents at all of the nursing homes she visited. The woman was ninety-nine years old and planning her hundredth birthday party, which would be in May next year, assuming that she made it. Ruby knew the woman would. She might be approaching one hundred, but she was full of energy and spunk.

As evidenced by the mermaid hair colors she'd just put in the woman's fluffy white hair. The purples and blues and greens brought out Mrs. Manthey's blue-green eyes, which sparkled as though she were still a teenager. Despite her age, the woman was as sharp as a whip, but her body was failing her. She couldn't walk anymore, and she struggled to use her hands, which were riddled with arthritis, but she didn't let that get her down. Every two weeks, she came in to get her hair done, and she always chattered merrily away, making jokes and giggling like a schoolgirl.

In a way, Ruby envied her.

Over the last couple of years, they had talked a lot, and she knew that Mrs. Manthey hadn't had an easy life. She had been one of twelve children, money had been scarce, and they'd gone to bed hungry more nights than not. She'd married at seventeen, lost her first baby when she was nineteen, her second when she was twenty, then her husband when she was twenty-two. After that, she'd spent a few years alone before marrying her second husband when she was twenty-eight. She had lost another two babies before finally carrying her one and only child—a little boy—to term when she was thirty-five. Her son was the light of her life, and after losing her second husband when she was forty, he was all she had had. But life wasn't done with her just yet, and at sixty-five, she had found love again and married her third husband, and inherited another four stepchildren and their families besides her son, three grandchildren, and nine great-grandchildren.

Gretel Manthey had lost a lot, but she'd also gained a lot, and despite losing three husbands—her third nearly a decade ago—and four babies, she had always looked for the positives in life and not dwelled on the negatives. She had lived through wars and recessions and a lot of losses, and yet, she was one of the sweetest people Ruby had ever met.

It made her feel like something was wrong with her.

She hadn't been able to do what Mrs. Manthey had. Instead of looking for the positives in life, her brain seemed to focus on the negatives. She knew that her circumstances were different than Mrs. Manthey's, but it frustrated her that she couldn't get over what had happened to her and move on with her life. It made her feel like there was something wrong with her.

Which kept throwing her into this negative spiral.

The more that she felt like there was something wrong with her, the more depressed she felt, and the more depressed she felt, the more she felt like the only way out was to end her life. The more she thought about ending her life, the more she felt like there had to be something wrong with her, and so the cycle went.

Forcing a smile she didn't feel, Ruby said, "Very hip. The colors suit you; they bring out your eyes."

"You do great work, honey." The woman beamed, then turned shrewd eyes in her direction. "You're a gem, Ruby, just like your name. Always remember that, and only ever associate with people who know it and treat you like you're something valuable. All three of my husbands knew how to love. They knew how to make me feel like I was special, they knew how to be partners. You deserve the same. I hope you find it one day."

She had.

She'd found exactly that in Judah.

He understood what it was like to think the world would be a better place without you in it. The way he looked at her made her feel like she was something precious. He made her feel all hopeful and happy inside, and yet ...

Those dark thoughts were still there.

Even knowing that she had a chance at happiness and a normal life with Judah couldn't erase the darkness.

There was definitely something wrong with her.

She just wished that she knew how to fix it because she was starting to feel like she was unfixable.

"Thank you for your kind words," she said, embarrassed. She wasn't comfortable with compliments, especially when she didn't believe that they were true.

Mrs. Manthey shook her head at her like she wanted to say more but didn't think it would do any good. "My chauffeur is waiting to take me back to my room," the old woman said. Ruby felt sorry for her. She knew that it was hard for Mrs. Manthey to live here. Although she had a lot of family who loved her, she required full-time care since she was no longer able to do much for herself. But most of the residents here suffered from Alzheimer's or dementia, and having to live with them could be difficult. Mrs. Manthey got lonely since other than the staff, she didn't have a lot of people to talk to, and she lived for her twice a month hairdressers appointment and weekend visits with her family. Ruby wasn't sure she wanted to live this long. Being old was hard.

"Have a lovely day, Mrs. Manthey," she said as she helped the woman into her wheelchair and pushed her over to the door where a nurse was waiting to take her back to her room.

"You too, dear." A young man walked over to the door and took control of the wheelchair, and Ruby turned and went to clean up and get ready for her next client. She was just grabbing the broom to sweep up the hair trimmings on the floor when Mrs. Manthey spoke one last time. "You are a strong woman, Ruby, even if you don't know it."

She didn't know it.

She didn't believe that it was true.

She had bouts of strength, perhaps. She had fought for her life and escaped hell, and she persisted through a lot of days when she didn't want to. She got up each day and went to work and did chores and hung out with her sisters, but that was it. It was just existing.

She knew that she had to find a way to make that strength last, and she knew that she had to do it herself. It wasn't something that anyone else could do for her. She could always go and see a psychiatrist again. She still had the numbers of the ones she'd seen before, and she was sure that Gideon would give her some names if she wanted to try someone new.

But she didn't want to see a shrink.

It wasn't that she thought badly of them. It was just that she always felt odd talking to a stranger. She always felt like they cared only because they were paid to care.

There was always someone else she could talk to, someone she knew cared about her.

Judah had made her promise him that when she was struggling, she would call him and tell him. She wanted to, but at the same time, she felt uncomfortable doing it. Not because she thought he hadn't meant what he'd said—she knew he meant it—but because she felt like she was bothering him. He was a cop. He was at work. He was dealing with things far more important than her.

"You think *everything* is more important than you," she whispered aloud. That was one of her problems. She didn't see herself as having any value, so it was easy to think that her death wouldn't really have any impact. Logically, she knew that wasn't true. She knew that her sisters would be devastated, but it was hard to believe it.

Ruby pulled out her phone and opened the contacts. She touched Judah's name and then sat and stared at his number.

She should call.

That's what he said she should do when those bad thoughts were creeping in.

He wouldn't think it was intruding on his day.

If she told him that she needed him, he would be here.

He'd said he would, and she believed him.

Right?

That little voice of inner doubt wanted to convince her otherwise. She shouldn't listen to it. Ruby knew that. It was the voice that convinced her she was worthless, and everyone would be better off without her. It was the voice that told her she was nothing and should just kill herself and end her suffering. It told her that she would always be defined by her past and that she could never escape it, so she may as well stop trying.

Ruby put her phone away.

Tears pricked the backs of her eyes.

Mrs. Manthey's voice echoed in her ears. *You are a strong woman.* Why couldn't she believe it?

She pulled her phone back out of her bag.

Call Judah.

It sounded so simple.

But it wasn't.

Reaching out to someone she cared about and admitting that she needed them was the hardest thing in the world to do.

~

10:45 A.M.

"Hello, Wilson," Judah said as he walked into the interview room. The teenager had been lounging in a chair—feet propped up on the table, his arms crossed behind his head against the wall, and his head resting on them. He looked like he didn't have a care in the world, but Judah wasn't buying it.

Right now, the kid thought that he was invincible, that they would never be able to pin any of this on him, but he was wrong. They had the connection to the school and the ghost costume, and once they got their warrant for his DNA, they would match it to the samples they'd found on Tiffany Kendrick. Once they had things sewed up with him, they'd push him to give up the rest of the gang.

"Please put your feet down. This isn't your home. This is a police station," he told Wilson as he took a seat at the table across from the cocky teen.

The kid rolled his eyes but put his feet down and crossed his arms over his chest. Getting information out of him wasn't going to be easy, but he and Zeb had already come up with a plan. They were going to go with their assumptions and hoped that the kid thought they knew a whole lot more than they actually did.

"Are you aware that you lost your high school dog tag?" Zeb asked as he took the seat beside him.

Confusion flashed through Wilson's eyes. It seemed he wasn't aware that he had left it behind at a crime scene.

"At the Kendrick house," Judah added. Then because he wasn't sure that the gang had even known the names of the people they had killed, he elaborated. "They were family number three. You know, the couple that you tortured and raped before putting a bullet through their heads."

All they got in return was a sullen pout.

"You know that you left something else behind at that crime scene," Zeb said. "Semen."

Wilson's cheeks tinted pink like he only just at that moment realized that he had made a mistake. Judah was positive that they had the right guy. Wilson was Ghost. They just needed to prove it.

"It wasn't the only thing left behind at that crime scene," he said. "The Kendrick baby was found hidden in some bushes. One of you didn't want to see the baby get hurt." Going on a hunch, Judah continued. "It was your girl, right? She's pregnant, and she couldn't stand the idea of your leader killing an innocent baby."

From the glare Wilson flung his way, he knew that he was right. "Let's say that what you're saying is true and I am part of some gang that killed some families, why would you think that I wasn't the leader?"

It was clear that despite sitting in an interview room in a police station having been arrested for committing multiple murders that the only thing they had said that bothered him was that he wasn't the one in control. They had thought that there was a power struggle going on between Skull and Ghost, and it looked like they had been right.

"Why weren't you in school today?" he asked, not answering the kid's question. They weren't here to give him information. They were here to get information from him.

"I was sick," he muttered sullenly.

"Your mother was under the impression that she had dropped you off at school on her way to work. She was surprised to hear that you were home," Zeb said.

"I got sick once I was there."

That was plausible, but Judah knew it wasn't the reason he was at home. He was at home because he wanted to be there to watch them discover the bodies, probably to see who was working the case, and maybe even to see his handiwork paraded out of the house as the bodies were taken by the medical examiner to the morgue.

It was clear from what they had seen at the crime scenes that the people they had been looking for got off on power and control, and in humiliating and hurting their victims. They knew that Skull was the one in charge and that it had been Ghost who was the one who really got off on inflicting pain. This was a dangerous man they were dealing with. He was no ordinary seventeen-year-old kid, and if they didn't find the evidence they needed to keep him locked away, he would never stop killing.

His phone buzzed, and he looked down at it. It was a message from Sapphire telling him that they had gotten the warrant for a DNA sample.

Perfect.

That was exactly what he had wanted to hear.

The DNA sample would conclusively prove that Wilson MacAvoy was one of their killers. Once they had him, hopefully, he'd see that giving up the others was in his best interest.

"That was a message from one of my colleagues," he told the teenager who was watching him closely. "A crime scene tech is going to be here shortly to collect a sample of your DNA. They're going to use that to prove that you were in the Kendrick house and that you were the one who raped Tiffany. We've already linked those murders through ballistics to the Cochrane and Lanely murders, which means you'll be going down for all of them. It's time to start thinking about turning the others in."

With that, he and Zeb collected their things and headed out of the room, giving the teenager time to think things over and hopefully realize that this time he had been backed into a corner and that his options were limited.

"We got him." Sapphire grinned at them as soon as they left the interview room. He knew that she wanted this case closed as much as he did. This was personal for both of them. If she hadn't been with Gideon that night, then she would have been in the house with Ruby when the gang broke in.

"As soon as we get confirmation that the DNA matches our samples, we'll go at him again," Zeb said.

"We need to get him talking because he's not the leader, and unless we get the leader, this won't be over," Sapphire said.

He agreed.

This would only end when they had all four members of the gang in custody.

Since Ruby needed to know that this was over and that these people wouldn't try to come back and finish what they started, he would make sure that they got Wilson to give up the names of his friends.

His phone buzzed again, and speak of the devil, Ruby's name flashed on the screen.

"I have to take this," he told the others and walked a few steps away. "Ruby? What's up?" he asked, worried. Had something happened?

"You said I should call you if I was thinking about ... you know," she said.

Relief that she was physically safe was quickly replaced by pride that she had reached out—he knew from experience how hard that could be —and happiness that she had reached out to *him*, and then concern that she was still having those thoughts. She regularly walked around with a razor. She wasn't just contemplating suicide, she was one step away from doing it.

"Are you at work or at home?" he asked.

"I'm at work, but I only have two more clients, and then I'll be going home."

"I'll meet you there in an hour."

"Really?" she asked.

"You already know the answer to that," he reminded her. "You wouldn't have called me if you'd thought I wouldn't be there for you."

"Thank you," she said, and he heard the mess of emotions behind those simple words.

"See you soon."

"Bye."

As soon as he hung up, he went back over to the others. "I have to go take care of something. I'll be back soon."

"Take care of what?" Sapphire demanded, already suspicious. "Is it something to do with Ruby? Did something happen?"

Since he didn't want her to worry unnecessarily, he said, "It was Ruby, but it's nothing to do with this case."

"Is she having suicidal thoughts?"

Judah wanted to be part of this family, and he knew that an important part of a family was trust. He wanted Sapphire and her sisters to trust him. "She is, but I asked her to let me know if she was, and she did. I don't think she's going to try anything,"

"Why is she telling you and not one of us?" Sapphire asked.

"Why does it matter?" Gideon asked before he could say anything. "Isn't the important thing that she reached out to someone?"

"Yeah," Sapphire reluctantly acknowledged. Judah could tell that she was struggling to accept that he and Ruby might soon be an item. He was pretty sure it had more to do with her own fears than him. "Tell her that we're all here for her and that Diamond, Amethyst, and I will check in with her later."

"I will," he promised. He wasn't here to tear Ruby away from her family or to divide the Hatcher sisters. He just wanted to be part of the family. He was prepared to prove to Ruby's sisters that he was in this with her for the long haul. This wasn't a fling or just some passing thing; he was serious about wanting to spend his life with Ruby.

In fact, he had never been more serious about anything in his life.

11:01 A.M.

"What are we going to do now?" Witch asked as she paced around Black Cat's bedroom.

Everything was spiraling out of control.

Wilson had been arrested.

Arrested.

If she hadn't seen it with her own eyes, she would never have believed it.

He'd texted her to come over, and she'd been on her way from school to his house. As she was turning the corner onto his block, she had seen him in handcuffs being put into a car. She had panicked and immediately called Skull and Black Cat to update them, and she'd been told to meet them here.

Instead of trying to figure out a plan and what their next move should be when she'd gotten to Black Cat's house, she'd found the two of them in bed right in the middle of sex.

Sex.

That was what they were thinking about right now?

At a time like this, when everything was crumbling around them, sex should be the last thing on their minds.

The man that she loved, the father of her unborn baby, was in prison. Who knew what the cops were doing to him right now. Was he okay? Had he been hurt? She knew that he wouldn't be scared. Her guy was a cocky one, and he knew that there was no way the cops could connect him to the crimes.

Right?

She'd thought so, but now she wasn't so sure.

"We're going to do exactly what we planned on doing," Skull said, relaxing in an armchair beside the bed. He hadn't bothered to put any clothes on after she'd walked in on them, neither had they bothered stopping what they were doing. They'd continued until they were finished and didn't seem to care that she was standing there watching them.

"Which is what, exactly?" she asked. She knew what the original plan had been, but so many things had gone off script that she was confused and had no idea where this was going to end. Not killing anyone at the Hatcher house—that wasn't supposed to happen, and then her saving the Kendrick baby. That wasn't supposed to happen either. Wilson changing things up and torturing people wasn't what was supposed to happen, and him getting dragged off by the cops absolutely wasn't supposed to happen. So how could they just say that they were going to do what they had planned all along? *None* of this was what they had planned.

"We're going to go back and tie up loose ends, and then we're going to proceed as planned," Skull elaborated.

"What loose ends?" she asked. She felt like she was so out of the loop now. For her, everything had changed the second she'd found out she was carrying another life inside of her. From that moment on, she had never intended to end this the way they had planned when they first came up with this idea.

In fact, had she known that she was pregnant, she would never have agreed to be part of this.

She doubted Wilson would have either.

Yes, she knew he was a dark, dangerous guy. He had *wanted* to hurt those people and had taken pleasure in their pain, and when he had been forcing that Kendrick woman to pleasure him, she couldn't deny she'd been jealous. She didn't want any other women touching her man. She suspected that if the cops let Wilson go, he wouldn't stop hurting people.

Was she prepared to live the rest of her life like that?

Witch touched a hand to her stomach and knew that she was prepared to put up with anything if it meant having her baby's father in their lives.

"The Hatchers and the baby," Black Cat said like it was obvious. She was curled up on Skull's lap—probably to make a point that it was two of them to her one—but at least she'd had the decency to slip into Skull's shirt so Witch wouldn't have to look at both their naked bodies.

"How are we going to do that?" she asked. "I thought you said there was a cop at the Hatcher house during the day, and one of the sisters *is* a cop. How are we going to get in there?"

"I have a few ideas on that," Skull said, a smug look on his face. He was happy that he was in control again, and Wilson wasn't here to challenge him. He hadn't wanted to mess with their original plan and had been so angry that Wilson had mixed things up. But now, with Wilson out of the way, he didn't have to worry about a leadership challenge. He was in control, and he loved every second of it.

"We don't even know where the baby is," she reminded them. She would go along with trying to kill the Hatchers again if there was no other option, but there was no way she was killing that innocent little baby.

"We can find out," Skull said confidently. He genuinely seemed to believe that everything should work out his way just because he wanted it to.

There was no point in arguing against that notion. They didn't even know where to begin looking, but that didn't seem to faze Skull or Black Cat. They'd already made up their minds that they would be victorious.

Moving on to the next thing she needed to know, Witch asked, "And after we do find the baby and kill the Hatchers, then what?"

"You know what," Black Cat said, stretching and then nuzzling her face against Skull's neck. All these two thought about was themselves and their sex life. Didn't they realize that the world as they knew it was about to come to an end—and not in the way they expected?

"So, once we tie up loose ends," she used their wording, "we're still going to kill ourselves?" Now that it was approaching time to follow through on what she had committed to do, she was wondering why it was she had ever allowed herself to be talked into it.

Why would she ever have wanted to die?

To kill herself, no less.

She was way too young to die.

She was pregnant, carrying a little baby inside of her that she already loved. She didn't want to die, and she didn't want to go to prison. She wanted to raise her baby with Wilson. She wanted them to be a family, even if they were dysfunctional and borderline insane, they could still be a family.

"Of course," Skull said. "Are you having second thoughts? Are you going to back out?"

She wanted to say yes, of course, she was having second thoughts. Any sane person would be having second thoughts about this craziness. Killing other people was one thing, but killing herself and her baby was quite another.

She couldn't tell them that, though.

If she did, she'd be signing her own death warrant.

No longer did she have Wilson to protect her. She was on her own, and she had to be smart if she wanted to remain alive.

"No," she said emphatically. "I'm still in. I just wanted to make sure that things hadn't changed now that Wilson has been arrested. What if the cops link us to the crimes now that they have him?"

"Wilson knows better than to talk," Skull said.

"So, there's no way they could know that we were involved," Black Cat added.

"How are we going to get Wilson out of jail?" she asked. She loved Wilson, and after she'd told him about the baby, they had talked about their future.

And that future hadn't included the way this had originally been going to end.

Wilson had been happy about the baby—all her worrying had been for nothing. He hadn't been angry with her; he'd been excited. When she admitted her secret, he had picked her up and spun her around the room, beaming with happiness, then he had kissed her stomach, and thrown her down on the bed and made wild, passionate love to her.

She wanted him back.

She wanted this to be over.

She wasn't a killer, and she wasn't a bad person. Okay, she'd done bad things, but that was because of the others. None of this had been her idea, and she wished she'd never been a part of it.

"We have to get Wilson out. He needs us. How are we going to get him out?" she asked again.

"We're not," Skull said simply.

"We're not?" she echoed, shocked.

"There's still three of us ... that's enough to finish this," Black Cat added, still lying sprawled all over her man. That was easy enough for her to say; it wasn't the love of her life rotting away in a jail cell.

These two.

What did she ever see in them?

Just days ago, she had admired them—maybe even worshiped them a little—but now, when she looked at them, all she felt was betrayal.

11:23 A.M.

Ruby felt nervous.

She was proud of herself for following through and calling Judah when those dark thoughts started creeping back in. She knew it was the right thing to do, and she hoped that he saw it for what it was—a step out in trust and the beginning of paving the foundation that a relationship could be built on.

That was what she wanted.

Fears or not, doubts or not, insecurities or not, she wanted a relationship, a marriage, a partnership. She wanted someone to share her life with. She had finally reached a point—one that for a long time she had thought she would never get to—where she was ready to say that her past was horrendous and would always be a part of her, but it didn't have to define her. For years, it had been ingrained in her head that she was just something to be used by men for their own pleasure, but now she thought she was ready to acknowledge that she was a woman who deserved better.

She wasn't there yet, but she was at least ready to try to get there.

That was massive progress.

And she almost couldn't believe that this was her thinking these things.

But she was, she *really* was.

After years of believing everything Igor and his men had told her and that it was safer to be alone, it was like a switch had suddenly been flipped. It wasn't that she thought she was now a brand-new person who could leave the past behind, but she was a person who wanted to find a new way of thinking

In a way, she supposed that *did* make her a new person.

"Ruby?" Judah called out as she heard the front door open.

Mug of hot chocolate in her hands, she turned to see Judah striding down the hall. His pace was brisk, and she could see the worried lines in his forehead, but his blue eyes were sparkling. She knew that sparkle was because he felt the same things that she did. They were building something that was going to last forever, and it was exciting. She was probably always going to struggle with suicidal thoughts; maybe Judah would too. She knew he would always struggle with his OCD, but that didn't mean that they couldn't be happy.

She hadn't been happy—really and truly happy—since she was seventeen. She was twenty-eight now. That meant about forty percent of her life she'd either been held prisoner by Igor or held prisoner by herself, and she was more than ready to find a way to shake off those chains.

Without overthinking anything, Ruby set the mug down and walked to meet him. When she did, she threw her arms around his neck and stood on her tiptoes to kiss him. She was never forward with men;

in fact, the opposite. Ever since she had escaped, she had avoided them because she was afraid, but she could never be scared of Judah.

"That wasn't the greeting I was expecting." Judah grinned at her when she broke the kiss.

"You were expecting me to be a crying mess, quivering in the corner?" she asked lightheartedly, mostly because she had found herself in that exact same position so many times before. But she was putting that side of herself away for good.

"Not crying or quivering in the corner, but I didn't expect you to be kissing me."

"The more I thought about calling you, the more I thought about the future, and the more I thought about the future, that kind of cleared the darkness that's inside me away," she explained.

"I'm so proud of you for reaching out to me." He curled a hand around the back of her neck and drew her closer. He kissed her and pulled her against his chest and held her.

This was nice.

She could get used to having a guy in her life.

Ruby felt so lucky to have met someone like Judah. He understood the insecurities that she battled daily because he battled something similar. Knowing that made her feel safe in a way that she wouldn't with anyone else. One of the reasons that she didn't have friends was because it was too hard to try to explain to someone else just what it was like to go through what she'd lived for four long years. Her sisters got it. It was easier to be around them. They didn't give her strange looks or whisper about what had happened to her.

Being a cop and working with her sister, Ruby knew that Judah knew about her past without her having to explain it. He had lived through his own ordeal, and she knew that he understood.

He'd been to that dark place.

And he'd survived.

They both had, and now they had a chance to make something beautiful grow out of the darkness.

"How soon do you have to be back at work?" she asked.

"I have a little time. Why?"

"Want to go upstairs? To my room?" she added. She wasn't quite ready for sex yet, but there were other things they could do.

Hands on her shoulder, he pulled her back so he could see her properly. "Are you sure?"

She smiled. This was exactly why she trusted Judah. Most guys wouldn't pause to take the time to ask a girl if she was sure when she asked him up to her room, but he knew that this was a big step for her and she was sure he didn't want her to think that he was using what was going on with the home invaders to take advantage of her.

"I'm positive," she assured him. She took his hand and led him to the stairs. She gasped when he scooped her up in his arms and carried her up the stairs.

They reached her room, and Judah laid her down on the bed and then stared down at her with a reverence that made her feel like she was something precious—just like her name. Rubies were hard, and they were beautiful. They were something that people treasured, and although she used to love her name when she was a teenager, the last few years she'd felt like she was letting it down. She was nothing like rubies were supposed to be, but when Judah looked at her like that with such open adoration on his face, that old feeling started to creep back in.

It wasn't just the adoration; there was some appreciation there too. She might not work out religiously like Amethyst and Sapphire, but she walked or ran on the treadmill every day, and most of the time, she watched what she ate—except for cupcakes, which were her weakness. To know that the man she liked found her physically attractive was definitely a confidence booster.

Ruby reached up and was about to drag Judah down and make him kiss her when there was a huge crash outside. His cop instincts were strong, and he immediately jumped off the bed and ran to the window.

She followed and then gasped when she saw what was outside.

A car had crashed into a telephone pole and burst into flames.

Was someone still inside?

She scanned the street and didn't see anyone, which meant that the driver and any passengers were probably trapped. Being stuck inside a burning car had to be one of the most terrifying things—being burned alive would be a horrific death.

"I have to go see if I can help," Judah said, already running toward the door. "Stay here, I'll be back as soon as I can."

Ruby watched from the window as people began to spill out into the street, having heard the commotion from their homes and coming to see if there was anything they could do to help. She didn't argue with Judah's orders for her to stay here. She wasn't a cop or a doctor, and there was nothing she could do to help. Plus, she didn't much like the idea of hearing the screams of the car's occupants if no one could get them out, and the flames claimed them.

She wasn't sure what made her turn around—instinct maybe, that sixth sense that people talked about sometimes—but whatever the reason, just as she spun around, she saw someone in a witch costume come running through the door at her.

With a cop for a sister, she'd been taught some self-defense, and she spun to the side just as the gun went off. The bullet whizzed past her, close enough that she felt a sting on her cheek.

Witch woman was close, so she grabbed the arm holding the gun and twisted, causing the woman to suck in a pained breath. Wrapping a hand around her wrist, she twisted that too and felt satisfied when the gun clattered to the floor.

Quickly, she snatched it up and then turned it on her would be murderer. She was breathing hard. The hand that held the gun was shaking, and she couldn't quite believe that this had almost happened. The car crash was a diversion, so the home invaders could make a second attempt at killing her.

But she'd stopped them.

Maybe she was a little tougher than she gave herself credit for.

"Please don't hurt me." Witch was crying quietly. "I'm sorry ... I didn't want to come here, but they made me. Wilson is in jail and it was just me against the two of them and I didn't know what to do. I was scared of them. Please don't hurt me ... I'm pregnant."

Pregnant? And she was spending her time breaking into people's homes and shooting them?

Ruby could tell by her voice that the woman was young, and she *did* sound fearful. She believed that Witch didn't really want to be here, but that didn't mean she was going to let the other woman go.

"Just stand there and don't move. I don't want to hurt you, but I will if you don't give me any choice. We're just going to stand here until my boyfriend comes back," Ruby said.

Boyfriend.

She hadn't meant to call Judah that, it had just slipped out, but it sounded just right; perfect, in fact. She had a boyfriend. She nearly squealed in excitement, even though she was holding a gun on a woman who had just tried to kill her. She felt like she was seventeen again, and it felt wonderful.

11:34 A.M.

"Someone call 911!" Judah yelled as he ran out the front door of the Hatcher house. He'd left his phone on the nightstand in Ruby's bedroom, right where he'd put it when he'd carried her up the stairs and laid her out on the bed, looking down at her and thinking about how lucky he was that this beautiful, strong woman actually liked him.

While he hadn't expected to find her crying and quivering in the corner, he also hadn't expected her to walk straight up to him and kiss him.

Not that he was complaining.

It was a wonderful greeting. He'd just expected her to be upset or worried—maybe with a razor blade in her hand—but he loved that she had surprised him.

He loved so many things about her, and he couldn't wait to get back to her, but right now, he had to help whoever had just crashed their car. As much as he wanted to spend a little time making out with Ruby, he couldn't stand by and not come to help someone in need.

The front of the car was scrunched up, and all of the doors were closed. No one in the street looked like they had just been in a car accident, so the driver was still in there, plus who knew how many passengers.

By the time he got outside and across the street, the car was a raging inferno. Judah knew whoever was in there—even if they survived the initial impact—had already been claimed by the fire, but he still had to check.

"Does anyone have a fire extinguisher?" he yelled out to the crowd gathering in the street.

"I have one in my kitchen," someone said.

"Get it," he ordered.

Getting as close to the car as he could—the heat was intense, and he could feel it prickling against his skin—he tried to look through the flames to see if he could find a body.

All he could see was fire.

"Here."

The fire extinguisher was shoved into his hands, and immediately, he aimed it at the car and pushed the lever. The fire was too strong, and the small emergency extinguisher couldn't do much to fight through the flames, but it did dim them a little—just for a moment.

But it was enough.

The car was empty.

There was no one there.

Immediately, Judah knew that he'd made a mistake.

This was a diversion.

So the home invasion gang could get to Ruby.

With Wilson MacAvoy in custody, they probably felt like they had nothing to lose and may as well try to tie up loose ends before moving on to whatever they had planned for their grand finale.

Judah dropped the fire extinguisher and ran toward the house. He had a key to the house and he'd locked the door behind him when he'd come running out to check the burning car—instinct maybe—and when he got to it, he found it still locked, he hoped that meant that whatever plan the gang had cooked up had failed.

Thankfully, he hadn't taken his gun off, and even though he thought that there was no one inside the house but Ruby, he pulled it out as he ran up the stairs.

She had to be okay.

She *had* to be.

The idea that the gang *had* gotten in here and they had already done something to Ruby—killed her—was something he did *not* want to entertain.

Judah's heart jumped into his throat as he entered Ruby's bedroom.

Ruby wasn't alone.

There was someone dressed in a witch costume standing in the room just a couple of feet away from Ruby, who held a gun on them. When he'd arrived here earlier, he had been so anxious to see Ruby and make sure that she was okay that he hadn't locked the door behind him and set the alarm. That meant that they could have snuck in here at any point while he had been carrying Ruby up the stairs and thinking about making out with her.

If she had been killed, he would have had no one to blame but himself.

"Judah," Ruby sighed with relief when she saw him.

As much as he wanted to drag her into his arms, he didn't. He had to stay in cop mode for the moment and make sure there were no other threats in the room and take care of the one that was here.

"Is there anyone else here?" he asked.

"No, I don't think so. I haven't seen anyone else, and she didn't say that there was anyone else," Ruby replied.

"Are you hurt?"

"No, I'm okay."

Briefly taking his eyes off the witch woman, he gave Ruby a quick once-over. She looked all right, and she didn't sound like she was in pain, so he returned his attention to the intruder. "Hands behind your back," he ordered, his gun still pointed at her head. He wouldn't hesitate to fire if he thought that she wasn't going to comply.

The witch did as she was told, and he had to say he was surprised. Given what they knew about the gang, he hadn't thought that she would give in so easily.

"Ruby, keep the gun on her," he instructed as he put his away, pulled out his handcuffs, and went to cuff the witch.

Once he had her under control, he turned to Ruby. She was watching his every move, and when she saw he was looking at her, she shot him a weak smile. She was holding it together, but her hands—

which still held the gun in a white knuckled death grip—were shaking, and she was as pale as paper.

"You did good," he said as he walked cautiously toward her. He wanted to keep things lighthearted, and since she still had the gun and she was understandably spooked, he didn't want her to accidentally fire it.

"Sapphire taught me some stuff ... she's going to be pleased that I was able to pull it off." Ruby gave a shaky laugh.

"She's going to love that when you tell her." He gently covered her hands with his and pushed down, so the gun pointed at the floor and not at the witch kid. Then he gently pried her fingers open and removed the gun, slipping it into his waistband.

"She's probably going to use it as ammo to get me to take a self-defense course ... she's been wanting me to for ages now." Her blue eyes lifted to meet his, and she shuddered. "I'm really glad you're here."

"Me too," he said, tucking a lock of blonde hair behind her ear, then tracing his fingertips down her cheek, curling them around the back of her neck and leaning down to kiss her, before resting his forehead on hers.

She was okay—better than okay. She had foiled Witch's attempt to murder her all on her own.

What a woman.

"You good?" he asked as he lifted his head, searching her eyes to make sure she wasn't going to lie to him.

"Shaken, but yes," she replied.

"I want you to grab my phone and call your sister. Tell her what happened and that we need backup here. But stay where I can see you," he added. Skull and Black Cat were still out there, and for all he knew, they were hiding somewhere in the house. He didn't want Ruby out of his sight until backup was here, and he knew that they were in the clear.

Judah waited until she had gone to retrieve his phone from the nightstand before he went to Witch, who he had been watching out of the corner of his eye while he allowed himself a moment with Ruby. The girl hadn't moved. She was standing right where he'd left her, and he could hear that she was crying quietly.

He pulled the witch mask off and saw that she looked much younger than he had expected. "How old are you?"

"Sixteen," the girl replied, but he wasn't convinced. She didn't look any older than fourteen.

"What's your name?"

"Nicole Trent."

"She said she's pregnant," Ruby said, coming to stand beside him. He wanted to tell her to stay as far away from this kid as she could, but he sensed that Nicole wasn't really a threat to anyone.

"You're pregnant, Nicole?" he asked.

The kid nodded.

They had Wilson, and now they had Nicole. That left only two others. So far, Wilson hadn't given them anything, but maybe Nicole would be more forthcoming with information.

"We have Wilson in custody. He was Ghost; you're Witch. Who are Skull and Black Cat?" he asked.

Nicole pressed her lips into a stubborn line.

Maybe he *wouldn't* be getting more information out of her.

"She's scared," Ruby said. "She said she didn't want to be here and that the others made her come. She begged me not to hurt her once I got ahold of her gun."

His heart beat erratically at the thought of her fighting for the weapon, but he quickly reminded himself that everything had worked out and focused on what Ruby had just told him. Nicole was scared. She wasn't the mastermind behind this, but she was an active participant. If she was afraid of the other members of her own gang, that really said something about them, and those two were still out there somewhere.

They had to find them because he suspected that they were going to continue to come after Ruby until they finished what they had started, and he was not going to let that happen.

❀

7:46 P.M.

. . .

"We need to upgrade our security system," Sapphire announced as she banged through the front door.

"You said that already when you were here earlier," Ruby reminded her little sister.

"I know, but now I've spoken to someone about it," Sapphire said as she dropped her bag on the kitchen table and dropped onto the sofa. She looked exhausted, and if Ruby had to guess, her sister had been helping out with the home invasion case as well as working her own caseload. "They're coming out to look at the place tomorrow. His name is Noah, and he's some sort of computer genius. I told him I wanted the best system he has."

"Isn't that going to cost a small fortune?" Ruby asked. With Sapphire moving out soon, that meant there would only be three of them living here. She didn't make a huge amount of money hairdressing. Amethyst was a firefighter, and she made a decent amount but not a lot. They mostly relied on Diamond's income as a graphic designer who worked in advertising and taught art classes on the side, as well as selling the occasional painting. Diamond's income made up about forty percent of the house's income, Sapphire's and Amethyst's twenty-five percent each, and hers only ten. When Sapphire left, they would be down a quarter of their money to pay bills. They couldn't afford a new security system right now.

"Yes, but it will be worth it. Once I leave, there won't be a cop here anymore, and Amethyst often works nights, so it's just you and Diamond. I need to know that you're both safe. Judah isn't going to be staying here forever. Don't worry about how much it costs. Gideon and I are paying for it."

"We can't let you do that," she immediately protested.

"We can't," Diamond echoed. "And you know Amethyst isn't going to like it either."

"Gideon and I already talked about it. He knows that moving out is a big step for me and that leaving you guys is hard, and he also knows that this will make it at least a tiny bit easier. Right?" Sapphire turned to her fiancé.

"Right," Gideon agreed. "We both want to do this."

"I don't think I can move out otherwise. I need to know that you guys will be safe here," Sapphire added.

"You're guilt-tripping us," Diamond said.

"Sorry." Sapphire shot them a completely unapologetic grin. "Noah will be here at eight tomorrow morning," she said like it was already a foregone conclusion.

Which Ruby supposed it was. Did she really want to argue about a security system when it *would* make her feel safer? Just because she and Judah were together now didn't mean they were going to move in together immediately or that they would be engaged next week. They were taking things slow, and when they were both ready, they would take that next step. When Judah moved back to his house, she would sleep better at night, knowing that they had the best security system money could buy.

"What are you guys doing tonight?" Diamond asked.

Although she had hung around the house all afternoon, answering questions about what had happened with Nicole Trent and reassuring Judah a dozen times—and then her sisters a dozen times—that she was fine, so far she hadn't made it into the kitchen to cook dinner. Nor did she really feel hungry. She *was* okay, but realizing that it was no longer just being cautious and that the gang really did want to finish what they started, had kind of zapped her appetite.

"Not much," Ruby replied. She was hoping that Judah would be home soon, but she knew he was busy, and if she didn't see him until tomorrow, it wasn't really a big deal.

Except ...

She hoped he was home soon.

"Gideon and I don't have plans, just hanging out here," Sapphire answered.

"We could hang out together tonight," Diamond suggested.

"I can leave if you guys want some family time," Gideon offered.

"No, you don't have to leave," Diamond assured him. "You *are* part of the family. It might not be official until you marry Sapphire, but we all already think of you as a brother."

Ruby nodded her agreement, thinking that hanging out with her sisters and soon-to-be brother-in-law could be a good way to pass away the time until Judah got here.

When had hanging out with her sisters become her backup?

Even though she had known Judah for months now, it was only in the last week that she had finally decided that she didn't really have anything to lose by giving dating him a try. How had he become so important to her so quickly?

Maybe all these months that she'd been telling herself that he was just an attractive guy who worked with her sister, he'd always been something more. Maybe she just hadn't let herself see it because sometimes it was just easier to let your fears control you than it was to fight them.

Realizing that everyone was looking at her, Ruby was about to say that family time sounded nice when the front door opened, and Judah came walking down the hallway.

Immediately, thoughts of spending time with her sisters were replaced by thoughts of spending time with Judah alone up in her room. Her little make out plans had been disrupted earlier, and she was eager for a second attempt. She didn't know how far she was ready to go, but she knew that making out with Judah filled her with excitement and not dread.

"Were you able to locate Nicole Trent's family?" Sapphire asked, immediately switching into cop mode.

"No. She's not speaking, and the school doesn't have a record of a Nicole Trent, which means she's either lying about her name or she goes to a different school," Judah replied as he joined them in the living room.

"Which do you think it is?" Sapphire asked.

"No one at the school seems to recognize her, so I'm guessing she goes to a different school. Hopefully, someone will report her missing, and we'll be able to find out who her family is." Judah sat beside her and gave her another assessing once-over. "How are you doing? No more incidents?"

"I'm fine, and so far, so good."

"We were just discussing hanging out together tonight," Diamond said. "You want to join us?"

"Actually, I'm kind of beat," Judah replied, giving her what she was sure he thought was a subtle glance, indicating he wanted to spend some time alone with her—no doubt to finish what they started earlier.

Ruby felt her cheeks heat and avoided eye contact with her sisters. "Actually, I'm a little tired too. Do you guys mind if we do family time tomorrow night?"

Sapphire looked like she was going to oppose the idea, but Gideon got in before she could say anything. "We don't mind at all. I'd love to take my beautiful fiancée out to dinner, and you can join us if you like, Diamond."

"Thanks, but I think I'll go get some more work done on a painting I've been working on," Diamond said. Her older sister's green eyes looked sad, and she sounded lonely. There was nothing worse than being the fifth—or third—wheel with another couple when all you did was feel like you were intruding. "See you in the morning."

Diamond made a hasty retreat to her art studio, and Gideon stood, taking Sapphire's hand and pulling her up with him. "Enjoy your night." He winked at them.

"Why can't we just eat here?" Sapphire asked him as he grabbed her bag and ushered her toward the door.

"Because I like to take you out, treat you like the princess that you are," Gideon told her.

Ruby could practically hear her sister's eye roll. "You're so corny," Sapphire said. "You just want me to leave, so I can't interrupt Ruby and Judah."

"Smart *and* a princess; I knew there was a reason I fell in love with you."

She could hear Sapphire laugh as the front door closed behind them, leaving her and Judah alone. He didn't waste any time. "I thought we could pick up the massage where we left off the other night. There were a few parts I missed."

Heat pooled in her stomach.

This was all so new to her. She hadn't felt this way about being intimate with a guy since she was seventeen years old.

As soon as Judah scooped her up into his arms, her lips moved to his like they were magnets. Upstairs in her bedroom, he laid her down on the bed, then stretched out above her, balancing his weight on one elbow while his other hand hovered at the hem of her sweater.

She knew what he wanted to ask, and it took her only a second to make her decision. "I think the massage will be better without the sweater."

Judah's cornflower blue eyes twinkled as he pulled the sweater up and over her head, then dropped it onto the floor beside them. His lips returned to hers, and his free hand began to brush lightly across her stomach. His fingertips tickled, but weirdly, not like when she and her sisters used to tickle each other when they were kids. This kind of tickling took that heat in her stomach and made it grow and reach out around her body until she felt like she was on fire. A good kind of fire.

As if he could read her body and her mind, Judah's hand rose until it was brushing the underside of her breast. She still had her bra on, and suddenly, she wished she was naked, so she didn't miss a single second of how good his hands were making her feel.

When Judah's hand closed over her breast and began to knead, Ruby moaned her pleasure into his mouth, and without realizing what she was doing, her body arched off the bed.

Time blurred into nothingness as they kissed, and Judah played with her breasts, giving attention to one and then the other. She offered no protest when his fingers found their way inside her bra and began to tease her nipples, making them turn into hard little pebbles.

This was how intimacy with a man should be. It *should* make her feel good and desirable. It should have her wanting more.

And she did want more.

She could feel that Judah wanted more too.

Proof of that was pressed against her thigh.

Even though she didn't want it to, her mind snapped back into what it had been trained to do. It wasn't her place to receive pleasure. It was her place to give it. That's what she was supposed to do.

Those thoughts pulled her out of the moment, and Judah noticed and instantly stopped kissing her, his hands lifting, so they no longer made contact with her body.

"Do you want to stop?" he asked her.

"That's hardly fair," she said, indicating his erection.

"It's fine." He smiled at her.

"You'll be uncomfortable," she reminded him. She was an expert at pleasuring a man. She'd learned to be if she didn't want to be killed. She could give him what he wanted. It wouldn't take long, and then he'd go to bed satisfied tonight.

"That's my problem, not yours," he told her, standing and picking her sweater up off the floor, carrying it to the en suite and dropping it into the hamper, before returning with the oversized T-shirt she slept in. "Arms up," he ordered.

Staring at him in shock, she did as she was told, and he slid the T-shirt over her head. Once she was covered, he slipped his hand inside, unfastened her bra and took her arms and put them through the sleeves, dressing her like she was a child. He picked her up and stood her beside the bed and removed her jeans before pulling back the covers, laying her down, and tucking her in. Her jeans joined her sweater in the hamper, and then Judah took off his own jeans—folding them neatly and hanging them over the back of the chair—and came and lay on the bed beside her, on top of the covers, spooning her. His erection pressed into her back, and yet, he didn't ask her to do anything about it.

"What are you doing?" she asked, confused.

"Going to sleep."

"But you need to come." Just because she knew that Judah wasn't like the men who had used and abused her when she belonged to Igor, didn't mean that she wasn't confused by his behavior. She was used to men taking what they wanted from her and not caring about what she wanted and needed. And yet, here was Judah, who was clearly turned on, saying that what he needed wasn't as important as the fact that she wasn't ready to take that step yet.

"I told you, I'll be fine holding you in my arms while we sleep. That's what I want. Everything else can wait. I don't want sex until you want it too, and I don't want you to do something because you were trained to think you have to. When you do that, I want it to be because it's something you want, something that brings you as much pleasure as it brings me."

She did want it.

She really did.

And yet at the back of her mind was a tiny niggling doubt.

"Judah?"

"Yeah?" he asked, his breath warm against her neck.

"How much about my past do you know?"

"I know that you and your sisters were sold by your parents to human traffickers."

"Do you know that they used me as a prostitute?"

Judah tensed, his arms inadvertently tightening around her. "I'm sorry."

She didn't want his pity; she wanted his understanding. "I was there for four and a half years ... that equals a lot of men." Fear and uncertainty and embarrassment almost had her stopping there, falling short of what she actually wanted to say. "After being used like that so many times, I don't think that I should like it," she blurted out.

"Sex?"

"Yes," she confirmed, then held her breath as she awaited his response.

"Why should that make you not like sex? I mean, that's fine if it did. I can see that messing with your head, but that doesn't make wanting it wrong. What those men did to you wasn't sex. It was rape. And when you're ready to take that step with me, that won't be sex either. That'll be making love. What you went through was horrendous, and I wish I could erase it from your past, but there isn't a right or wrong way to deal with it. You are strong and sweet, and you care about others. As far as I'm concerned, you're already a survivor, whether or not you ever want to have sex again. Ruby ..." His fingers traced up and down her arm. "I care about you, and I want to be here with you. I don't care about anything other than you. I'll wait as long as you want to. This is about developing something real, not about a hot night between the sheets."

"You're amazing, you know that?" she said, as tears began to drip from her eyes.

"You're the amazing one." Judah pressed a kiss to her neck and then pulled her closer.

It was still early, but she was drained and tired, and being snuggled in Judah's arms like this had sleep already lapping at the edges of her mind. Ruby gave into it, secure in the knowledge that she and her heart were safe in the hands of the man who held her.

10:57 P.M.

"And then there were two," Skull said as he locked Black Cat's bedroom door. He didn't want anyone interrupting them tonight.

Not that he minded an audience.

It had turned him on knowing that Nicole was watching them earlier, but she wouldn't be the one interrupting him tonight. She was in prison, and the only people who might walk in were Black Cat's parents. They wouldn't just stand quietly and watch as Nicole had done because she was too afraid to turn around and leave after he'd ordered her to stay.

If Black Cat's parents found him doing their precious little daughter, they would throw him out. And while he could always just kill them, he knew that wouldn't make his pet happy, and he loved his little pussy cat.

At the moment, she was stretched out on the bed. Her shoulders were propped up on some pillows, and her legs were crossed at the ankles. She had her phone in her hands, and she was flipping through it, no doubt scrounging up every piece of news she could find on their crimes. She liked to follow it all, soak up the attention. He, on the other hand, couldn't care less about the attention. The only attention he wanted was from his beautiful cat, his loyal followers, and his victims.

But tonight, there would be no more victims. They were nearly finished with what they started, and it was too late to bring anyone else into it. His loyal followers were both in prison now, and he knew they were both too smart to turn on him, so he wasn't worried about them saying something they shouldn't.

Which just left him with his cat.

She was naked, and her pale skin looked stunning against the black quilt. Her dark hair was fanned out across the white pillows, and her dark eyes were riveted on the screen in front of her.

But he wanted those eyes somewhere else.

On him.

"I said, and then there were two," he repeated, stalking over to the bed. Sometimes it drove him crazy that his girl didn't quiver in fear when she was in his presence. He loved fear. He loved it even more when that fear was directed at him. Wilson hadn't understood why he didn't want to torture their victims, but it wasn't that he didn't want to; it was that he didn't *need* to. He already had what he wanted. Their fear was enough to sustain him, invigorate him, give him a rush like nothing else could—not even Black Cat.

But his girl wasn't like anyone else.

"Mmhmm." She nodded like she was only half listening to what he was saying.

He didn't like that.

He wanted her attention riveted on him and him alone.

He reached out and twisted one of her nipples between his fingers until she squawked and finally stopped what she was doing to look at him.

"That hurt." She pouted. He loved that whenever it was just the two of them, they walked around naked. Her parents didn't know that, but they also didn't know that most nights, as soon as they went to bed, he scaled the house to sneak into their daughter's second-floor bedroom where he spent the night. What they didn't know couldn't hurt them, but easy access to Black Cat's body was going to hurt her if she didn't stop playing with her phone.

"And it'll hurt worse next time if you don't put that away," he warned. He wasn't above hurting the girl he loved if it was the only way to get what he wanted.

"Fine." She sighed and rolled her eyes dramatically as she set the phone on her nightstand and fixed him in a sharp stare. "Happy now?"

"No, not yet," he said, reaching out to take her hand and wrap it firmly around his already hard length, encouraging her to squeeze. He always concentrated better when she was touching him.

Black Cat began to purr as she rearranged herself onto her knees, so she had better access to him and began to stroke him with a mixture of harder and softer, faster and slower movements.

"We need to decide our next move," he told her.

"I thought it was finishing what we started."

"It was ... it is ... but Nicole messed up, and now it's going to be harder to get to the Hatcher house, and we still don't know where the baby is." He was still angry with Nicole for snatching the infant and hiding it so he couldn't finish off the Kendrick family. He hated loose ends, and now, because of that stupid safe room and that idiot Nicole, he had two left that needed to be attended to. If that girl was here, he would have given her a lesson she would never have forgotten. She and that guy of hers seemed to enjoy forcing others to perform sexual acts against their will, so maybe he would have done that to her, seen how she liked it.

"You'll figure something out," Black Cat purred.

He should be flattered by her words, but he was getting to the point where he could no longer form a coherent thought.

The heat was building inside his body, ready to send him bursting into flames any second now.

Flames.

Fire.

They'd stolen a car, turned the engine on, put a brick on the gas pedal and sent the car slamming into a telephone pole where it burst into flames.

It was just meant to be a distraction so Nicole could kill Ruby Hatcher, who would now no doubt be under constant police supervision so they couldn't get to her.

But maybe they didn't have to get to her.

Maybe they could blow the house up, taking out Ruby and anyone else who happened to be there.

Satisfied that he had indeed figured out a way to get what he wanted, he grunted as he came. Black Cat's skilled hands drew out every last drop of pleasure until he was spent and empty.

"You have a plan," she said as she stretched back out on the bed.

"I do," he agreed.

"And then, once we finish, we can finally end things," she said, a relaxed look floating across her face.

Killing others was his part of the plan, but killing themselves was hers.

That was how much he loved her.

They were a Romeo and Juliet of sorts. Young, in love, obsessed with one another to the point where it had consumed them.

When the Kendrick baby and Ruby Hatcher were dead, then they would end their own lives. That way, the two of them would be together forever. Nothing would be able to separate them—not the cops, not Black Cat's parents, not Wilson and Nicole, not even life. In death, they would remain united for all eternity.

"I love you. You know that, right?" he asked as he scooped her into his arms and lay down on the bed on his back, draping Black Cat across his front.

"I know," she said, twirling her fingers through his hair.

Sometimes he was afraid that she didn't. That his obsession with his plan, and taking from her without always giving her something in return, that she might not know that she was the best thing that had ever happened to him.

He didn't have the same kind of family that she did.

He hadn't been loved by his parents.

His dad was a former military man who ran his house like they were his soldiers—not his wife and kids. Three basic meals a day, no toys, no video games. When they weren't at school, they were expected to be doing chores or learning some skills he thought was necessary. There was no fun, no warmth, no guidance—just orders to be followed.

His mother was a loyal soldier who obeyed her husband's every command. She didn't speak out of turn, she kept the house as though it were a museum, she had no friends, limited contact with her family, and zero interest in being a real mother to her children.

His brother was the good son, the one who did as he was told, who followed those orders as though he felt it was his place in life. He got perfect grades, mastered every skill their father asked of them, never spoke back, never complained, and he never fought to be his own man.

But *he* was different. *He* was his own man. *He* was in control of his destiny, and *he* was going to make sure that he was as far from the man his father wanted him to be as he possibly could.

There was only one thing that destroyed a man like his father.

Disgrace.

He didn't have a smart, obedient, loyal son. He had a cold-blooded killer for a son.

His father could take his stupid rules and stuff them. He was getting what he deserved. He would be dead, and his father would have to live the rest of his life, knowing what his son had done.

Stroking his hand up and down Black Cat's spine, he let himself drift off to sleep, anxious for the next day to arrive so he could finish what he'd started and then step out of this world and into the next.

CHAPTER

Ten

October 25th
9:17 A.M.

"I think I found Nicole Trent's family."

Judah looked over to his partner, who was grinning back at him. Finding who the kid was had proved difficult. There were a lot of Trents in the area, and all of the Trents they'd contacted had denied having a teenage daughter named Nicole. While it had been frustrating—especially now that they knew the gang did indeed intend to come back for Ruby—as soon as he'd gotten back to Ruby's house last night and spent time with her, all that frustration melted away.

He'd had the best sleep of his life last night, just holding Ruby in his arms, her warm body snuggled against him, feeling her chest rising and falling evenly with each breath she took, knowing that she trusted him.

That was more important to him than that she had feelings for him.

He had always known that she liked him, no matter how much she wanted to avoid those feelings, but given what she'd been through, to know that he had earned her trust meant something.

When he'd left for work this morning, he made sure that there were two cops with Ruby. One would stay outside, and the other would stay inside—neither would leave her for anything. There would be no more distractions to try to lure them away and leave Ruby unprotected.

"Who are they?" he asked.

"Looks like they have different last names," Zeb replied. "Eric Mariano reported his sixteen-year-old stepdaughter Nicole Trent missing late last night. Whoever took the report obviously didn't take it very seriously because if they'd looked into it, they would have seen we had the girl in custody."

"They probably thought she was just another runaway." It was sad, but that was the way it usually went—most teenagers ran away; they didn't get kidnapped. "But at least we know the family is looking for her. Mom not in the picture?"

"According to the report, the stepdad said that he thought there was a chance that Nicole had gone looking for her biological dad. Apparently, he ditched her and her mom when Nicole was a baby. Mom remarried but sadly passed when Nicole was four. The stepdad has been raising her ever since; that's why when we were contacting people with the last name Trent, we didn't find her family; she kept her name when the mom remarried. The stepdad remarried when Nicole was seven and now has three kids of his own. He says Nicole often talks about feeling left out and like she's not really wanted or really part of the family, and he thought she might have gone to find her place in the world with her biological dad because she talked about him a lot."

"If she felt like she didn't really belong anywhere and like she didn't have a family of her own, that would have made her susceptible to being lured into this gang. From the way she talked to Ruby at the house yesterday, she was afraid of the other two and worried that someone was going to hurt her. I think she's not talking now out of fear, but once we find Skull and Black Cat and get them in custody, I think that she might be more willing to talk."

"I agree. Now that we know who Nicole's family is, we should bring them in and see if they can get her to start talking."

"If she already doesn't feel connected to them, then I don't think she'll be any more willing to talk to them than she is to talk to us."

Judah thought that the only person the girl truly felt cared about her was Ghost—Wilson MacAvoy. He was assuming that the boy was the father of Nicole's baby. He also thought that part of the reason that Wilson had kept quiet and not said anything about the other members of the gang when he knew that they had proof he was involved was that he didn't want to bring Nicole into it. Judah believed that despite everything they had done and the kind of people that they were, the two truly loved each other. After all, they had teamed up against Skull and Black Cat if the torture was anything to go by.

"What are you thinking?" Zeb asked.

"That maybe we should let Wilson and Nicole see each other."

"You think that might get them talking?"

"When Nicole was examined by a nurse when she was booked, they found bruises on her chest. It looked like someone beat up on her. I don't think it was Wilson. She seems to trust him, and the only time she's talked has been to ask if he's okay. But she's afraid of the other two. Maybe if we let them see each other and remind them that the other two are still out there, we could suggest that once the baby is born and it goes to live either with Nicole or Wilson's family or enters the foster care system, it could be in danger, then they might be willing to give up the other two names."

"The other option would be to tell Wilson that we have Nicole in custody and that she's in the hospital," Zeb suggested. "If he thinks that Skull and Black Cat hurt her again, especially if he does know that she's pregnant, then he might be angry enough to turn on the others."

Judah liked both plans; both had merit, and either could end up getting them the information that they needed. They would need to talk them through and figure out which one gave them the best chance at getting Wilson and Nicole talking because right now, that was the quickest way they were going to get the others in custody and ensure that Ruby stayed safe.

He was about to start a list of pros and cons when something occurred to him. "Zeb, what's Nicole's address?"

"2988 Gerrard Place."

Turning to his computer, he quickly brought up the crime scene files for the Kendrick and Cochrane murders. "Bingo."

"Bingo?"

"Wilson MacAvoy and his family live opposite the Lanely house. Nicole Trent and her family live opposite the Kendrick house," he said, excitement starting to buzz inside him. A link. Finally, they had something tangible to look into. "Who lives opposite the Cochrane house and Ruby's house? I'll bet anything that it's kids from the high school."

Nicole didn't attend the high school, but she had briefly before dropping out shortly into her freshman year because she had been bullied. He got that. He knew firsthand how badly that hurt, and how many times he had begged his parents to let him change schools or even to homeschool him. Nicole had managed to convince her stepdad to send her to a different school—a small private school about an hour away—but that didn't mean the other kids didn't go to the high school.

"The house directly opposite the Cochrane house has a couple and their two sons. The older one is away at college … he's twenty. The younger one is seventeen and a senior at the high school. His name is Jimmy Weston," Zeb said.

"I'm pretty sure there's a kid in the house across from Ruby's too," he said. He'd been staying there for a few days now, and he'd been there to visit several times over the last few months as well, and he was pretty sure he had seen a family living in that house.

"The Dwyer family," Zeb said, tapping away on his keyboard. "They have two daughters. The oldest is eighteen, but it looks like she's ill. She hasn't attended school in over a decade. The younger one is fifteen, a sophomore at the high school. Her name is Stephanie."

"That's perfect," he said. "We knew we were looking for two couples. We have one, and the houses opposite our other crime scenes have a male and female who both go to Van Nielson High, right?"

"Right," Zeb confirmed a moment later.

"So it has to be these two. Skull is Jimmy Weston, and Black Cat is Stephanie Dwyer. That must be how they chose their victims. They went after the family in the houses opposite theirs. That way, they could keep track of the investigations. And that's probably why the witness never saw any cars she didn't recognize. They didn't have to drive to the crime scenes. They could just meet up at their own houses. We have to go straight to the Weston and Dwyer houses and pick these two up."

"The houses they live in aren't going to be enough to hold them for long," Zeb warned.

His partner was right. The locations were merely circumstantial and weren't enough to get arrest warrants, but they were enough to bring the two in, and once they had all four of the gang members here in the station, he was sure they could get someone to flip. The first person who wanted to make a deal just had to turn on the others. While he would hate to see one of them get off lighter on a deal after what they had done to Ruby and the other families, at least this would be over, and Ruby would be safe.

~

10:01 A.M.

Her dreams were odd.

Bright colors, floating balloons, weird sounds, and cats.

Always cats.

Stephanie had loved cats from the time her parents had put her first kitten in her arms when she was three years old. Ever since, she'd been hooked. It wasn't a coincidence that she had chosen a black cat costume for the murders; she had chosen it on purpose. She couldn't really explain it, and as crazy as it sounded, it was kind of like she was part cat. It sounded insane, but it was what it was.

A large ball of wool appeared before her.

She batted at it and watched it roll across the floor.

She pounced, her cat feet moving with agility and ease as she careened over a couch, a table, and a pile of shoes, and landed with a thud on the ball of wool.

Rolling over onto her back, she began to bat the ball of wool from side to side. As she did, it started to unravel.

Curious as to where the growing thread of wool was going, she lazily got back to her feet and began to follow it.

It led her out of a house and into a garden, weaving through beds of colorful flowers and up a tree.

Something began to tickle her.

She wriggled, trying to get away from it.

But she couldn't.

The more she squirmed, the more she was tickled.

Something warm and soft settled on her lips. Her paws suddenly morphed into hands; the garden faded away and was replaced by four walls and a glow around the curtains covering the window.

Her bedroom.

Stephanie woke and realized that it was Jimmy's lips on hers, and the tickling feeling was his fingers running over her bare flesh. She knew that she had fallen asleep in his arms, but she had expected him to be gone by the time she woke up. He didn't usually spend the night because they both knew that if her parents found out that she had a boy sleeping over in her room, they would go ballistic.

Her parents were clueless. They had no idea that she had a boyfriend and that she was sexually active, let alone that she snuck out of the house at night to break into other people's homes and kill them.

What idiots.

She didn't think particularly highly of her parents. It wasn't that she hated them because she didn't. She did love them in her own way, but they had a complicated relationship, and most of the time, she just thought they were stupid.

"You shouldn't be here," she told him. Just because her parents were mostly oblivious, didn't mean that they couldn't come in here to see how she was spending her day.

"I couldn't leave," he told her, one of his hands finding its way between her legs. "We didn't give you a turn last night."

"No, we didn't," she agreed, sucking in a breath as he touched her right in that sweet spot.

Loud voices suddenly filled the air.

People.

Her parents, no doubt.

Why did they always have to ruin things?

"My mom and dad are coming," she whispered.

"Door's locked," Jimmy said.

Stephanie rolled her eyes at him. "When they try to open the door and find they can't, they're going to know something is up. They aren't *that* stupid."

"So, tell them that you want to be left alone." Jimmy shrugged.

"They'll never buy that. They'll know something's up, and if they come in here and see us naked and in bed, they're going to freak out." It wasn't that she really cared whether or not they freaked out, she just wasn't in the mood to deal with melodramatic parents today. While she had enjoyed it, it had been a busy week, and she wanted to chill out this morning before tonight when they would have a third go at killing Ruby Hatcher. It wasn't like she was going to have many more mornings where she could just lie in bed and make out with her boyfriend. In a couple of days, she was going to be dead, and while she was excited about what lay beyond this world, she still wanted to enjoy these last days.

"Let them freak out," Jimmy shot back, his face getting that stubborn look that she was getting so used to. It wasn't like she hadn't known what kind of guy he was when they'd gotten involved, but sometimes that evilness surprised her. He didn't care about anyone but himself, and her to an extent, but given the opportunity, she was pretty sure he would throw her under the bus to save himself. She would just have to hope things never came to that point.

"Okay, then," she agreed. She supposed it would be kind of fun to see what her parents would do when they found her lying naked in her bed with her boyfriend touching her.

"Our daughter is a good girl. There's no way she's done what you're saying," she heard her mom say. Her voice was loud and just on the other side of the door.

"Someone else is out there," Stephanie said, pushing Jimmy's hands away and sitting up. Who would be here in her house on a Saturday morning? And why were they discussing her? "Do you think it's the cops?"

"Why would it be?"

Why did Jimmy always have to be so deliberately obtuse? Did he really believe it was outside the realms of possibility that either Wilson or Nicole would give them up to the cops? Surely, he couldn't be that stupid, and yet, the confidence that was flowing off him said that he was.

"We should get dressed ... you should sneak out," she said, climbing off the bed and scrambling for the nearest clothes. If it *was* the cops, then it would look worse if they came in here to find the two of them together. They didn't know what the cops already knew or what Wilson and Nicole had told them, so her best bet was just to play the innocent little girl and hope that things worked out because she was going to be pretty angry if things got messed up when she was this close to getting what she wanted.

"No," he said, wrapping an arm around her waist and dragging her back down onto the bed. Why was he behaving like this?

"Ma'am, please move out of the way and let us do what we came here to do," a man's voice said. It wasn't her father's voice, so there was definitely someone else out there, and she knew it had to be the cops. There were no other options, and the man even sounded like a cop.

"Chase, go call our lawyer," her mom said. "He'll put an end to this."

"You do what you feel you need to do, ma'am, but we will be talking with your daughter. Stephanie, open the door." The order was accompanied by a sharp rap on the door.

"Who is it?" she called out sweetly, trying to sound like she had just been woken up.

"It's the police," came the reply.

"Oh," she tried to sound shocked and hoped it worked. "I just need to get dressed."

"Whatever you're wearing is fine," a different male voice said. So there were at least two cops out there.

"Let me go," she hissed at Jimmy. Now wasn't the time for him to go off on one of his ego rants.

"No," he said again.

She shoved him off her. "They already know it's us. The best we can do is for you to get out of here and let me deal with them alone. I can convince them that they're wrong about me, but as soon as they see you and see how angry you are, they're going to know they're right."

"Open up, Stephanie," the first cop ordered.

"Honey, open the door," her mom echoed.

"Go." She threw Jimmy's clothes at him, then grabbed her robe and walked toward the door. Despite the cops telling her to stay in whatever she was wearing, she didn't really want them to get a look at her naked body.

Hoping Jimmy was going to listen and do as she said—but accepting the possibility that he was going to stubbornly sit right where he was—she opened up the door and found her mom and two cops standing there. The cops didn't have their guns out, but they looked like they were ready to pull out their weapons at any second.

"What's going on?" she asked, twirling her dark hair around her finger and batting her eyelashes.

The cops wasted no time. The one with blue eyes grabbed her and shoved her up against a wall, yanking her hands behind her back and cuffing them. Although she was more angry than afraid, she let tears well up in her eyes and trickle down her cheeks.

"Mommy? What's going on?" she asked.

"It's okay, baby, we'll get this sorted out," her mom promised.

"Hey," Jimmy growled. "Let go of her."

His protective instincts kicked in, and with a muffled scream, he launched across the room. Everything erupted into pandemonium. She was dragged out of the room, crying and screaming, and led down the stairs and out of the house. As she was walked toward the car, she couldn't quite keep a smug little smile from settling on her lips. She had just chastised Jimmy for being overconfident. It seemed she suffered from the same affliction because she was positive that she was walking out of this unscathed.

∽

11:16 A.M.

As relieved as he was, and as much as it felt like things were finally over, and he could relax and know that Ruby was safe, Judah knew that now, more than ever, he needed to remain focused. Things *weren't* over yet. In fact, they were at that critical stage where they could pull it all together and mark this case as closed, or everything could all fall apart.

That, he wasn't going to let happen.

There was too much riding on keeping these four dangerous teenagers behind bars where they belonged.

"We have the DNA found on Tiffany Kendrick's body to prove that Wilson MacAvoy was one of the home invaders. The ballistics ties him to the other crimes as well; we have enough to put him away for this," he began. "He's not walking out of here a free man. And we have Nicole Trent for the attempt on Ruby's life at her house yesterday. She's not walking out of here a free woman either."

"That leaves us searching for something to tie Jimmy Weston and Stephanie Dwyer to the crimes," Zeb said.

"Sapphire and Elijah are going through Stephanie's room, and then they'll go to Jimmy's house. We could get lucky and find something there." He wasn't sure what the odds of that were. Jimmy was seventeen, and Stephanie was only fifteen. Both were just kids, so they might not have had the forethought to make sure that they didn't leave any evidence behind. Then again, on the whole, they'd been fairly good at keeping physical evidence to a minimum, so they very well might have gotten rid of anything that would tie them to the crimes. So, while he was hoping for something like the costumes they'd worn with blood still on them or the guns, he wasn't counting on it.

"We still have another way of getting what we need to hold all four of them and have them all charged with the crimes," Zeb said.

His partner was right. It wasn't all or nothing with the forensic evidence.

There was one other way they could get what they needed.

"We need to get one of them to turn on the other," Judah said.

"So far, Wilson and Nicole haven't caved and given anything up."

"And I don't think that we're going to get anything out of Jimmy. He was furious that we dared to arrest Stephanie, and he's adamant that we're making a mistake by arresting him and his girlfriend." Back at the house, it had taken his partner several minutes to wrestle the kid under control and get him handcuffed and outside into the car.

"From what we heard from Julie Johnstone, and from what it looks like, Jimmy is the one in control, so I think the chances of him giving up anything and giving us a confession is completely out of the question," Zeb said.

"I agree. Which is why I think we should focus our efforts on Stephanie. She's only fifteen and the youngest of the group. I think if we can get anyone to flip, it's her." The kid had been crying by the time he got her in handcuffs, and she cried the entire way back to the station, then cried all through booking and when they put her in an interview room where she was currently sitting waiting for them.

"It's worth a shot," Zeb said. "It's not like we have anything to lose. If she won't flip and turn on the others, we're only going to be right where we are right now."

They were still going to need something else to keep Jimmy and Stephanie in custody, but he was fairly confident that he and Zeb could persuade the fifteen-year-old that she would be in a better position if she confessed to everything and made a deal before they got enough to nail her to the wall anyway.

"Let's go," he said. He wanted this case wrapped up today, so when he went back to Ruby's tonight, he could give her the good news. Then, there would be nothing hovering over them, and they could just focus on their budding relationship.

When they stepped into the interview room where Stephanie was waiting for them, along with her lawyer, the girl turned a tear-stained face in their direction. She was pale with red splotches on her cheeks, and since she hadn't been wearing anything under the robe when they arrested her, she was dressed in jail clothes. Stephanie was small, and the clothes were several sizes too big for her. With her long dark hair tangled around her head, she looked much younger than her fifteen years.

While his natural instinct as an adult looking at a kid was to feel sorry for them when they found themselves in a predicament where they were in way over their head, he had to remind himself that she had put herself in this position. She and the others had cold-bloodedly murdered eight people. She wasn't an innocent little kid. She was a killer—a cunning one at that—and had to be approached with caution.

"Hello, Stephanie," he said as he took a seat at the table.

The girl just sniffed and looked at the lawyer her parents had sent to represent her. She looked like she had no idea how to get herself out of this mess. Hopefully, her lawyer was smart enough to see that her best option was to give a full confession and then make a deal. He still hated the idea of one of these people who terrorized Ruby and made her feel unsafe in her own home getting a lighter sentence, but if it got all of them off the streets, he'd go along with it.

"We have Wilson MacAvoy and Nicole Trent in custody," he said. He was sure she knew this but wanted to remind her that they didn't necessarily need her to close this case. If she wanted to make herself a deal, she had a limited time to do so. "Or perhaps I should call them Ghost and Witch ... that's what they dressed as when you committed your murders, right? And you and your boyfriend were Black Cat and Skull."

"You don't have to say anything, Stephanie," her lawyer informed her. Stephanie just looked at them with big, round eyes.

"That's true, but we already have enough to charge Wilson and Nicole, and we know that you and Jimmy were involved. You *will* be going to prison for these crimes. How long you spend there is up to you. You want a deal, then you write out a confession that details everything, including what the others did," Zeb told her.

Stephanie looked to her lawyer, who nodded at her. "It could be your best chance."

The teenager looked back at them, her lips still pressed into a thin line, but tears were brimming in her eyes again, and he was sure that she was going to cave soon.

"If you don't take this opportunity, one of the others might. You're fifteen, but you will be tried as an adult, and given the cold and calculating way you shot those innocent people ... and tortured them ... you'll likely get a life sentence—possibly multiple life sentences, one for each victim."

"I didn't torture anyone," the girl mumbled under her breath.

"Speak up, please," he said sharply. He had little patience with this kid, and she was already working his last nerve. He wanted a confession. Now.

She took another glance at her lawyer, and when he nodded reassuringly at her, she burst into tears. "I'm sorry. I didn't want to do it. It was all Jimmy's idea."

"What was Jimmy's idea?" he asked. This had to come from her. It couldn't be them putting words in her mouth because that could get the whole confession deemed inadmissible.

"The costumes, breaking into those people's houses, the murders, all of us killing them so that no one could back out and turn on the others. It was all his idea," Stephanie sobbed.

"How did you meet Jimmy?" Zeb asked.

"I ran into him one day at school—literally. He thought I was pretty, and we started talking, and then, before I knew it, we were together."

"How did he bring up the idea of the murders?" Judah asked. It wasn't like that was something you could just bring up to someone else. You had to know that they were going to reciprocate your desires and not just turn you into the cops.

Stephanie's gaze dropped to the floor. "He knew that I wanted to commit suicide, and he threatened that if I didn't help him, he would make sure he got me committed to a psychiatric hospital."

"Why were you suicidal?" he asked, his tone softening. Both he and Ruby had walked that path, and if things had been different, maybe they would have ended up in Stephanie's position.

"My family is kind of messed up."

He knew a little about the Dwyer family, but he wanted to know more. "How is your family messed up?"

"My sister is sick. She was born with kidney dysplasia, where the kidneys don't develop properly. She used to have dialysis, but she needed a transplant. So, my parents had me. Not because they wanted me ... just because they wanted my kidney. I donated when I was ten. Normally, you're not supposed to donate to someone so young, but my parents found a doctor who would do it. The transplant didn't take, and my sister is still very sick. She's dying, I don't think she has long left. I never felt like I was important or wanted, and it just got to be too much. I wanted to punish my parents, and what better way than to make them lose both their daughters?"

Judah couldn't imagine growing up feeling like he wasn't wanted and only existed to help someone else. His parents had been there for him throughout his life, especially after his suicide attempt. But despite how her parents had made her feel, that wasn't an excuse for what she'd done. It didn't give her free reign to act out her anger and frustration.

"I'm sorry to hear that, Stephanie, but you knew that what you were doing was wrong. Jimmy couldn't have gotten you committed. You should have told someone what was going on," he said.

"I know ... I'm sorry ... I was scared. Jimmy has a temper, and I was scared about what he would do to me. I'm sorry. I know that doesn't fix anything, but I am. I'll tell you whatever you want to know." The girl's tears started up again.

"Write it all down," Zeb said, setting paper and a pen down in front of her.

"We'll come back to you soon," Judah said. Once they saw what Stephanie wrote, and if she had anything to back it up besides just her word, then they would discuss a deal, but he wasn't making one until he knew that whatever she was giving them was enough.

None of these kids were walking for this.

They did the crime, and now they were going to do the time.

12:49 P.M.

His partner was buzzing about the room frenetically.

Sapphire had been hyped all day, and her agitation and anxiety were starting to make him anxious.

It wasn't that he didn't understand why she was on edge. Her sister had been attacked twice in less than a week, but if she continued on at this pace, she was going to miss something important.

"Would you calm down, please?" Elijah asked as she started rifling through Jimmy Weston's closet.

"I *am* calm," Sapphire said.

"You're not," he contradicted. He and Sapphire had been partners for years now, and although he was a couple of years older than her, it often felt like she was decades older than him. Sapphire was intense, and one hundred percent committed to her job. Before she'd met Gideon earlier in the year, work had been the only thing besides her sisters that she had in her life. While she had mellowed ever since her fiancé had come into her life, she was still intense most of the time—today, in particular.

"I just want to make sure we have enough to keep these kids in prison where they belong. Moving out is hard enough as it is without having this hanging over my family." The last sentence she mumbled quietly under her breath, but he heard her. Elijah knew what Sapphire and her sisters had gone through, but they'd never discussed it. Despite the fact they'd been partners for years, they had only in the last few months become friends, but this wasn't the kind of thing that you just openly talked about. Elijah didn't even think Sapphire talked about it much with Gideon.

Walking over to his partner, he rested a hand on her shoulder, stilling her. "We got this, Sapphire. We'll find what we need, and these kids will pay for what they did."

She shot him a strained smile and took a deep breath, clearly trying to calm herself down.

As they both resumed their search of the room, his thoughts lingered on Sapphire and her sisters. What they had gone through was horrific, and all of them still bore the scars. Sapphire was learning to manage hers, and Ruby appeared to be taking the first step to moving on by starting a relationship with Judah. Emerald was still missing, and Amethyst had her gym and her bodybuilding.

That just left the oldest sister—Diamond.

Diamond.

She was every bit as beautiful as the gemstone she had been named after, and every bit as precious. He'd been attracted to her for a while, and he knew that she liked him too. He had intended to ask her out earlier this year around the time he'd been shot, and Sapphire had met Gideon. But then, his life had kind of gone off the deep end, and he'd decided that, for the time being, it was best to keep his distance. The last thing he wanted to do was hurt her. She'd been hurt enough in her life, and he wasn't going to add to that.

Turning his attention to the laptop that sat on a desk in the corner, he walked over, pulled out the chair, and sat down, then pressed the power button. It took a moment for the computer to boot up, but eventually, a picture of Jimmy and Stephanie popped up on the screen. Luck was on his side, and the computer wasn't password protected.

Not really sure what he was looking for, Elijah began to flip through folders. They were really here to look for something like the guns or bloody clothes or shoes or something like that to tie the kids to the crimes, but sometimes computers turned into goldmines, so he wasn't going to leave this one untouched.

There were papers that Jimmy had written for school and dozens of photos of him and Stephanie. That could be an angle to pursue. So far, all they had to tie Jimmy to the crimes was the statement that Stephanie had given, but the two had been naked in Stephanie's room when Judah and Zeb arrested them. They were obviously sexually active. Maybe they were into taking pictures of each other. Stephanie was only fifteen, so technically that could be deemed as creating child pornography, which was something they could use to hold him until they got something else.

As he was flipping through the photos—most of which were completely innocent—he noticed a couple of videos. Maybe they were more into film than photography.

Elijah opened up the first one and immediately knew he was on to something.

It was Jimmy's bedroom. The light was on, but the curtains were open, and he could see that it was dark out, so he knew this had been filmed at night.

"Sapphire, come watch this," he called out.

"What is it?" she asked as she stopped what she was doing and walked over, standing behind him.

"A video ... filmed in here. Look, there's Stephanie." He pointed to the screen as they saw someone in a black cat costume—obviously, Stephanie, since they knew that was what she'd worn when she and the others committed the murders—walk from the desk where the computer was over to the bed. She lay down and arranged herself a specific way, and once she was done, she just lay there.

A couple of minutes later, Jimmy appeared, it looked like he had come from the bathroom. Over the next few minutes, they watched Jimmy order Stephanie to stand and strip, then the two of them had sex.

After they were done, they lay down together and appeared to go to sleep.

"Fast forward a bit," Sapphire said.

He started fast forwarding through the footage, the two tossed and turned in their sleep, and then just as dawn was coming, Stephanie slipped off the bed, tiptoed to the laptop, and then the screen went black.

"Stephanie was the one who filmed that," Sapphire said. "She was the one who turned the camera on and turned it off."

"And she didn't want Jimmy to know. She waited until he left the room before starting the recording, and then made sure she turned it off while he was still asleep."

"Why wouldn't she want him to know?"

"I don't know. From what Zeb and Judah said, she told them that she was afraid of Jimmy. She said that all of this was his idea and that she only went along with it because he threatened to get her committed, she was contemplating suicide and she was afraid that he would hurt her if she didn't." From what they had just watched, it didn't appear that Stephanie was afraid of Jimmy. It looked like she was attracted to him.

"When was this filmed?" Sapphire asked.

"Good question," he said as he opened up the file's information. "It was filmed five days ago, October twentieth."

"The night of the first murder."

"Time stamp is eleven fifty-one at night. That means it was just after they committed the Cochrane murders."

"So, Stephanie was forced to find a gun and take it with her while she and three friends put on costumes, broke into someone's house, tied them up and shot them, all against her will because she was afraid? But the first thing she does afterward is come and turn on a camera and film herself having sex with her boyfriend, the one who she's supposedly terrified of? I don't buy it."

"I don't either," Elijah said. There was no way that this girl was afraid for her life. The look on her face as her boyfriend made her come was plain to see. If she was scared for her life—even if Jimmy had brought her here, and even if he had forced her to have sex—there was no way she would have turned the computer on and started a recording.

"Jimmy isn't the one in charge. He's not the ringleader."

"Stephanie is. She let Jimmy think that all of this was his idea. She probably let the others think that too, but she was the one who no doubt came up with this whole thing. She wanted Jimmy to think that he was in charge so that if we ever managed to find their identities, she could just cry and claim that she was forced to do it. She's only fifteen. If she got in first and made a deal, told her sob story about being suicidal and manipulated, then she could probably walk out of this with at most three years in a juvenile facility, being let out when she turned eighteen."

"The girl is diabolical," Sapphire agreed. "We need to get this video to Judah and Zeb before they let the DA make any deals with Stephanie. She's the mastermind, and she's not going to slide."

Elijah couldn't agree more.

These kids had broken into Diamond's home, and she could very easily have been there at the time. Just because he didn't intend to start a relationship with her any time soon—possibly ever—that didn't mean he wanted her to get caught up in this. He would make sure that Stephanie, and the others, paid for what they had done and spent the rest of their lives where they belonged—behind bars.

2:12 P.M.

This case just kept getting more and more complicated.

Just when he thought that they had everything under control—they had all four of the home invasion gang in custody and a statement from one of them implicating everyone else—they found out that they had been played.

They had fallen right into Stephanie's trap.

"The girl is good," Zeb said, as though reading his thoughts.

"She is," he agreed. "Those tears and fear. She made them sound real, but they were nothing but a tool she was using to get what she wanted." Although he didn't say it out loud, the fact that she had spoken of wanting to commit suicide had definitely swayed him and convinced him that she was another victim in all of this.

He had let his emotions and his own personal struggles get in the way of his objectivity, and it very nearly could have let a dangerous killer walk away practically free.

He wasn't going to make that mistake again.

"So do we want to show Stephanie our hand and see what she says, go to Jimmy and tell him that his precious girlfriend is pinning all of this on him, or use it to try to get Wilson and Nicole to talk?" he asked. Choosing which path to take right now was imperative. They had to make sure that they played this right if they wanted to ensure that all four kids stayed right where they were.

"I think we should leave Stephanie for now, let her think that everything is still playing out the way she planned," Zeb said. "Let's take a go at Jimmy, then if that doesn't work, we can go and speak with Wilson and Nicole."

"Sounds like a plan," he agreed. "Let's do this." Picking up the laptop that Elijah and Sapphire had brought back from Jimmy's house, he followed Zeb toward the interview room where Jimmy Weston was waiting for them.

When they entered the room, they found the kid lounging in his seat. He had it tipped back against the wall, his fingers threaded together behind his head. He looked bored, but not in a cocky way—just like he was literally bored. He didn't appear to be concerned that he was sitting in a police station. Obviously, the time he'd spent in here after he'd been arrested at the Dwyer house this morning had calmed him down.

The kid had a partially healed scratch on his arm that matched with the position of the wound that Ruby had inflicted the night the gang had broken into her house, but since they didn't have the razor they hadn't had any DNA to run to prove that it was Jimmy who Ruby had cut.

So, they were doing this the hard way.

"Good afternoon, Jimmy," he said as he took a seat.

Jimmy nodded but didn't say anything.

"Put your chair down," Zeb commanded as he also took a seat at the table.

Judah expected the kid to argue or ignore the instruction, but he didn't. He lowered the chair back down, so all four legs rested on the floor then simply looked at them. However, he'd seen the kid glance at the laptop, and Jimmy obviously knew it belonged to him and wanted to know what was going on, but he didn't want to ask.

"We searched your room, found something interesting," Judah said slowly, opening the laptop and taking his time opening up the video file.

Jimmy still didn't say anything, just sat there and waited.

The kid had certainly developed some patience and self-control since the scene he had put on at the Dwyer house this morning. It seemed that if Stephanie wasn't involved, he was able to remain in control of himself.

"You're not interested in watching?" he asked.

Jimmy shrugged. "There's nothing all that interesting on my laptop."

"Oh, I disagree," he said with a small smile. "When you weren't looking, your girl set you up."

"Stephanie?" Jimmy looked like he thought the idea was preposterous.

"See for yourself." Judah turned the computer around so Jimmy could see the screen, then started the video. The teenager was able to school his features while he watched, not giving anything away. He wanted to figure out what was going on inside the kid's head, but it was hard to get a read on Jimmy.

"Nothing to say, Jimmy?" Zeb asked when the video ended.

The kid shrugged again.

"You know when this video was filmed, right?" Zeb asked.

"It was the night that you, Stephanie, Wilson, and Nicole committed your first murders," Judah supplied.

"So, what?" Jimmy said. "So we had sex that night. No big deal. That is not proof that we committed any murders."

"Let's set aside the fact that Stephanie is wearing a black cat costume, and we know that's what one of the killers was wearing," Judah started. "And just focus on the fact that Stephanie already told us that you two, along with Wilson MacAvoy and Nicole Trent, murdered the Cochrane, Kendrick, and Lanely families, and broke into the Hatcher house."

That finally got a reaction out of Jimmy Weston. "I don't believe you."

"Well, that doesn't change the facts," Zeb said.

"When she got here, Stephanie gave us a whole confession. She told us that the four of you chose your costumes. Each stole a gun from a family member and how you decided to each hit the houses opposite yours because it would make things random. She told us how you broke into the houses, how you were supposed to just tie up the people inside and kill them, how you would each shoot someone because that meant you were all in. She told us all about how you got angry when Ruby Hatcher was able to foil your plan, and that Wilson didn't like you yelling at him and Nicole, so he decided to go off script. She told us how you beat Nicole up after she saved the Kendrick baby, and she told us that the endgame was that all four of you would commit suicide and that the only reason you hadn't already was that you wanted to tie up loose ends and kill Ruby Hatcher and the baby."

Jimmy stared at him, a scowl on his face.

"All of that fits with the crimes," Zeb said. "She isn't making that up. Her times and days and descriptions are in line with what we already know, and some of it wasn't released to the public. The only way she could have known it is if she was involved."

"Here's the thing that's going to interest you, though," Judah said. "She says that all of this was your idea."

"Stephanie wouldn't say that," Jimmy said confidently.

"Oh, but she did," he said. "She had a whole sob story prepared. How she was unwanted by her family and wanted to kill herself, that you knew this and used it against her, threatening to have her committed, then threatened to hurt her if she didn't go along with your plan. She says she was afraid of you."

"Stephanie isn't afraid of me," Jimmy scoffed.

"That's not what she says," Zeb said.

"She has a lawyer in there with her. She's already written out her statement, and she's ready to pin all of this on you and take a deal, probably to serve only a few years before being free to go about her life, while you rot in prison. This is your chance to clear things up. This is your chance to tell things from your point of view. When we found this video, we knew that Stephanie was lying. She's the mastermind, she just set you up to take the fall. So, help yourself, Jimmy," he said. While he didn't want this kid to walk free, he also didn't want him to take an unfair portion of the blame.

Jimmy looked sullen now, but there was a stubborn glint in his eyes. "You're trying to trick me into telling you what you want to know, but I'm not going to fall for it. I love Stephanie, and she loves me. There is no way that she would have done what you said she did."

"This could be your only chance, Jimmy. If we don't get corroborating evidence that Stephanie was behind all of this, then she's going to walk away with only minimal punishment. I know you love her, but she was just using you," he pleaded. If they couldn't use Stephanie's statement, then they still didn't have anything concrete on Jimmy, so they needed someone to talk. If it wasn't going to be Jimmy, then it would have to be Wilson and Nicole.

"This is it, Jimmy," Zeb warned. "When my partner and I walk out this door, then your chance to tell your side of things is gone."

The teenager just crossed his arms across his chest.

Sometimes love blinded you, and you couldn't see what was happening, and it looked like Jimmy Weston was choosing to be deliberately blind.

That meant that cracking Wilson and Nicole was their last chance.

3:37 P.M.

It was such a gorgeous afternoon.

It was like summer had decided to make one more play before it fully gave way to fall and then the winter, that was only just around the corner.

In deference to the mild day, Ruby had the windows and the doors open, she was wearing sweatpants and a T-shirt, and her feet were bare.

Her long, blonde hair was hanging loose around her shoulders and wafting in the gentle breeze. The sunshine was warm on her skin as she sat on the front porch, ready to start carving Halloween jack-o'-lanterns.

Halloween wasn't one of her favorite holidays. There was something about all the costumes that just creeped her out a little, but carving pumpkins was something that she loved to do. Since her sisters didn't enjoy it, she was always the one to make them, and although she was running a little late this year—given everything that had been going on —this afternoon she was going to make a few before she headed off to work at five.

She had nine pumpkins, and she didn't think she could get all of them done today, but she could probably do at least four before she left, then finish the rest tomorrow. When they were done, she was going to put them on the ends of each of the three porch steps and then arrange the other three at the front door.

The fall wreath on the front door rustled in the wind. Besides the jack-o'-lanterns, it was really the only decorations they put up for Halloween. Although they had a large front yard with two huge trees that made the house nice and cool with their shade in the summer, theirs was the only house on the block without gravestones and ghosts and witches and monsters. She liked to focus more on the fall side of Halloween than the spooky side.

She loved this time of year—the cooler weather, the changing leaves, the crisp nights, and milder days. Fall had been her favorite season ever since she was a little girl. As a child, she'd loved the leaves. She would ask every weekend for a rake, so she could make huge piles and then jump and roll and play in them. Sometimes her sisters would join her, and occasionally, her mom would make them mugs of hot chocolate with marshmallow polar bears when they came inside. Sometimes they'd sit around the fireplace and talk or play board games, or sometimes, her dad would read them stories. Those were some of the happiest times of her youth. Although her parents hadn't been abusive and had never done anything to hurt them before selling them, they'd both been cold and distant, not the warm, involved parents that most of her friends had.

While she didn't rake up piles of beautiful red, yellow, and orange leaves and play in them anymore, she still loved raking them up. There was just something about the chore that sent her back to that happy time.

With a wistful smile, Ruby busied herself, cutting the top of the first pumpkin and set it aside ready to put back on when she was done, then she started scooping the guts out. This was her least favorite part, and her nose scrunched up as she took a huge handful and dumped it into the large bowl. Amethyst loved roasted pumpkin seeds, so she always kept them and set them aside for her sister to use later.

Once she had all the goopy stuff out, she moved the bowl aside and picked up a permanent marker. This was her favorite part. Sometimes she liked to go with a theme, carving farm animals or insects or flowers, but this year she didn't feel like that. This year, she was just going to draw the traditional smiley jack-o'-lantern faces.

Ruby was just finishing drawing the face when she noticed a car pull into the driveway of the Dwyer house.

That fifteen-year-old, Stephanie—a kid she knew and talked to— was one of the four people who'd broken into her home was still a shock. She'd brought in the mail for them when they'd gone on vacation last year, helped them get their cat down from a tree when it got stuck a few months ago, she'd thought they were a nice family. It still didn't seem real. Stephanie was just a kid. How could she have taken her grandfather's gun and used it to kill innocent people?

The whole thing was surreal.

She hadn't expected that when the home invaders' identities were found that they would include someone that she actually knew. She'd thought that they would be strangers who had just picked a house at random—not one of her neighbors.

Edna Dwyer climbed out of the car, and whether it was because the woman knew she was sitting on the porch or not, she looked right across the road, and their eyes met. Ruby couldn't read the expression in the other woman's face, but she couldn't help but shudder, suddenly cold. She couldn't imagine what Edna Dwyer and her husband were going through right now, learning what their daughter had done and the impact that Stephanie and her friends' actions had on her.

Ever since she and her sisters had moved out of their aunt's house and into this place, it had been her sanctuary—the one place that she didn't have to feel the prying eyes of the world trying to look deep inside her mind. But a shadow had been cast over it. Now, she scanned the rooms upon entry, searching for anything that shouldn't be there. She didn't know when, or if, that feeling would ever pass. Her sanctuary had been breached, and she wasn't sure if she would ever have another one. She was one of the lucky ones; at least, she was still alive. The Cochranes weren't, and Marcus Kendrick was going to grow up without his parents, as were the Lanely kids.

Should she go over and talk to Edna?

Part of her wanted to ignore the woman. Ruby blamed her, in part, for her daughter's actions. She also knew that the woman was suffering, too. She had lost her daughter because while Stephanie was still alive, she was going to spend the rest of her life in prison. Ruby didn't know a lot about the Dwyer family. She and her sisters tended to keep to themselves, but from what they did know, they worked hard to support their daughters, one of whom had a terminal illness. They seemed like just a normal family. She would have never in a million years guessed that things would turn out like this.

She should go over there, offer whatever comfort she could. She didn't particularly like speaking with people she didn't know, but she couldn't just sit here and do nothing.

Just as she was setting down her marker and looking for where she'd left her shoes, Edna Dwyer turned abruptly and hurried inside. Ruby felt relieved, and yet at the same time, she knew that neither of them was going to feel better until they talked. She didn't want the Dwyer family to blame themselves for Stephanie's actions. She may only be fifteen, but she had known that what she was doing was wrong, and from what little Judah had told her when he'd called earlier, the girl was the mastermind behind it all.

Maybe tomorrow she'd stop by, but right now, she just wanted to relax a little. It was nice not to need to have cops hovering around her house anymore. Now that the four gang members were in police custody, there was no reason for her to be babysat.

The downside to that was that Judah would be going back home now. When he'd called earlier to update her on the case, they hadn't had a chance to talk for long because he'd been busy, so she wasn't sure if he was leaving today or spending one last night here.

She hoped it was the latter.

Maybe she was a little more ready to take things all the way with Judah than she'd thought that she was, because she wanted him here, sleeping in her bed tonight.

Ruby picked up the marker again and finished drawing a cute face on her pumpkin. She wanted nothing dark or scary this Halloween. She'd had enough of that to last a lifetime. So, this Halloween was just going to be about having fun, no horror movies or costume parties, or anything like that. She'd hang out at the house with her sisters; they'd eat candy apples, Halloween party mix, and more candy than any person needed to eat in one night.

She hoped that Judah would join them.

She hoped that he would be there for all the special days going forward.

Birthdays, Christmases, Easters, Fourth of Julys, her sister's wedding —Ruby wanted Judah by her side for all of them. She'd found something that she'd thought would forever allude her, and even though she knew she might battle suicidal thoughts for the rest of her life, she knew that that didn't have to stop her from being happy.

Judah made her happy.

He gave her something that she wanted to live for, someone she wanted to be strong for, and a future that could be bright enough to end the darkness her ordeal had trapped her in.

She wanted to spend the rest of her life with Judah.

4:44 P.M.

Judah picked up his phone but didn't call.

Zeb had to pop out for a moment to take care of something, so he waited for his partner to return so they could go and interview Wilson MacAvoy and Nicole Trent. He wanted to call Ruby and speak with her about tonight. Now that they had the four gang members in custody, she was no longer in danger. He had only been staying at her house to make sure that should they return, they couldn't hurt her. Now that that reason was obsolete, there was no reason for him to stay.

No reason, except he didn't want to go.

He didn't want to leave Ruby.

Falling asleep last night with her in his arms and waking up with her warm body pressed up at his side was what he wanted. That was how he wanted to spend the rest of his life.

Judah knew that she wanted the same thing, but he also knew that they had only been dating—kind of, although they hadn't made it official yet—a couple of days, it was way too soon for them to make such a big step like living together. He would be as patient as she needed him to be. That wasn't an issue as far as he was concerned, but he wanted to make this official. He wanted them to be a couple, and he wanted everyone to know that they were a couple.

He wanted to call her and ask about tonight—if he should stay or if he should pack up his things and go home. He wanted to do whatever she was most comfortable with.

And yet, he didn't.

Maybe because he was afraid of her answer.

It would be easier to just take the decision out of her hands and make it for her. Going home tonight was probably the better option. He didn't want her to think that him spending another night when it wasn't strictly necessary was him trying to pressure her for sex. As good as sleeping with her would be, it would only be good if she wanted it as much as he did, and he didn't think she was there yet.

He put his phone back down.

Ruby was probably already on her way to work anyway, so there wasn't really any point in calling her.

"Liar," he muttered to himself under his breath.

"Did you say something?" Zeb asked, walking up to their desks.

"Uh, no, nothing important. I was just talking to myself," he replied. He didn't want to discuss his relationship with Ruby with his partner. Not because he didn't trust Zeb or his opinion. He considered his partner a friend, but he was over thinking things already, and the more he dwelt on it, the more he was going to overthink. "You ready to go interview Wilson and Nicole?"

Zeb arched a brow, his brown eyes sharp. "If you're thinking about Ruby, then we all know that you like her and that she likes you. I think you two getting together is the only good thing to come out of this whole mess. If you want some advice, don't let this pass you by; grab hold of it and make it happen. Ruby is stronger than you think, stronger than she thinks. She can handle this—all of it—so go for it and don't hold back."

He took what Zeb had said and stored it away.

His partner was right. Ruby was strong—stronger than most people. Not only had she survived four years of hell, but she had saved herself. She had done what was needed to make it through those years, and then she had done what was needed to escape. He wasn't sure that anyone was stronger than she was.

He just had to remember that and not let his doubts get in the way.

He would never doubt Ruby, but doubting himself was something he'd done for most of his life. The bullying he'd endured as a child had changed who he was; it had made him not like himself. It was like those words—which had hurt him so much more than the fists had—had gotten inside him, taken hold of a part of him, and made him spend the last seventeen years not liking himself.

But that had to change.

If he wanted a relationship with the woman who owned his heart, he had to find a way to like himself again. He needed to put the past in the past just as much as Ruby did. Maybe because they had both been to that same dark place, they could help each other.

"You ready to do this?" Zeb asked.

"Ready." He and Ruby had the rest of their lives to figure things out and find a way to make things between them work. Today he had to make sure this case was sewn up.

Together he and Zeb went to the room where Nicole Trent was waiting for them. Given that she was pregnant and had some injuries from Jimmy Weston beating her for saving the Kendrick baby, she had spent the last couple of days in the medical ward at the jail.

"We have a visitor for you," Judah told the teenager as they walked into the interview room. The sixteen-year-old looked so young in her prison wear, without makeup, and her hair pulled back in a simple ponytail. Of the four kids, he felt like Nicole was the one who wasn't truly evil. She was dragged into a situation she hadn't known how to get out of, and now she was going to spend the rest of her life paying for that.

"My stepdad?" the girl asked. So far, her family had refused to come and visit her, and Judah felt sorry for her.

"No. Wilson," Zeb said as the door opened, and a cuffed Wilson MacAvoy was led in.

"Wilson." Nicole's eyes lit up, and if she hadn't had her cuffs attached to the table, he was pretty sure she would have thrown herself into his arms.

"Are you okay?" Wilson asked as the guard led him to the table and sat him down beside Nicole, then attached his handcuffs to the table as well.

"Uh-huh, are you?" Nicole asked.

"Fine. Why are we here?" Wilson demanded, turning his attention on them.

"Here's what we know," Judah said, taking a seat. "DNA evidence connects you, Wilson, to the crimes. And, Nicole, at the very least, we have you for the attack on Ruby. We also have Jimmy Weston and Stephanie Dwyer in custody. We know the four of you were the gang that was breaking into people's homes and killing them. Right now, Stephanie has written a statement implicating all four of you and claiming that she was pulled into this by Jimmy, who threatened her, but we know that's not how it happened. We know that Stephanie was the mastermind. What we want from you two is proof that you all committed the crimes, so she doesn't make a deal and walk away from this." He laid all of their cards on the table.

"What's in it for us?" Wilson asked.

"We'll put in a good word for you when it comes to sentencing," Zeb replied. "We'll tell the judge that you cooperated, and that will work in your favor. Maybe you'll get out in time to see your baby get married and have kids of their own."

The teenagers exchanged looks, and when Nicole nodded, Wilson sighed but started talking. "We have proof that all four of us were involved. It was our insurance policy."

Perfect.

That was exactly what they wanted.

"What is it?" Zeb asked.

"We have the gloves. The right ones from the pairs we all wore for the first murder. They'll have DNA, right? Our DNA on the inside and blood on the outside because we all touched the victims. Jimmy and Stephanie have the left ones."

"Where are they?" Judah asked. They would send officers there immediately to pick them up and take them straight to the forensics lab.

"They're in a plastic bag inside a box in the tree house at Nicole's house."

"We also need motives," Judah said. He wanted this case to be a slam dunk when it went before a judge.

"Stephanie wanted to punish her parents for only wanting her to save her sister; Jimmy wanted to punish his dad for the way he treated him, and Nic just felt like she didn't belong anywhere. She wanted to find her dad, and her stepdad wouldn't let her, so she wanted to punish him."

"And you?" Zeb asked when Wilson didn't mention himself.

Wilson said nothing.

"You may as well tell them," Nicole said, touching her shoulder to her boyfriend's.

He rolled his eyes but averted his gaze. "Just angry, I guess. Some stuff went down at summer camp a couple of years ago. I was tired of being the victim. I wanted to be in control, I wanted to be the one to inflict pain and cause fear for a change."

The teenager didn't need to elaborate. Judah could assume that the "stuff that went down" was that he had been sexually abused and humiliated, probably in much the same way that he had tortured the Kendricks and Lanelys. They had motives. They had forensics. All they needed was confirmation that Stephanie was the one in charge, so she didn't use her sob story when it came to sentencing. "Whose plan was it?"

"Stephanie's," Nicole said immediately. "We've been friends for years. We used to live next door to each other before my family moved. She's been talking for as long as I can remember about killing herself to punish her parents. Then, it changed to killing others and then ourselves, because then our parents would know what we'd done when the gloves were found. That way, there was nothing they could do about it. They'd have to live the rest of their lives knowing what their children had done. I guess Wilson, Jimmy, and I all had our own reasons for wanting to end our own lives, and that's how this all started," she finished softly.

Four angry kids, all with their own reasons for wanting to die, had caused more pain and suffering than they could ever understand. So many lives taken, so many forever changed. It just went to prove how destructive anger could be.

He should learn something from this.

It was time for him to let go of the anger he still harbored toward those who had bullied him. He had a bright future ahead of him, and he wasn't going to let anger steal it from him.

9:58 P.M.

She stifled a yawn as she parked her car in the garage and climbed out.

The stress of the last few days and knowing that someone might want her dead, had drained her. Ruby hadn't really realized how much until it was all over, and the kids were all in custody. Now she just wanted to put on her pajamas, curl up in bed, and start on her new book.

Well, okay, maybe that wasn't *all* she wanted to do.

If Judah was still here, there were some other activities she wanted to try out in bed.

If he was still here.

They hadn't spoken since this morning, and she didn't know what his plans were. When she walked inside, she could find him sitting in the living room waiting for her—maybe with a candlelight dinner prepared

or with a beautiful bouquet of flowers or a box of her favorite chocolates. Or she could find that he'd already packed up his things and gone
back to his place.

While she hoped it was the former, she knew that just because Judah
went back to his place didn't mean things between them were over. It
just meant that they were very early in their relationship and that she'd
been the one who wanted to take things slow. He was just doing what
she'd made clear she wanted.

Only now, she wasn't sure it *was* what she wanted.

"Be smart," she told herself as she grabbed her bag, closed the door,
and locked her car.

It was smart to take things slow, right?

She wasn't sure.

If she wanted something, shouldn't she just go for it?

After all, she had spent so many years hiding in the shadows. She
didn't want to waste any more time. Her parents had stolen enough
from her, but they couldn't steal her future.

With a mess of nervous fluttering butterflies in her stomach, Ruby
opened the door that led directly to the laundry room, slipped off her
shoes, and headed for the door that opened onto the living room. She
liked doing the evening shift at the nursing homes. Since it was later at
night, there weren't as many of the high care residents, and most of the
ones that stopped by the hairdressers were the ones who still led active
lives, and they usually chattered away with her and made the hours
fly by.

Tonight, though, she'd spent the whole time counting down the
minutes until she could come back home. That wasn't necessarily
unusual. She often craved the quiet safety of her home when she was
out in the real world, but tonight, the reason she wanted to leave had
nothing to do with that. Tonight, it was all because of Judah.

It was kind of scary how important he had become to her in just a
few days.

But scary, in a good way.

It was nice to have something good in her life; it was nice to feel like
the shackles of her past were loosening, and it was nice to feel like after
so long thinking that all her life would consist of was books, work, and

her sisters, she just might be about to get her own happily ever after. As a girl who had read literally hundreds of fictional happily ever afters over the years, it was beyond exciting to be teetering on the edge of hers.

A HEA.

Her own HEA.

She was buzzing with excitement.

Too many romance books read over the years, when she opened the door to the living room, she expected to see the room filled with thousands of twinkling candles, rose petals strewn all over the hardwood floors, music playing softly in the background, a home cooked meal he had prepared especially for her and set on the table, and her prince charming waiting for her with a bunch of roses in his arms.

But that wasn't what she found.

When she walked into the living room, what she saw was a stack of dirty dishes sitting in the sink—a clear indication that Amethyst had cooked dinner—the TV playing some reality show she didn't know the name of since she didn't watch a lot of TV and her twin lounging on the couch.

Amethyst looked over. "There's fried rice in the fridge if you want to heat some up."

"Why are you watching TV?" she asked, trying to hide her disappointment. Usually, her twin was working out in her gym on the nights where she wasn't at the fire station. For her to be lounging on the couch meant something was wrong. She really didn't want any more bad news right now, but she steeled herself for it.

"Just didn't feel like working out tonight; no big deal." Amethyst shrugged, trying to look nonchalant, but failing. Still, if her twin didn't want to talk, she wasn't going to push her.

"Where's everyone else?" she asked, now she was the one trying to be nonchalant.

"Sapphire and Gideon are at their place, and Diamond is teaching a late class. Judah packed up his stuff, so it's just the two of us tonight. Want to watch TV with me?"

So, he *had* gone.

Ruby knew her face fell, but there was little she could do about it. How could he just leave without telling her? It wasn't like she didn't know that he'd be going back to his place now that he didn't need to be here to protect her, but for him to just pack up and leave without a word ... that hurt. And it immediately made her doubt him, herself, and the choices she had been making the last few days.

Had she just gotten caught up in the moment, romanticizing the whole Judah being her protector idea?

Had she misread things with him?

Had she made a fool out of herself when all along, he was just being nice?

Maybe he felt sorry for her.

That made her angry. She didn't want anyone's pity.

"I think I'm just going to go up to bed," she told her sister, already turning and hurrying for the stairs. She didn't want to cry, but tears were burning the backs of her eyes, and if she was going to cry, then at least, she wanted to do it alone.

"Okay, night," Amethyst called out after her.

"Night," she mumbled back, already on the second floor and running for her bedroom door. Just a couple more steps and then she could let go, maybe shedding a few tears was just what she needed right now

Ruby threw open her bedroom door and froze.

Candles.

Rose petals.

Music.

And Judah standing there with a bouquet of beautiful white moon-flowers.

How had he found out that those were her favorite flowers?

Tears had already been brimming in her eyes, and they started to tumble out, but now they weren't tears of pain. They were tears of happiness.

"Are you all right?" Judah's brow creased with concern as he hurried over to her, setting the bouquet down on top of her dresser.

"Mmhmm." She nodded, brushing away the tears.

"Then, why are you crying?"

"I thought you left without saying goodbye," she admitted. She needed an honest relationship, and she needed Judah to know that there wasn't anything they couldn't say to each other. They both needed a safe place, and she wanted to be that for Judah as well as wanting him to be hers. That safe place had to be based on honesty, so she wasn't ever going to hide how she was feeling—not when she had someone who actually understood.

"You know I'd never do that," he rebuked.

"I know, but when I came home, and you weren't waiting downstairs, and then Amethyst said that you'd packed up your things, I thought I must be wrong."

"I did pack up my things," he said, pointing to his bag sitting in the corner of her room. "I wanted to surprise you, sorry. If I'd known it was going to upset you, I wouldn't have done it." He hooked an arm around her waist and drew her against him, and then touched his lips to her cheeks, catching her tears.

"No, this was perfect," she said, wrapping her arms around him and pressing closer. She couldn't have planned this out any better if she was writing her own romance novel.

"I don't want you to think this is me trying to pressure you," Judah told her. "This is just me showing you how much I care about you, and how special I think you are. We can make out a little or we can go straight to bed or we can just sit here and talk. Whatever you want."

She knew exactly what she wanted.

She wanted to not be afraid anymore.

"I don't want to talk, and I don't want to go to sleep," she told him, her hands moving to his shirt, where she began to unbutton it.

As though knowing that he didn't need to check with her that she was sure, Judah's hands also moved. One settled on her bottom, and the other began to stroke her back. She appreciated so much that he didn't baby her, coddle her, treat her like she was some broken doll that had to be handled with the utmost of care.

She wasn't any of those things.

She had been crushed by what life had thrown at her, but she was fighting her way out of that place.

She was fighting for her future, and her future very prominently featured Judah Willow.

When she finished unbuttoning his shirt, she took a moment to just look at him. Okay, he was pretty drool worthy, and she had read about a lot of drool worthy heroes, but none of them were as hunky as the man standing before her. Her fingers traced over those rock-hard abs. She'd always thought it was a little weird when heroines did that in romance books, but there was no way she could look at that chest and that six-pack and not touch it.

Letting her hands run up to his shoulders, she pushed his shirt off and let it fall to the floor. Then she unbuckled his jeans. Her fingers curled into his waistband as she tugged his jeans down his legs. When she had them down around his ankles, she undid his sneakers and he kicked them off. He stepped out of his jeans, leaving him in just a pair of boxers.

Ruby didn't even hesitate.

The time for hesitating was gone.

She was seizing her future with both hands and making it happen because that was the only way she was going to get what she wanted.

She shoved his boxers down and then just stood and looked at him.

He was naked.

She was standing in a room with a naked man.

And she didn't fell even a little bit afraid.

"Things seem a little unbalanced," Judah said, a bemused smile on his face.

"I guess they do," she agreed, reaching around to unzip her dress.

"Uh, uh, uh." Judah stopped her. "You had your fun; now, I get to have mine."

Taking her by the shoulders, he turned her around, brushed her long blonde hair over her shoulder, then very slowly unzipped her dress. His fingertips lightly brushed along her bare skin, making her break out in a mass of goose pimples. She liked this—undressing each other—she hadn't thought that would be sexy, but it was.

Judah's hands went back up to her shoulders and slid her arms out of the dress, letting it join his clothes on the floor. He unzipped her knee-high boots and lifted her legs one at a time, slipping the boots off. Then he knelt in front of her, his fingers tugging on her stockings as he very slowly inched them down over her hips. She wanted to grab his hands and make him hurry up, but the slower he went, the more that tingly feeling in her stomach grew, so she sucked in her bottom lip and let him tease her.

When he had her stockings down around her ankles, instead of letting her step out of them, he hooked his fingers into the waistband of her pink panties and took his time pushing them down, leaving her naked.

He was naked.

She was naked.

This was the first time since she was seventeen that she had voluntarily been naked with a man, and she had expected that her pulse might be rising and her heart hammering in her chest, but still, she felt more excited than anything else.

Judah would never hurt her. That was the difference between her and the men who had paid to use her. This was voluntary. She wanted to be here doing this. She wanted to be doing a whole lot more than this.

Judah lightly kissed her stomach, making her shiver, and he grinned up at her. Standing up, he cupped the back of her head in his hand as he walked her backward until she was up against the wall. Without pausing, he moved his lips to her neck and began to nuzzle as his hands explored her body. He teased her nipples before going between her legs and teasing her there too.

Ruby tipped her head back as she moaned. Inexperienced sex at seventeen wasn't like this. It was just straight to the main course—no appetizers—but this was all about building the tension until neither of them could take it any longer.

Not wanting to just sit back and let Judah take control, she reached out and took him in her hands. He was big. *Really* big, and she was a little nervous about how he was going to fit inside her. It had been seven years since she'd had sexual intercourse, so her body wasn't used to it anymore. What had been a part of her daily life while she was Igor's prisoner was then something that had terrified her, but now it was beautiful because she was sharing it with someone she loved and who loved her in return.

She had never touched a man like this before. It hadn't been her place when she was just a sex slave. It was her place to stand there and let the man do whatever he'd paid to do to her.

Ruby wasn't sure she was doing it right until she heard Judah moan. The sound was pure pleasure, and it bolstered her confidence. She touched him, and he touched her. They teased each other, they made each other feel amazing, and just when she could tell she was close, Judah's hands wrapped around her waist and he lifted her up. She wrapped her legs around him and kissed him as soon as his lips touched hers.

He carried her to the rose petal covered bed and laid her down, rolled on a condom, then stretched out on top of her. Before he entered her, he flipped them over, so she was the one on top, the one in control. Straddling him, she took him inside her slowly, inch by inch, partly because her body needed the time to adjust to his size, and partly because she liked the heat in his eyes as he watched her.

When he was fully inside her, she started to move up and down. Judah's fingers dug into her hips as he met her thrust for thrust.

As she came on a rush of pure unadulterated pleasure, she screamed Judah's name. Had she not been so stuck in a world of bliss that seemed to go on and on, she probably would have been embarrassed knowing that Amethyst had probably heard her and knew exactly what they were doing up here, but she wasn't. She didn't feel anything but wonderful emotions that ranged from pleasure to gratefulness, to wanting to do that again, to love.

"Thank you," she whispered as fresh tears filled her eyes. "Thank you for making this perfect."

"You're perfect," Judah told her, catching her tears on his thumb as he brushed them away. Lifting her off him, he scooped her up into his arms and stood up. "Want to take a shower with me?"

If by shower he meant more of what they'd just done, then her answer was a resounding yes. She wanted to do this with him every day for the rest of their lives.

CHAPTER
Eleven

October 26th
5:24 A.M.

She had barely slept a wink all night.

As tired as she was, she was just too happy to sleep.

Ruby's mind was whirring at a million miles a minute, thinking about last night, and about the future.

Last night had been amazing. They'd made love three times, their first time in the bed, then once in the shower, which had been slow and sensual, they'd connected on an even deeper level now that the first time was out of the way. The third time had been in bed again, and that one had been hot and passionate as they moved on to the next stage of intimacy.

Then Judah had spooned her against him and drifted off to sleep. She had tried to sleep, too, but her body was still tingling with the last residue of pleasure, and she kept thinking about how she really could have this for the rest of her life.

Nothing was standing in the way of her and Judah finding happiness together.

Nothing.

Not a single thing.

In a way, it was daunting. She had used her fears as a shield to stop anyone from getting close to her. She'd thought she was too damaged to ever make anyone else happy. She had been afraid to let anyone else in because they could hurt her like her parents had. Men were bigger and stronger than her, and nothing was stopping them from doing to her the same things that those men at Igor's had.

Judah was nearly a foot taller than she was, and he had a good hundred pounds on her—most of it muscle. If he wished, he could do anything he wanted to her, and there wasn't anything she could do about it. And yet, lying here in her bed in his arms, she knew that she was the one with the power. Judah had let her take control last night, just another way for him to remind her that she never ever had to be afraid of him, and she knew that underneath his tough exterior, he was just as afraid of being hurt as she was.

That's what happened when you'd been hurt so deeply that it left scars on your heart. You were forever wary of letting yourself be that vulnerable again. But with Judah, she wanted to be vulnerable. She wanted him to know that sometimes she wasn't as strong as she hoped she could be because she wanted to draw strength from him. She wanted to give him her strength, too. They might have been hurt and tortured in very different ways, but their pain was the same.

Pain.

That was a thing of the past.

She knew that there would be pain in her future, but it wouldn't be the same kind of pain.

Ruby rolled carefully over so that she was facing Judah. He looked so peaceful while he was asleep. He was a serious guy, and although she knew it was to mask his hurt, she didn't want him to keep a mask on with her. She had lowered hers for him, and she wanted him to be able to do the same. They were partners now, and they had the whole rest of their lives to help each other grow stronger.

It almost seemed to be too good to be true.

If this was one of her romance books, then she would be expecting a plot twist right about now.

Whenever it looked like the hero and heroine were about to get their happy ending, some other obstacle was thrown their way.

As if her thoughts came to life, she heard footsteps clattering up the stairs, and a moment later, her bedroom door was flung open.

"Ruby, Judah," Sapphire called as she ran into the room.

"What's wrong?" Ruby asked, bolting upright.

Although he had been fast asleep just seconds ago, Judah bolted upright along with her, already that serene look gone from his face, his eyes alert, and his cop persona firmly in place. "What's going on?" he demanded.

"I found something. You two need to come and see it immediately. Throw some clothes on ..." She averted her gaze, so it was fixed firmly on the wall. "And come meet us in the living room."

Without waiting for a reply, Sapphire disappeared, leaving the two of them alone. The spell that had encapsulated them in a little bubble of fairy tale happiness last night had vanished, and Judah had already jumped out of bed and begun throwing his clothes—which he had folded neatly and left on a chair before they went to sleep last night—on.

Reluctantly admitting that it was time to go back to the real world, but also content in the knowledge that tonight she and Judah would have another chance to do this all over again, Ruby also got out of bed. Since it was cold this time of the morning, she grabbed a pair of pink leggings and a blue sweatshirt that matched her eyes, then shoved her feet into a pair of fuzzy unicorn slipper boots.

Judah was already hurrying out the door, and she trudged after him, wishing that she could have stayed in her happy place a little longer.

"Oof," she grunted as she walked straight into the wall. No, not the wall, Judah. He'd stopped at the top of the stairs and turned around to wait for her.

"Sorry," he said as he leaned down and kissed her. "That wasn't how I wanted to start our day. Good morning." He kissed her again, deeper this time, and she knew that both of them wished they could have started the day with a little time alone together.

"We're waiting," Sapphire called out from downstairs.

"Your sister is moving out soon, right?" Judah groaned as he straightened.

"That one," she giggled, "but the other two will still be here. We could always spend some nights at your place where we can have a little more privacy."

"I like the way you think." He grinned, his blue eyes sparkling in a way she hadn't seen before in the few months they'd known each other.

Taking her hand, Judah led her downstairs, and the farther they got, the more that pit of anxiety that had settled in her stomach when Sapphire came bursting into her room, started to grow.

Something was going on, but she had no idea what. Was it something to do with Emerald? That her baby sister was still out there somewhere was never far from her mind. Or maybe something had happened to Diamond? She'd been upstairs with Judah all night, so she didn't know if her older sister had made it home safely last night. It couldn't be something to do with the home invasion case, though, could it? That case was closed; all four people were in custody, so there shouldn't be anything else going on here.

"What's up?" Judah asked as soon as they joined Sapphire, Gideon, Amethyst, and Diamond in the living room. Well, at least she knew that her older sister was okay.

"Sapphire found something," Gideon answered.

"I thought you two were spending the night at your new place," she said as she and Judah took seats at the table with the others.

"We were," Sapphire replied. "But I realized I left my watch here, so I had to come to get it."

"At five in the morning?" she asked.

Sapphire shrugged. "I feel weird starting my day without it on. Gideon and I were going to go running early, so we were up anyway. Besides, it was lucky I did forget it and come over here to collect it, or I wouldn't have found this." She lifted up a small black camera that was inside a plastic bag.

"Is that a camera?" Judah asked.

"Yep," Sapphire nodded bleakly.

"Where did you find it?" Judah asked. Ruby could feel panic rolling off him. It looked like this case wasn't as over as they'd thought that it was.

"It was over there, on the bookcase, partially hidden behind a photo." Gideon pointed.

From the place he indicated, the camera would have been able to capture everything that happened in this room.

This room where Stephanie Dwyer and the others had intended to tie her up and then shoot her.

"None of the other crime scenes had cameras," Judah pointed out.

"But none of the other crimes turned out like this one. Ruby messed things up by getting away. They panicked. Maybe they forgot to get the camera before they split," Sapphire countered.

"I don't understand. Why would they need to film what they were doing?" Ruby asked. She was starting to feel shaky, and her head was spinning. She'd thought this was over, but now it wasn't.

"Maybe they wanted to re-watch it," Gideon suggested.

Judah shook his head. "Their plan was to kill themselves when this was all done so there would be no need for them to keep something that they could use to relive the crimes."

"There's only one other reason I can think of that they would need to record this," Sapphire said grimly. Everyone else looked just as grim, but so far, her brain hadn't connected the dots.

"What?" Ruby asked.

"There was a fifth member of their gang," Judah said, reaching for her hand and squeezing it so tightly it hurt, but she didn't pull away. "One that wasn't here but wanted to watch what was happening."

So, it wasn't over.

Which meant she wasn't safe.

Which meant her perfect happy ending was in jeopardy.

∾

7:47 A.M.

. . .

To Judah, this whole mess seemed like a way for the universe to laugh in his face at him, thinking that he had found happiness and that he could let go of the past and be a better person going forward.

The cruel words that his tormentors had thrown at him when he was a boy had stuck. They had become a part of his psyche and had pushed him to the place where he had thought that he and everyone else would be better off if he was no longer a part of this world.

But he had fought back.

He had worked out religiously so he would never again be that tiny, skinny kid who couldn't defend himself. He had gone to therapy to learn how to control his OCD so that he mastered it, and it didn't master him. He'd become a cop so he could stand up for those who needed someone in his corner because there had never been someone in his when he was alone and scared.

Then he had fallen in love with the most beautiful woman, who had captured his heart with her own battles and the way she had risen above them.

Now it seemed like the universe wanted to remind him that no matter how big his muscles were, how much control he thought he had, or what his job was, he could still lose everything in one single second.

Control was an illusion.

The more you thought you had it, the more it seemed to slip through your fingers.

This morning, he should be waking up slowly with Ruby snuggled against him. He should be kissing her and taking her out for breakfast and starting to talk about the future and what it held for them.

But he wasn't doing that.

Instead, he was at the police station, trying to figure out who this fifth mystery member of the gang was. Ruby was at home. Again, there would be a police officer standing at her front door until this situation was resolved, and he hated that. Her home should be just that, a place to relax and be happy, not a place to hide out with a guard on your door so no one could kill you.

"Stephanie is going to tell us what we need to know," Judah growled the second the door opened, and Zeb walked in.

"We'll get her to talk," his partner promised.

They better, because there was no way he was going back to Ruby's tonight to have to break the news to her that this still wasn't over and that she still wasn't safe.

The look in her big, blue eyes this morning when Sapphire had shown them the camera, and she finally realized what its discovery meant had been like a punch in the ribs. It had physically hurt him that she was hurting. They had both been through a lot. They both knew what it was to doubt yourself to the point that you truly believed you were worthless, and they both knew what it was like to fight your way out of that web.

He *would* give her the peace she needed. Nothing else was acceptable.

Tonight, he wanted to make love to her again, then fall asleep, holding her in his arms.

This was supposed to be over. They had the kids; they had the gloves with the DNA evidence; they had the confessions. It should have been a slam dunk case. Now, it was like having to start all over again from scratch.

"Do we have any ideas who we're looking for?" he asked Zeb.

"I guess someone related to one or more of the four kids," his partner replied thoughtfully.

"The gang was two couples, is it possible that there is more than one more person involved, perhaps another couple?" Judah hated the idea, but he had to count it as a possibility.

"Could be," Zeb agreed, looking as unhappy about the prospect as he was. "Do you think we can expect more murders?"

"I don't think so. Whoever this other person—or persons—are, they weren't active participants in the home invasions, but they could have been intending to be involved with the suicides."

"Which means there's a chance that they've already committed suicide."

"I don't think so," he said again. "They're a group; they're in this together. I don't think they would have moved onto the suicide pact unless they were all ready to do it together. Since we have Stephanie, Jimmy, Nicole, and Wilson in custody, I don't think the other gang members would have killed themselves." This fifth person was out there somewhere, and he was terrified that they would make another attempt on Ruby's life. Part of him had wanted to stay with her as though he was the only one capable of protecting her, but the other part had wanted to be here because he also felt like he was the only one who could close this case.

Someone knocked on the conference room door, then a moment later, it swung open. "Stephanie Dwyer is in interview room four waiting for you," a young officer announced.

"Thank you," he said as he stood. They had played nice for long enough. Now, Stephanie was going to tell them what they wanted to know.

"Take it easy," Zeb said quietly as they walked to the room where Stephanie was waiting. "I know that you care a lot about Ruby, but pushing too hard is only going to make her shut down. We have to play this smart, not hard."

He knew that his partner was right, but all he wanted to do was grab the teenager and shake her until the answer that he needed came tumbling out.

But that wouldn't work.

It would just make Stephanie arc up and get stubborn and refuse to talk.

Judah drew in a deep breath, then mumbled to himself. "Smart, not hard." Then he opened the interview room door and walked in. What he saw wasn't what he had been expecting. Gone was Stephanie's cocky, overconfident demeanor, her dark eyes were now full of fear, and she looked like she had gotten younger overnight. Her plan to walk away, having spent only a couple of years in a juvenile facility, had not panned out, and now she would be spending at least the next couple of decades behind bars.

Stephanie was afraid now, and that was something they could use to their advantage.

"You guys made a mistake," he told the teenager. While he might have had sympathy for her last time they had spoken, now that he knew the truth about her and what she had done, he felt nothing but anger when he looked at her. She was suffering, but she had brought it all down upon herself.

This time there was no attitude. She just looked at them and waited to hear what they had to say.

"You left the camera at the Hatcher house," Judah informed her.

Her eyes grew wide, and if he'd needed confirmation that the camera was there because of the gang, he had it.

"You guys panicked when Ruby got into the safe room, and you couldn't get to her. After Jimmy threw a tantrum trying to break in, you guys ran, leaving it behind. We know that. What we don't know is who the camera was there for," Zeb said.

"We know it was there for someone else to watch what you were doing, but who? Who is our mystery person? And what was their costume? We already have a skeleton, a black cat, a ghost, and a witch. Nothing fun or cute, so a monster, maybe? A mummy, zombie." On the word zombie, Stephanie's eyes dipped, indicating that he had the right answer. Zombie. The fifth person was a zombie. Who could it be?

It hit him quickly.

The answer was in the question.

Zombie, the living dead.

It was Stephanie's older sister, Kimberly.

Kimberly Dwyer was eighteen years old, had been sick her whole life, missed a lot of school, had no friends, and these days never even left the house and was now dying. According to Stephanie's parents, their older daughter had been given only months to live. The diagnosis had no doubt been the catalyst for Stephanie's entire plan, including the suicide pact.

"It's your sister, isn't it?" he demanded.

"No," Stephanie said sullenly, pouting like a petulant toddler.

"Was it your idea or your sister's?" he asked.

Had they read this whole situation wrong? Stephanie had claimed that Jimmy was the mastermind, but the video and Wilson and Nicole's statements had said otherwise, but maybe Stephanie had only been following what her big sister told her to do. She *was* suicidal—all three other teenagers had backed that up.

"Stephanie, was it your idea or your sister's?" he repeated.

He needed to know.

If Stephanie was the one in control, then Ruby was probably safe. It would be unlikely that Kimberly would try to do anything to hurt her.

But, if this was all Kimberly's idea, then she was still out there, and Ruby was in danger.

∼

8:03 A.M.

"I'll get it," Ruby called out to her sisters when the doorbell rang.

"Should you be getting the door?" Amethyst stuck her head out of her gym.

"There's a cop out there, so it's not going to be anything bad," she reminded her twin. "It's probably some paperbacks I ordered."

"More books." Amethyst rolled her eyes. "Do you really need *more* books?"

"Hey, you used to love reading too before you turned into a gym junkie. And these ones aren't *just* books; they're signed paperbacks from one of my favorite authors."

"You have about a million favorite authors," her sister said with a smile.

Ruby shrugged. "What can I say, it's part of the bookworm life."

"Enjoy your new babies," Amethyst said as she went back into her gym.

Babies.

The idea immediately brought to mind something other than some new books to add to her every growing collection.

One day real babies might be in the cards.

The idea of a little person running around who was half her and half Judah was exciting.

She hadn't really thought much about being a mom after she got home from her ordeal. Just existing was hard enough, let alone thinking about taking on the responsibility of another human being. Then she was too afraid of men and too scared of being hurt and too sure that she wasn't worthy of being loved, that the idea of having kids just never really entered her mind.

It wasn't like she had thought she was missing out on anything. She'd thought that she and her sisters would just live here together for the rest of her lives. But then, Sapphire fell in love with Gideon, and she started wanting to find someone to share her life with. And now that she had fallen in love with Judah, the idea of having a baby suddenly seemed like something that might actually happen.

Ruby knew she had a big grin on her face as she opened the door, expecting to find either the delivery guy waiting with her package or the cop who was watching over her standing there with it, having already signed for it.

Instead, she found Kimberly Dwyer standing beside the cop. The girl was so pale, she looked like a ghost and was as thin as a skeleton, but she had a big smile on her face. In addition to holding the handle for her oxygen trolley in one hand, she also had a plate of cookies.

"Hi, Ms. Hatcher. I made these for you. They're kind of an *I'm sorry* gift, you know, because of my sister. I know it's not much, certainly not enough to make up for what Stephanie did, but I just wanted to do something." Kimberly gave her a shy smile.

Smiling back at the teen, she held the door open wider. "Come on in."

"Are you sure? I don't want to interrupt your day."

She had already called in sick for work. She just didn't think that she could settle down, knowing that this case wasn't over, after all, and she didn't want to be distracted and jittery and accidentally ruin someone's hair. So, staying home had been the plan. She'd been going to spend the day reading and waiting for Judah to call her with news, then spend the night with her boyfriend. They might not have officially decided to be boyfriend and girlfriend, but they both knew that they were in a relationship now.

"You're not interrupting my day," she assured Kimberly. She had intended to stop by the Dwyer house to check in on them today anyway, so she may as well do what she could to reassure Stephanie's sister that she wasn't responsible for anyone else's actions but her own.

She led the girl down to the living room, she wanted to offer her a hand, but she wasn't sure the independent teen would like that. So, she kept her hands to herself and entered the kitchen.

"Would you like something to drink to go with the cookies?" Ruby opened the fridge and pulled out a carton of milk. "Are you too old for milk and cookies?" she asked with a grin as she turned around, only for the smile to fall off her lips.

Kimberly had put the plate of cookies down and replaced them with a knife.

The knife was pointed directly at her about two inches away.

"You make a fuss, and I kill Amethyst and Diamond when they come to see what you're screaming about, and then I'm going to kill Sapphire, too," Kimberly hissed.

Ruby didn't move a muscle.

Amethyst was just at the front of the house in her gym, and Diamond was upstairs getting ready for work. She wouldn't do anything to risk them getting hurt, even if that meant letting Kimberly do what she'd come here to do.

Sorry, Judah, she threw the words out into the universe like they could somehow find their way to him, and he would know just how sorry she was that there wasn't a way she could stay alive but also keep her sisters alive.

"Smart," Kimberly smirked. "Where's the safe room? The one you used to escape that night. You thought that you had escaped your fate, but you were wrong."

Over the years, she had thought a lot about fate.

Was it fate that she had been sold into sexual slavery?

Was it fate that she had escaped?

Was her fate to die young and alone?

Ruby didn't know, but she pointed to where the safe room was, accepting that until she found an opening of some sort to use to escape Kimberly's clutches, this *was* her fate.

"It's over there."

"Let's go."

Keeping the knife poised right above her heart, Kimberly shuffled sideways as they walked over to the safe room.

"Open it up," Kimberly ordered.

Knowing that this was a bad idea but unable to come up with an alternative, Ruby punched in the code and stepped inside

Kimberly slammed the door shut and then turned to face her.

Ruby tried to stay strong even though her insides were quivering. It was hard to keep her cool. They were locked in here, and the only way in was to have the code, and the only people with the code were her and her sisters, and they had no reason to know that she was trapped in here with a killer. She knew without a shadow of a doubt that Kimberly was just as involved in the home invasion gang as the other four, even if she hadn't been here that night. She was the reason the camera had been put here, so she could watch everything.

Only now, it seemed she wanted to be a little more active.

Judah would figure this out.

He had to.

He knew that he was looking for someone else, and he would have to put the pieces together and figure out that Kimberly was the woman that he was looking for.

If he didn't, she was a dead woman walking.

No.

She could do this.

She could find a way to save herself.

She had done it once before, so she could go it again. Especially since she had so much riding on this, so much to live for.

"You don't have to do this, Kimberly," she said, backing up until she was against the wall. She knew she could take Kimberly if given the opportunity, but as long as Kimberly held the knife, her options were limited. Even given the girl's frailty, she could still slice through an artery if she got within striking distance. For now, she thought talking and keeping her distance were her best options.

"I want to do this. I'm tired of just being the sick girl, the one who's dying, the one who is so frail, so fragile, so vulnerable. I hate that. Hate it. I'm not going to be that girl anymore. I'm dying, and I want to have some fun before I do."

So, all of this was about dying?

Maybe that was something she could use to bond with the girl. If she could buy some time, distract Kimberly, maybe she could make it around to the door and sneak out of here, closing the door and trapping the teenager in here until Judah could get here.

"I know what it's like to be afraid of dying," she said softly.

"Because you were sold as a teenager?"

She hadn't realized that the Dwyers knew that much about her past. Maybe the kids had actually looked into the people they intended to kill. "Yes. I spent four years battling wishing I was dead and being terrified that I'd be killed."

"Do you still wish you were dead?" Kimberly asked, looking intrigued.

"Some days," she admitted. "And some days, I'm glad I'm still alive."

"I was seven the first time I really thought about killing myself," Kimberly said, lowering the knife a little, so it was no longer held out in front of her like a pointy shield. "I couldn't take it anymore. The pain, the hospital visits, the isolation—was hard. I just wanted to be a normal kid."

That was something she could relate to.

How many times over the last seven years had she wished that she was just a normal woman?

Millions.

Countless millions.

And for Kimberly, it had been something she had lived with ever since she could remember.

"I've tried a few times to kill myself; have you?" Ruby asked Kimberly.

"I asked a doctor once, but he told my parents, and they made me get counseling. Then I talked to my sister about it. We both hated our parents. She hated them because they only had her to save me, and I hated them because they wanted to keep me alive because it was what *they* wanted, not because it was what *I* wanted."

As Kimberly was talking, Ruby was edging her way around the room, hoping the teenager was too busy venting to notice.

It seemed to be working.

She was getting close to the door, and the temptation to speed up and make a run for it was strong. The only reason she hadn't was because Kimberly was still between her and the door, and she still had that knife.

"I wanted to leave something behind when I died," Kimberly was saying. "I wanted it to be something that would never be forgotten that my parents would forever be burdened with, knowing that if they had just let me die, none of this would have happened. But they didn't, and now Stephanie is in prison, and I'm about to be dead."

Kimberly turned slowly, awkwardly, and Ruby froze. The teen pulled a mask from her pocket and put it on. A zombie mask. She was sure that in Kimberly's mind, that had some kind of deep meaning, she probably saw herself as someone who should—and wanted—to be dead, but was still alive. The living dead, a zombie.

"Today we both die in this room," Kimberly announced, an odd sort of serenity seeming to surround her.

Ruby knew it was now or never and hoped that she could outrun the dying teen to the door.

She moved.

Kimberly shoved the oxygen trolley out in front of her.

She stumbled.

That was all the advantage Kimberly needed.

The knife seemed to swing through the air in slow motion.

The lights that turned on automatically when the door opened reflected off the blade, momentarily blinding her.

There was no pain when the metal sliced through her neck.

There was only sadness.

Against all the odds, she had found her prince charming and her happily ever after. Now it was over.

Blood gushed down her chest.

Her hands lifted instinctively to press to the wound.

Dizzy, she sank to the floor.

She was going to die alone in this room while two of her sisters were in the house, no idea what was going on.

She wished that Judah wasn't going to have to find her lifeless corpse, but she knew the chances were he would be the one to open the door to this room.

At least, if she was going to die, it was after she'd had the most amazing night of her life. Judah had made her feel all the things she thought she wasn't—special, desirable, important—and she hoped he knew that was how she thought of him as well.

Tired now, Ruby let her eyes flutter closed.

8:27 A.M.

Judah hammered on the Dwyer front door, then looked anxiously over his shoulders.

His instincts were telling him to go to Ruby's house, that she needed him, but he could see the cop standing on her front porch, so he knew that she was okay.

There were two cars parked in the Dwyer's driveway, so he also knew that they were in there, so why weren't they answering?

He hammered again.

"Something feels wrong," he said to his partner.

"I'm getting a bad vibe, too," Zeb agreed.

"Do you think she did something to her parents?"

"If we're right and she's the mastermind behind all of this, then I wouldn't put it past her."

"We're right," he reminded his partner.

Just as he was about to give up and head over to Ruby's house, the door was finally flung open by a disheveled looked Mrs. Dwyer.

"Detectives," the woman looked surprised to see them. "What are you doing here?"

"Where's Kimberly?" he asked. He wasn't here to answer questions. He was here to take the eighteen-year-old into custody.

Mrs. Dwyer's hand flew to her mouth. "Did something happen to her?"

"Why would you think that? Isn't she here?" From his understanding, the teenager was dying and didn't have the strength to leave the house. So, why did her mother think something had happened to her?

"No, when we got up this morning, she was gone," Mrs. Dwyer

said, clearly panicked about what had happened to her daughter.

Judah didn't have to wonder.

He knew where Kimberly Dwyer was.

He should have trusted his gut and gone straight to Ruby's place when it told him something was wrong.

Without waiting another second—because he didn't know how many Ruby had left—he turned and ran across the street.

Diamond was just walking down the porch steps toward her car and startled when she saw him coming running. "Judah? What's wrong?"

"Is Ruby home?" How was Kimberly planning to kill Ruby when she was inside her house with two of her sisters and a cop at the door?

"Yes. Why?"

"What's she doing?" Maybe he was overreacting, and Kimberly wasn't here. Maybe she was trying to figure out how to get inside when she'd realized that the house was being protected.

"I don't know. She was going to spend the day reading, but Kimberly Dwyer stopped by with cookies," Diamond explained.

If Kimberly was already in the house, then he might be too late.

"Where were they when you left?" he demanded, more forcefully than he should have because he could tell he was scaring Diamond, but he was terrified.

"I don't know; I didn't pay any attention. What's going on?"

"Kimberly was the fifth gang member," Zeb filled her in.

Judah was already running up the porch steps and tried to open the locked front door when he realized that he didn't have his key. "Diamond, let us in," he yelled over his shoulder.

She hurried up to join him, her hands shaking so badly that she couldn't get the key to slide into the lock. He took it from her, shoved it in, and opened the front door, pulling out his weapon and screaming Ruby's name as he went.

"What's wrong?" Amethyst appeared in the hall, but there was no sign of Ruby.

"Where's Ruby?"

"She and Kimberly Dwyer from across the street were going to have cookies," Amethyst replied.

"Kimberly was in on the home invasions," Diamond told her

younger sister.

He ran down the hall, scanning as he went. This girl was dying and was on oxygen. He didn't think it was likely that she was lurking somewhere and was going to jump out at them, but she could have a gun. The living room was empty, but he could see the plate of cookies on the counter and a carton of milk.

Kimberly had Ruby; that was obvious, but where would they go?

"I'll check her bedroom," Zeb said, heading for the stairs.

"I would have heard them if they'd gone into Ruby's library as its right across from my gym, but I'll check to be sure," Amethyst said.

"Diamond, you should go wait outside," he said. He didn't want to be worrying about anyone else's safety right now. "Tell the cop at the door to call in backup and an ambulance, then stay with him."

"Judah, the safe room," she said, walking over toward it. "Look, here," she pointed to a small panel on the wall that he remembered seeing the night of the home invasion but not while he was staying here. "The panel is hidden unless you open it to put the code in so you can go inside. Kimberly must have taken Ruby in there because that's where she escaped that night."

He should have thought of that.

"She wasn't up there," Zeb said as he came back downstairs.

"Not in the library," Amethyst said at the same time.

"They're in the safe room," he informed the others. "Can I get in there even though Ruby is inside?" He wasn't sure that the safe room would open from out here once someone had barricaded themselves in there.

"You need the code," Diamond told him.

"What is it?"

"Three, one, one, seven, nine, four," Amethyst rattled off.

"Thanks, now both of you go outside," he told the sisters. He needed Ruby to be his focus right now, and he couldn't guarantee that one of them wouldn't do something to put themselves in danger as soon as this door opened.

Amethyst looked like she was going to argue, but Diamond shot him a stricken look, then grabbed her sister and dragged her down the hall. When he heard the front door close, he pushed the code in.

The door swung open, and his eyes immediately fell on Ruby.

She lay on the floor.

Her blue sweatshirt was drenched in blood from a gash on her neck.

Her hands were pressed against her wound; her head turned in his direction at the sound of the opening door.

She was alive.

Relief flooded through him, but it was dampened by the amount of blood puddled around her.

She could still be bleeding out.

If Kimberly Dwyer had only just cut her throat before they got in here and had nicked an artery, then Ruby might have only minutes left to live.

Anger burned through him as he focused his gaze on Kimberly.

She stood above Ruby, the knife—from which droplets of Ruby's blood dripped down onto the floorboards—poised above her victim, but when she saw them, she quickly moved it so that it was pressed to her own neck.

Judah was tempted to let her kill herself if that was what she wanted, but instead, he went with doing the right thing. "Put the knife down, Kimberly," he ordered.

"I don't think so." She grinned back at him.

Although he had his gun pointed at Kimberly, the oxygen tank that she had beside her rendered it virtually useless. If he fired his weapon in here, the tank could explode, killing Kimberly, Ruby, Zeb, himself, and since he wasn't sure how big an explosion there would be, possibly Diamond and Amethyst too, as well as anyone else nearby.

"It's over, Kimberly. We know you're involved, put the knife down and let us take you down to the station," Zeb said.

"What's the point? I'm dying. I'll never make it to the trial. It should end this way, the way it was supposed to." With that, she sliced the blade of the knife deeply through her neck. Blood gushed, and the knife clattered as it fell from her fingers and hit the floor. Kimberly dropped promptly down beside it.

Leaving Zeb to deal with the teenager, Judah ran to Ruby and dropped to his knees at her side. He yanked off his shirt and balled it up and then gently moved her hands away from her neck and replaced them with the shirt.

How could one person lose this much blood and still be alive?

And yet, she *was* still alive. For now, at least.

At his touch, her long eyelashes fluttered on her deathly pale cheeks before her eyes opened slowly, as though it required more effort than she had strength.

"Judah," she said as her lips lifted in a small smile.

"Don't talk," he admonished gently. "Just try to stay as still as you can, an ambulance is coming, and the stiller you stay, the less you bleed."

"Don't care," she whispered.

"Well, you better." He tried to joke, forcing his mouth to obey him and smile. He wanted to reassure her, but he was panicking like he had never panicked before.

She smiled back, her blue eyes—painted with pain—locked onto his. "Love you."

Tenderly, he brushed a lock of her hair off her cheek and away from the blood, then reached down to take one of her ice-cold hands in his. "Yeah, I love you, too, so you just hold on, okay?"

"'Kay," she murmured.

He pressed the shirt more firmly against her wound, trying desperately to stem the flow of blood. Ruby winced, and he hated that, in trying to save her life, he was hurting her. "I'm sorry," he said. It was so unfair that he was losing this beautiful, amazing woman when they had only just found each other. He didn't want her to go. He didn't want her to leave him. He wanted to force his own blood, his own life, inside her, giving her what she needed to live.

But sometimes in life, you didn't get what you wanted.

Ruby's eyes—that were still locked onto his—began to dim, like her soul was fading away, moving on to what lay beyond this world.

"Ruby," he said sharply. He released her hand and tapped lightly at her cheek.

The only response was her eyelids falling closed.

"Ruby," he said again, more desperately this time.

This couldn't happen.

Maybe if he refused to believe it, then it wouldn't.

How he wished that was all it took to save her life.

Still holding the shirt to her wound, however pointless it was, he wouldn't stop. Judah lowered his forehead and rested it on Ruby's.

Tears came, and he didn't bother holding them back; they dripped down onto Ruby's cheeks as steadily as her blood dripped onto the floorboards.

~

9:12 A.M.

He hated white walls.

That was what Judah decided as he sat in the surgical waiting room, staring at the horrid white wall.

The white was dirty, and it glared in the stark florescent lights. The more he sat and stared at it, the more he hated it.

Diamond and Amethyst were sitting beside him. None of them had spoken since Ruby had been taken from the ER to surgery.

No one had told them anything.

Was Ruby still alive?

He'd thought that she wasn't going to make it until the paramedics showed up. But she had. He'd thought that she wasn't going to make it through the ambulance ride to the hospital. But she had. Now he had to believe that she could make it through surgery as well.

She had to.

He didn't know what he was going to do if she didn't.

Judah didn't even want to think about it.

Maybe if he didn't think about it, he could stop it from happening.

Closing his eyes, Judah started praying. There was only one person who was going to save Ruby's life, and that was God. He prayed like he had never prayed before, begging, pleading, bargaining, repeating his plea over and over.

Please, God, don't take her from me.
Please, God, don't take her from me.
Please, God, don't take her from me.

"What happened? Where's Ruby?"

The words startled him out of his prayers, and he looked up as Sapphire, with Gideon behind her, came running into the waiting room.

He stood along with Diamond and Amethyst and walked over to her.

"Kimberly Dwyer was the fifth member of the gang," he explained. Sapphire and Elijah had gone to deal with one of their cases this morning, so she didn't know they had figured out who the camera had been put there for. "Before we could tell anyone, she got into the house and took Ruby into the safe room where she slit her neck."

Sapphire gasped, her hands flying to her mouth, and when Gideon put his hand on her shoulder, she lifted one of hers to cover his. "She's okay, though, right?"

"She lost a lot of blood. Diamond and Amethyst both donated in the ambulance." He'd wanted to, as well, but they didn't share the same blood type. So, all he'd been able to do was sit there, impotent, unable to do a single helpful thing. "She's in surgery. There's a chance that she won't make it through." As much as he hated saying the words, Sapphire needed to prepare herself for the worst.

"No," Sapphire sobbed. Her knees buckled, and Gideon caught her before she hit the floor, then turned her around and drew her against him. She buried her face in his chest as she wept.

As horrendous as this was for everyone, at least Sapphire and Gideon had each other. They had someone to hold them, someone to comfort them, someone to support them if the worst happened.

He had no one.

His only connection to this family was Ruby, and if she didn't make it, the Hatcher sisters and Gideon would pull together, grieving as a family, and he would be left out in the cold, to grieve alone.

Leaving the others together, he wandered back to his chair and dropped heavily down into it. Everything had been so perfect last night. Just hours ago, he and Ruby had been together, making love, and he'd been thinking how amazing it would be to do that every night for the rest of his life. The future had seemed so bright. It was like he had gotten everything he could ever want and more.

And now, he had nothing.

A hand touched his shoulder, and he jumped, looking up to see Sapphire standing there. Her eyes were red rimmed, her cheeks splotchy, and she was trembling. She looked like a piece of her might be gone forever, and he could completely empathize with that.

"Can I sit?" she asked.

"Of course."

Sapphire dropped into the uncomfortable plastic chair beside his and began to twist her hands together in her lap. "I'm sorry," she said at last.

"For what?" he asked, confused. She had nothing to do with Kimberly Dwyer getting to Ruby. That was on him. The first thing he should have done was call Ruby and the cop guarding her to let them know, not go to the Dwyer house to arrest her. He hadn't thought the kid was physically capable of doing anything, that was why she hadn't participated in the murders, just watched them via the camera.

"For being so rough on you the last few days." She chanced a quick look at him before her watery eyes darted away. "I shouldn't have been. I like you, and I'm glad that you make Ruby happy. It wasn't personal; it wasn't anything to do with you at all. It's me. I always felt guilty that I was rescued so quickly. I was only gone for a few days, and being back home, living with my aunt and uncle, knowing that my sisters were still suffering, the guilt was crushing. And it never really went away. Now I feel like I have to protect them, make sure they never get hurt again, and I had to be sure that you really loved Ruby. You do. I can see it in your eyes. You're just as scared of losing her as we are; that means you're already a part of our family. I promise I'll ease up on you," she said, turning to look at him again, and giving him a half smile even as tears began to trickle down her cheeks.

That Sapphire had opened up to him, trusted him with her fears, made him feel like maybe he was already part of the Hatcher family, and he knew without a shadow of a doubt, that even if Ruby didn't make it, he wouldn't be left to grieve alone.

Ruby had brought Sapphire over here to tell him that. It was like she was looking out for him even as she fought for her life. For a second, that scared him, as though Ruby were already gone and was now his guardian angel looking out for him and making sure that he would be all right.

Despite the fear that was still living inside him, he didn't feel that Ruby was gone yet. He knew that she was strong—strong enough to survive hell and escape—and he knew she was strong enough to live through this.

"Ruby will be okay," he told Sapphire, hoping that his confidence was well founded.

"I hope so," she said, throwing her arms around his neck and squeezing.

Judah squeezed her back. He liked that Ruby had a sister that would test him to make sure that he was good enough. He liked knowing that as awful as what she had lived through was, Ruby had a wonderful support system, and when she pulled through it, he was going to be part of that system.

"Guys, the doctor is here," Gideon announced.

Immediately, they both sprang to their feet. Sapphire went straight to Gideon and wrapped an arm around his waist, and he stood with the family, confident now that he *was* a part of this family.

"You're Ruby Hatcher's family?" the surgeon asked. He was dressed in scrubs, and although Judah tried to read the answers he sought in the man's face, he couldn't.

"Yes," Sapphire said firmly, shooting him a quick glance.

"Is she okay?" Amethyst asked.

"She made it through surgery," the doctor told them.

They let out a collective sigh of relief. Sapphire and Gideon hugged, Diamond and Amethyst hugged, then Sapphire held out a hand to Judah and pulled him closer, and the five of them held on to each other.

"Can we see her?" Diamond asked.

"She's very weak, and still sedated, but you can visit her one at a time."

As much as he ached to see her, he didn't want to prevent one of her sisters from seeing Ruby, but Sapphire had other ideas. "Judah should go first. I think that if Ruby could choose, he's who she'd most want to see right now."

Shooting her a grateful smile, he followed the doctor through a couple of corridors, and then finally, he saw her.

She was lying in a bed, a tube threaded across her face from ear to ear, helping to deliver additional oxygen, a machine behind her bed displayed her heart rate and pulse, and her neck was heavily bandaged.

But she was alive.

And that was all that really mattered.

"Can I touch her?"

"Yes." The surgeon smiled at him. "She won't wake up for a while, but I'm sure she'd be happy to know that you were sitting there with her."

Alone with the woman he loved, Judah pulled up a chair beside her bed and picked up her hand, carefully avoiding the Pulse Ox cable attached to one of her fingers. He brought her hand to his lips and tenderly kissed it. Her hand was warm, and her vitals all looked good considering what she'd just survived. He hated that she would forever have a scar on her neck as a reminder, but he hoped that she looked at it as a symbol of strength and resilience. Survival.

He'd thought the universe was going to mock what should have been his happy ending with the woman he loved by snatching her away from him, but it seemed that even the universe couldn't take away something so pure.

3:40 P.M.

She hurt and felt exhausted, but she also felt wonderful.

Ruby gave a content sigh and opened her eyes.

The first thing she saw was Judah's face hovering above her.

For a second, she thought she was still in the safe room, but then she realized she was lying on a soft bed, and there were white walls around her. She was no longer cold, and there were the quiet sounds of a hospital.

If she was in a hospital, then she was alive.

That alone was enough to make the pain and discomfort more than worth it.

She beamed up at Judah, who was watching her cautiously like he wasn't quite sure if she was all right or not.

Wanting to reassure him, she opened her mouth to tell him that she was fine and that she was so glad he was here, but before she could talk, he touched a finger to her lips to stop her.

"Your neck got pretty banged up, you can't talk," he told her.

She couldn't talk?

Had her voice box been damaged?

How was she going to live the rest of her life unable to speak?

Noticing her panic, Judah ran a hand over her hair, then brushed his knuckles across her cheek. "I meant you can't speak while the wound is in the first stage of healing, not that you won't be able to speak ever again. A couple of days, and you'll be talking up a storm."

Ruby relaxed and lifted a hand, searching for Judah's. A couple of days wasn't so bad, not compared to the rest of her life. Because that was what she and Judah had, the whole rest of their lives to be together.

There was still a lot about Judah she had to learn, and there was a lot that he didn't know about her too, but the prospect of finding out those things—what made him laugh, what scared him, what made him cry, did he have hobbies when he wasn't working—and she couldn't wait to find out the answers to all those questions and many more.

Right now, though, there were a couple of pressing questions that were too important to wait. Gesturing at Judah that she needed pen and paper, he stood and looked around, producing one and handing it over.

Kimberly?

"She's dead." Judah answered her written question.

No doubt, the teenager had killed herself. Ruby knew the girl was dying anyway, but she was sad to know that Kimberly was dead. She didn't know how the Dwyers were going to cope with everything that had happened.

Sisters?

"Your sisters are all here at the hospital. They're in the waiting room. They've been in and out of your room while we were waiting for you to wake up. Do you want me to go and get them?"

No. Not yet, she added. She wanted to see them, but first, she wanted a little time alone with Judah. After just those few words, her hand was starting to tingle, and although she knew the pain in her neck was there, it should be worse, whatever drugs they had her hopped up on were doing a good job of keeping her comfortable.

"I'm so glad you're okay." Judah kissed her forehead and began to stroke her hair, the fingers of his other hand still curled around hers. "When I saw you lying on the floor in the safe room, covered in blood, more blood than I thought anyone could lose and still be alive, I was more scared than I've ever been before. Losing you wouldn't just be losing you, it would be losing the future that we should have had."

Future.

That was what she wanted to know.

What exactly *was* their future?

So much of her life had been uncertain. Would she make it through another day? Would her life ever be normal? Would she always have suicidal thoughts even if she got to a place where she was happy with her life? She needed something certain, something to hold on to, something concrete to build on.

Future?

"What's our future?" Judah asked. When she nodded, something she quickly realized wasn't a wise thing to be doing right now, he replied, "Well, I hope it's us, together, building a life that we share. I want us to get to know each other, find out what we have in common, and what differences we have that complement one another. And then, when we're ready, I want to propose and marry you in front of our families and friends. I hope that one day we'll have kids, but if we never did, it wouldn't make our family any less of a family."

That was exactly what she had wanted to hear.

Ruby wanted to know that they wanted the same things out of the next phase of their lives.

All she could do was grin—a goofy grin—at him.

"Whatever drugs they have you on are making you all dopey," he teased.

She tried to mock frown at him, but she was just too happy.

"You must be exhausted. You should close your eyes, get some rest,"

Judah suggested. "I'm sure a doctor will be in to check on you soon."

She shook her head; sleep was the last thing she wanted to do right now. She just wanted to lie here, holding hands with her boyfriend, basking in the joy of being alive that you could only ever really know when you had come so close to death you could feel it.

"Honey, I know that you are just enjoying being alive right now, and I'm right there with you, but you need to sleep. When you wake up again, you can see your sisters, and we can talk some more. While you sleep, I'm going to be sitting right here beside your bed, just like I was when you were sleeping before."

Ruby knew he hadn't left her side. The tension that was still visible on his face as a testament to that. He was wearing hospital scrubs in place of the clothes he'd put on this morning, which had no doubt been stained with her blood.

As much as she didn't want to admit it, he was right. She was drained like her energy had left her body along with her blood, and it was only her relief at being alive and her love for Judah keeping her awake at the moment, but even that couldn't keep her awake much longer.

Back at the safe house, when she'd thought that she was going to die and it might be her only chance, she'd told Judah that she loved him and he'd said it back. Although she didn't think he'd only said it because he too had thought she was dying, she wanted them to say those words to each other now—now that there was no death sentence hanging over them.

Picking up the pad of paper that was resting on her lap, she wrote the three words that had become so very important to her. *I love you.*

"I love you, too, my precious Ruby," he said, and love shone from his eyes as he looked down at her. Dipping his head, he very lightly touched his lips to hers, sealing their love with a kiss, just as they would do at their wedding one day in the not-too-distant future.

Her life had been filled with some very low lows—times when she had honestly wished that she were dead, and times where she had actively tried to make that happen—but for the first time, she felt like she had left the dark behind for good.

It was such a wonderful feeling.

Hope was a double-edged sword.

On the one hand, it gave you something to live for; on the other, it gave you something to die for.

Finally, she had found herself on the something-to-live-for side, and her hope was that her future would remain bright. She and Judah might have dark days, days where the clouds covered the sun, but no matter how many clouds there were in the sky, the sun was *always* there. It never disappeared. It was just that some days you couldn't see it.

That was exactly how she felt about the rest of her life.

Ruby curled her fingers tighter around Judah's trying to convey without words just how much he meant to her.

The smile he gave her said not only that he understood but that he felt the same way about her.

That was a pretty great feeling, to know that the person you loved loved you back.

Content, she settled down against her pillows and closed her eyes. She didn't even care about the tight pulling on her neck where her stitches were. Who cared about a few stitches and some pain and discomfort when she was this happy?

She had heard the saying the darkest hour was just before dawn, and she'd never really got it, but today she did. Being in that safe room with Kimberly knowing that the chances of her making it out alive were slim, that had been the darkest day of her life because she'd had happiness dangled before her only to have it snatched away.

But today was the dawn.

The dawn of the beginning of the rest of her life.

As teenagers they were sold to human traffickers, now the Hatcher sisters have to rebuild their lives. To find out what happened to Diamond Hatcher continue with book three in this gripping romantic suspense series now!

Fractured Diamond (Broken Gems #3)

Also by Jane Blythe

Detective Parker Bell Series

A SECRET TO THE GRAVE

WINTER WONDERLAND

DEAD OR ALIVE

LITTLE GIRL LOST

FORGOTTEN

Count to Ten Series

ONE

TWO

THREE

FOUR

FIVE

SIX

BURNING SECRETS

SEVEN

EIGHT

NINE

TEN

Broken Gems Series

CRACKED SAPPHIRE

CRUSHED RUBY

FRACTURED DIAMOND

SHATTERED AMETHYST

SPLINTERED EMERALD

SALVAGING MARIGOLD

River's End Rescues Series

COCKY SAVIOR

SOME REGRETS ARE FOREVER

SOME FEARS CAN CONTROL YOU

SOME LIES WILL HAUNT YOU

SOME QUESTIONS HAVE NO ANSWERS

SOME TRUTH CAN BE DISTORTED

SOME TRUST CAN BE REBUILT

SOME MISTAKES ARE UNFORGIVABLE

Candella Sisters' Heroes Series

LITTLE DOLLS

LITTLE HEARTS

LITTLE BALLERINA

Storybook Murders Series

NURSERY RHYME KILLER

FAIRYTALE KILLER

FABLE KILLER

Saving SEALs Series

SAVING RYDER

SAVING ERIC

SAVING OWEN

SAVING LOGAN

SAVING GRAYSON

SAVING CHARLIE

Prey Security Series

PROTECTING EAGLE

PROTECTING RAVEN

PROTECTING FALCON

PROTECTING SPARROW

PROTECTING HAWK

PROTECTING DOVE

Prey Security: Alpha Team Series

DEADLY RISK

LETHAL RISK

EXTREME RISK

FATAL RISK

COVERT RISK

SAVAGE RISK

Prey Security: Artemis Team Series

IVORY'S FIGHT

PEARL'S FIGHT

LACEY'S FIGHT

OPAL'S FIGHT

Prey Security: Bravo Team Series

VICIOUS SCARS

RUTHLESS SCARS

Christmas Romantic Suspense Series

CHRISTMAS HOSTAGE

CHRISTMAS CAPTIVE

CHRISTMAS VICTIM

YULETIDE PROTECTOR

YULETIDE GUARD

YULETIDE HERO

HOLIDAY GRIEF

Conquering Fear Series (Co-written with Amanda Siegrist)

DROWNING IN YOU

OUT OF THE DARKNESS

CLOSING IN

About the Author

USA Today bestselling author Jane Blythe writes action-packed romantic suspense and military romance featuring protective heroes and heroines who are survivors. One of Jane's most popular series includes Prey Security, part of Susan Stoker's OPERATION ALPHA world! Writing in that world alongside authors such as Janie Crouch and Riley Edwards has been a blast, and she looks forward to bringing more books to this genre, both within and outside of Stoker's world. When Jane isn't binge-reading she's counting down to Christmas and adding to her 200+ teddy bear collection!

To connect and keep up to date please visit any of the following

www.ingramcontent.com/pod-product-compliance
Lightning Source LLC
Chambersburg PA
CBHW031940240626
47153CB00003B/805